Required Reading from the *New York Post*

PRAISE FOR *ONE HUNDRED MILLION HEARTS*

"Sakamoto's words seem painted rather than typed. Her writing is simple but not simplistic; each image feels painstakingly assembled. Metaphors—of resilient cherry blossoms and the thousand red stitches that comprised kamikazes' sashes—weave through a dense narrative."
—*Minneapolis City Pages*

"An elegant and thoughtful meditation on history, family, and personality, nicely packed into a tautly mysterious domestic drama." —*Kirkus Reviews*

"With fluid shifts in time and simple yet poetic language, the story blossoms. . . . Sakamoto is a gentle storyteller who never forces the point, but rather lets the details slowly surface. She gracefully, but skillfully, paints the story with words." —*Booklist*

"Deft evocation of Japanese culture and . . . grave examination of a tragic episode in Japanese history."
—*Publishers Weekly*

"A dazzling, multilayered novel of loss and regret, of love and death . . . Sakamoto writes with a keen, almost merciless eye for detail, a painter's eye for scene and setting."
—*The Ottawa Citizen*

"In a novel where history could have easily overtaken fiction, Sakamoto invests in each of her characters so fully they seem to live their own lives, struggle with each other through real conflicts, and dance beautifully around the give and take of love." —*Quill & Quire*

"Evocative . . . Poignant . . . In Miyo, Sakamoto has created a marvellously complex, compelling character who is transformed . . . from a brave but helpless cripple to a woman

P9-DVY-728

who runs and dances and loves, not in innocence, but in full, terrifying knowledge." —*The Gazette* (Montreal)

"Sakamoto really shines." —*National Post*

"What Sakamoto does well is draw the reader into the debate. . . . Nothing is as simple as it seems, appearances do not always represent truth. This is a strong, rich and often complicated tale. . . . It's worth the read."
—*The Hamilton Spectator*

"A compelling and sensitively drawn story."
—*The Winnipeg Free Press*

"Simple, achingly beautiful and deeply spiritual."
—*St. John's Telegram*

PRAISE FOR *THE ELECTRICAL FIELD*

"Hums with suppressed violence and delicate mysteries."
—*Los Angeles Times*

"With precision, Sakomoto has invented a riveting modern narrator, who seems on the periphery but is actually at the center of the story." —*The Washington Post*

"An irresistible, high-tension read . . . Will long haunt its readers, from its electrifying opening to its crackling, thunderstruck conclusion." —*The Oregonian* (Portland)

"[I]t's refreshing to see a first novel as ambitious as this, its writing sure and honest." —*Seattle Weekly*

"[A] novel that will galvanize readers with its portrayal of a memorably enigmatic set of characters."
—*The Boston Herald*

"Sakamoto is a master of repressed tension. . . . [A] writer to watch." —*Chicago Tribune*

ONE HUNDRED MILLION HEARTS

ALSO BY KERRI SAKAMOTO

The Electrical Field

One Hundred Million Hearts

—

Kerri Sakamoto

A HARVEST BOOK
HARCOURT, INC.

*Orlando Austin New York
San Diego Toronto London*

First published in Canada by Alfred A. Knopf Canada.
An earlier version of chapter one appeared in a
slightly different form in *Toronto Life,* August 1999.

www.HarcourtBooks.com

Library of Congress Cataloging-in-Publication Data
Sakamoto, Kerri.
One hundred million hearts/Kerri Sakamoto—1st. U.S. ed.
p. cm
ISBN 0-15-101037-4
ISBN 0-15-603004-7 (pbk)
1. World War, 1939–1945—Veterans—Fiction. 2. Fathers and daughters—Fiction.
3. Fathers—Death—Fiction. 4. Kamikaze pilots—Fiction.
5. Women—Japan—Fiction. 6. Sisters—Fiction. 7. Japan—Fiction. I. Title.
PR9199.3.S163O54 2003
813'.54—dc22   2003057064

Text set in Fairfield Light

Printed in the United States of America
First Harvest edition 2005
A C E G I K J H F D B

For Richard and for Laurie: my water and my blood

ONE

DURING THE WAR my father learned to shoot a rifle, lunge with his bayonet and march the perimeter of Okayama Second Middle School, knees high and arms swinging. He had been born in Vancouver but sent to Japan for schooling, then to a farther away place he called Manchukuo. I couldn't find it on my map of the world. Manchuria, he said when I asked, but he never uttered it again. He never spoke Japanese except to count *ichi ni* to me, one two, when I woke up in the middle of night afraid, which rarely happens these days.

No one would look after me the way my father did. He laid me down when my breath twisted like a rope in my throat, or doubled me over when my heart pounded and raced and rattled my whole body. When the headaches came, he pressed his fingers into my left temple until I fell asleep. He rubbed my back, slapped my leg when the blood didn't flow. *Good blood*, he'd say when it came back. He saved me, just as he might have saved others as a soldier in the Japanese army had he ever been sent into battle.

Every day he'd drive me to and from school, pulling up by the doors after the other children had gone in. He was still a young man in those days, a young man not much older than my thirty-two years; a young man with chances. His hair was very thick and very black; his limbs were strong as he carried me up the steps I couldn't climb back then, my feet bouncing in thick-laced ortho-pedic shoes over the crook of his arm. He could have found someone, someone to keep him company, to take my mother's place. I remember him pausing for a moment to catch his breath, eyeing the other children around me, sizing up the differences. He was a giant among the dwarfs seated at their miniature desks, elbows out, hands in cups and saucers as Miss Whitten instructed: little fists planted in open palms. I remem-ber my father towering over them, I remember him handsome, the way people look in old pictures when they were young, their faces still an open road.

Setsuko first came knocking when I was seven. She was like him, a nisei, Canadian-born Japanese. She was younger than him, a tough woman who'd weathered the internment camp as an orphan. So many times he broke their bowling dates at the last minute when I needed prescriptions from the pharmacy, books from the library; a snowsuit when it suddenly grew cold. My father even bought me my first brassiere, my first sanitary pads, and later on tampons, when I wanted to be like the other girls, though we didn't know if they'd work because of how my insides are shaped. A woman could have helped with those things but Setsuko had no feeling for me. One time my stomach started to ache just as she arrived, and he left her at the door to drive to the drugstore.

I stood there staring up at her and she didn't say a word; finally I went to my room until my father came back.

By the time I was eight she gave up, seeing how little was left for her. One night weeks later, when he put me to bed and went to close the door, I saw him in that lonely light from the hall, and felt sorry for him. I said the only words I could think to say: "Thank you, Daddy."

"For what?" he shot back. It isn't in him to say much; he flailed for words. "What?" He was angry at my feeling sorry for what he'd lost. "Who am I?" he stammered, poking his chest with his thumb. I shrank under the covers, ashamed. "I'm your father," he said, almost shouting, "that's what I do!" He slammed the door, muttering to himself.

At Wellington's, where I copyedit legal documents, everyone seems bored, they want out; they have ambitions I overhear a cubicle away. I like the fact that my carefulness gets rewarded; that's why I've stayed ever since high school. Somewhere out in the world things happen to other people, decisions get made and written and arrive on my desk. It's a mystery. I have a window overlooking the parking lot in a valley amid blocks of steel that shimmer like knife blades but, like mountains, seem too big for people. In between, there are lawns vast as wilderness. Every so often, I see a man scamper out and squat with a cigarette, like the cooks I glimpsed in Chinatown alleys on drives to church with my father as a child. In the lot, people park their cars close together in the same spots every day, leaving it empty on one side.

One day my father doesn't show up. He's never late; he's early, always. It's past the usual five-thirty and I sit in my spot in the glass foyer watching for the green Chevrolet. Any minute now, I tell myself. People swing their briefcases, leave in twos and threes, then one by one, until I notice the music because it has stopped and, for the first time, I miss it. The lights dim to match the sky outside; my reflection melts away. I'd sit until morning if not for the guard, who taps me on the shoulder. "Excuse me, ma'am," he says in his slate-blue uniform, his face so fresh that I realize I've gotten older; ten years have gone by and my father has never not come.

I arrive home breathless from a careening taxi ride that has slid me from side to side on the cold cracked seat. In the driveway, the green Chevrolet is crushed on one side, one eye out. I find my father in the kitchen, a bandaged cut on his cheek. He's studying his hands, holding them close, then far away. He barely glances up. "Daddy," I start to say, then stop myself, harness my breath. I wonder how I'll survive; if he goes away, leaves me, dies, I may too.

For the first time, I must take the subway to work. I have no choice; my father's dizziness from the accident hasn't gone and his eyesight, I now learn, has long been deteriorating. His licence has been taken away and won't be given back. I plan which trains to take in which direction, try to guess where the escalators are. I lie awake the night before, practising.

In the morning, my father is all dressed up with no place to go; he's in his usual work clothes for the auto shop but seems like a man out of uniform. It's different leaving him at the door. Glancing up from the street, I see him in the window, watching me make my way toward the station. I know he's keeping count for me, an old habit. I remind myself that I have my own rhythm, my own pace that will get me where I need to go. I'll be just another body going from here to there.

On the train, there's a vicious rush to get out; I find myself pushed on all sides, wobbling; my left knee buckles. I step out just before the doors clamp shut. But my shoulders snap back, my knapsack is caught and the train starts to move. I'm pulled along, slowly at first, then faster. I scream but there's no one here for me. My feet are tumbling fast so I lift them. I see the blur below and the wall at the end of the station looming; beside it a long dark hole. I close my eyes and feel my hair whisked back, my face cold and bare with only eyes. This is what it feels like to move, to fly, for once.

Then suddenly arms are grappling for me, my body is yanked and jolted to a standstill; the train screeches to a halt. The ground is under my feet once more, and I crumple to it. The ride is over.

I open my eyes to passengers squished in against one another, staring at someone else's mishap from inside the train, their arms hanging from handles though they aren't moving. Down a few cars my knapsack is dangling, a little black pouch with my new subway tokens, my medications, my keys: a funny mole on the sleek silver body of the train. A man crouches close to me, watching with probing eyes, arms around but not on me. My legs are splayed in front, and at the sight of them I sob, I haven't left them behind, especially the crooked one, brittle as a cane. I'm crying for the first time in years. It makes me remember the last time, though the wetness on my cheeks feels unfamiliar. He touches my tears.

"Does it hurt?" the man asks, and it seems an odd question. My father has never asked; the doctors never did. Something is lurking in this man's eyes, as if he himself were the one hurt, and this kindness is both for himself and for me. It occurs to me that he is searching for signs of pain that aren't physical.

"Does it hurt?" he repeats, with a gentleness that makes me shove his hand aside.

"I'm fine," I say, aware that what I say, and my hand that fends him off, are quashing his gentleness. I struggle to my feet, pushing the stranger still farther aside.

The stranger's name is David and finally, because he is persistent and because I am alone, I let him bring me home in a taxi. I see my father looking helpless, what I saw in the window for the first time this morning. David towers over him. He's tall and thin, everything within reach of his long arms; my father is short and square, empty-handed. "Dave," my father calls him right off, to trim him down to size.

"It's David," I chide, as if to someone else, not my father. When my father looks up through new thick glasses, his eyes are jittery circles where there used to be oval calm. I thank David and show him the door we haven't stepped away from. We haven't had a visitor since Setsuko stopped coming.

This David calls me on the phone again and again. Afterwards, not a word is exchanged between my father and me. It's business as usual but he makes a point of showing his face, those changed eyes behind glass, which I choose to ignore.

"Miyo? Is that you?" The sound of David's voice, my name coming through the line, a simple sound, the person it summons; it's a different me. I have to pause to hear it, to wait for my father to disappear into the next room.

"Yes," I answer after seconds pass, "it's me."

In spite of what my father's silence tells me, I go. Nothing to lose, I say, though this David may be playing a cruel joke. I know that. I try to think of the man as a wily child because I know wily children. "Stay back," my father used to warn me whenever they came close. It wasn't because he was ashamed; he could have despised me just for being alive. He saw me for what I was and still he took care of me, fed me, helped to dress me because I was clumsy, not used to my body. I had to learn how to coddle its weak parts, to compensate for my left with my right. When the boys in the playground jeered at me, he chased them off with a branch and called them mutts. He protected me, and I learned. "Think you're prettier?" he yelled at them. "Go home!"

Sooner or later David will show himself. That much I know as I sit with him in a dimly lit restaurant. Anything more I can only imagine. I imagine he chose dimly lit on purpose. I make myself look into his eyes just as steadily and deeply as he did in mine, daring him to flinch from me. I search for the slightest glimmer but find nothing. He does most of the talking. He's in human resources, he tells me. He meets a lot of people. His hands are clasped, his slender fingers interlaced like tall people embracing. "You learn to read them," he says, "what's below the surface. What's behind them." I give a backward glance at whatever might sneak up on me. He laughs at my little joke. "I mean their past. What resources people use to survive a situation." I nod to let him know I understand.

The other day on the subway platform, he saved my resources, however inhuman they may have seemed coming out of my mother's womb. It was a blessing that she died, I've always told myself.

"How did she die?" David leans in very close, scanning for the hurt, as before. Like a doctor pricking my skin, probing for patches that aren't numb, that can be cut out and grafted. "In an accident," I say, "not long after I was born." That's the little story I tell him. I don't tell him that my birth was the accident.

"I have a good feeling," David tells me when we part. He takes off his leather glove to shake my hand. I give him mine and, as I do, see that my glove is still on.

A good feeling. I think about this phrase over and over as I lie in bed. I try to sleep but the words roll back and forth on a thick carpet in my head until I hold myself; I squeeze and stroke, my body grasping for their meaning. Something has begun and there is no going back. Inside me, tiny flaps swell open and don't quite close.

David calls and again we meet. This time a movie, an old one in black and white at a theatre where the seats sink low to the floor and make my buttocks ache. A plump woman with thick eyebrows and a cruel mother is transformed once the mother dies. "Oh, Jerry, don't let's ask for the moon," she implores her married lover, "we have the stars." Just then David's hand lands on mine like a friendly furless animal that is warm and sweaty. It's different from my father's touch, his dry callused hand on my back, rubbing my sore spots. I feel David looking at me in the dark as the unwished-for moon flickers on the screen. He's seeing how I am feeling this, a man's hand on mine for the first time. I like his moistness on my skin, as if his friendly animal is breathing, resuscitating mine, as if something intricate and chemical is going on between our palms. I turn to him and smile as the moon fades, not knowing if he's seen, then cover my silly smile with my other hand.

In a café, we sit by a wall of mirrors. "Can I take your order?" the waitress asks her reflection. She serves us guided by what she sees in the glass. It's a special trick, the constant challenge of placing cups and saucers just so and reversing your first impulse. I like how she greets herself smilingly each time she returns with more coffee.

David seems not to notice until the girl misses and tips the coffee onto me. She gives a startled cry and our glances meet in the mirror. Instantly David is crouched by my side as before, this time with a napkin, blotting the spreading stain. Dabbing gently, he must feel through the napkin how small and diminished my breast is beneath my blouse, and yet how responsive. I draw away but find myself red-faced in the mirror, the warmth stealing up and, at the same time, a shiver at my nipple. David returns to his seat, careful with the hand that has touched my breast.

I wait for the wily child, the boy in the playground to come out and jeer, the one who has uncovered your terrible, ugly secret to give to the world.

❤

David tells me about the people who come to him, who sit in his visitor's chair and talk about themselves. What their strengths are. "What do they say?" I ask.

"Oh, getting along with others, taking the ball and running with it, that sort of thing." It's not so much David's words that draw me but the lull of them, his mastery of the world they come from. Then he asks the visitors their weakness. "This is the most important question," he says. "The answer tells you everything." He smiles knowingly. "If they're smart, they'll describe a weakness that is actually a strength. They'll say, 'Well, Ms. Mori, I've been told I work too hard.'"

A moment passes in which his smile falters and he reddens. "No," he says, shaking his head and waving his hand as if erasing a blackboard. "No, that's not true." He peers at me and in this shadowy drooping light I can picture him older, his cheeks slouching close to each side of his long thin nose, his eyes sloping down at the far corners, kindly and sad. "They stopped asking that question years ago because everyone knew how to answer."

David reaches for a lock of my hair and brushes it back from my temple and the dip there. "You see, Miyo?" Our eyes meet and his grow dim, mirroring mine. "You hardly notice it," he says. "Your hair suits you like this." He brushes strands with his fingers, those long slender people sliding the length of my hair, gently busy, and I close my eyes, let them do what they want to.

David is growing accustomed to how quiet I am, believing that he is coming to know me, that this partic-ular silence of mine is me, whole and complex—and maybe it is. At the end of the evening, sitting in his car in front of the house, I glance up at the empty window as my final destination. The words *thank you* and *good night* are on my lips, waiting for him to taste and swallow them whole. Instead, he gives my hand a moist squeeze and says the words himself.

One night, before he can drive off, my father comes onto the porch and waves at David.

"Come in," he barks. "Sit down." He watches David come up the driveway and into the house. He's searching for defects, wondering what the man wants with me, doubting that he would take care of me properly or at all.

David knows to be quiet; maybe he's already picked that up from me. When my father leaves the room, he studies the old photograph of my teenaged mother visiting my father in that schoolyard in Japan long before they married. My mother stands neatly, expectantly, hands clasped behind her back. I expect David to mention her, her beauty.

"Your father fought in the Japanese army?" David asks. I shrug at the photo that has sat in our living room for as long as I can remember. It strikes me that my father's brief utterances have begun to sound like commands lately.

"Not fought," I say, just as my father returns and sets down a tray of green tea and beer. He takes the picture out of David's hands and without a word replaces it on the cabinet. He sits apart from us, close to the television because of his bad eyes, and flicks between a baseball game and the news. Before long, he stands abruptly, signalling the end of the evening.

I walk with David down the empty crumbling driveway back to his car. My father's Chevrolet is parked in the garage now, rakes and shovels piled around it. Our footsteps echo beneath a starless sky. There's a sliver of a moon. David slips into the car, rolls down the window and leans out. *We can't have the stars tonight*, I'm tempted to say, when I hear the screen door scrape open and see my father's shadowy figure raise a hand. "Goodbye," he calls to David, who waves back.

"Your father must have a strong sense of duty, being in the Japanese army, don't you think?" David waits for a moment but I don't answer. "Is it me or is he always like that?" he asks anxiously, and I'm reminded of his sweaty palms, his small breathing animals: the wet that doesn't go with the dry.

"It's him," I say, "not you." I surprise myself with that. Overhead, one dot of light pierces the clouds. I hear the screen door drag shut, realizing my father's been there until now. I lean forward with my eyes closed so I'll only feel, not see. It shocks me, this soft rim of flesh meeting mine, the roiling wetness; that there is nothing between us, only the slick dark air inside his mouth and mine, sour but sweet, a faint taste and the tiny rivets on his tongue.

David calls the next morning, and as I hear him talking I try to imagine the movement of his lips. But then "Miyo," he whispers and I remember. I like the sound of my name, because it now has a taste and a texture.

David asks again about my father, what it's like between us. What my father thinks of him and if he said anything about last night. "He didn't say a word," I reply.

"Is he kind to you?" David suddenly asks. "Does he ever tell you he loves you?"

I want to tell him how silly his questions would sound in our house. I glimpse my father at the window looking out. His shoulders have grown sloped and rounded like a woman's without me noticing. He could never carry me now. David's words linger like sweet candy on a tongue that craves salt. Abruptly my father turns to face me, his glasses off. I'm not sure how much he sees with or without them.

"Miyo? Did you hear me?" David isn't content with my silence, not this time. I should try to explain, to enumerate the things my father has done for me day in and day out as far back as I can remember—a man alone, saddled with a needful infant. Things I don't have a name for.

But in fact I do, David has given it. Duty, he called it. His strength that is a weakness. All these years, I have been my father's duty.

"I love you," David suddenly whispers into the phone. I want to laugh but can't. My eyes fill hotly, in shock, gratitude. I don't know what else.

That night David and I have sex for the first time. The half-moon casts a sickly, bluish light through his bedroom window. I am grateful when David closes the drapes and turns out the lamp on his night table. When he takes my clothes off I shiver. I try to explain how new this is to me, but "It's all right," he whispers, touching me with lips that seem strange again.

Go home, I half expect David to say as I struggle to stand straight in the dark before him. *I made a mistake.*

But he doesn't. He lays me down carefully on the bed and cradles my right breast; then, as if to prove himself to me, he licks the hollow in my chest by my left. I feel the chill his tongue leaves behind, as if my skin glistens with his spit. He traces the scar down my side that has grown with the rest of me, from surgery as an infant, his tongue like the knife I have no memory of. Every so often he pauses to see if I'm all right. I can't help but feel a terrible dread that makes me want to rush on.

He prods my legs open with a tongue that's become a muscular animal, prodding until I feel my hole gaping, hurt and burning. I know what's coming. When he tries to push his penis in, I swallow my scream. It won't go in and he keeps whispering in my ear, "It's all right, it's all right," and all I can do is count in my head. Until I give in to my own animal's instinct and ease myself to the left, and he veers to the right along my crooked passageway. In the dark I hear him groan as he moves up and down, see-sawing through my middle. It hurts but it would hurt more not to be filled, and I let myself go with the way of nature, I lift my legs as if the ground is rushing under me and I'm in the air. I hitch them up onto his shoulders, him helping with the left, and in the dark I can't see them the way I did the day he saved me, I can't see that thin raggedy one. "Say something," he coaxes, moving and plunging. I hear my voice, a surprise, words that make no sense, noises from my mouth. "You sound beautiful," he sighs. "You look beautiful." I imagine his eyes wide open, drinking in what light there is in the dark, but I can't see. I hear the count; I'm marching away, faster and faster.

He collapses on me for a few moments, drained and heavy, his head next to mine. His curls are on my cheek, a funny tickle. He rouses himself and starts to pull away but I grab hold of him, it feels unnatural to come apart just yet. It feels to me the way we were meant to stay, a puzzle corked together. "Don't," I say, and clamp my legs tight around him, "please," and I don't let him go. We stay like that for some time, until I feel a widening cave between our bodies and the sweat chilling his; he wants to be let go. When he pulls his penis out of me, I feel pried open and frayed, never to be closed. Nothing the same.

"How are you?" David whispers, as if someone besides ourselves might overhear. He draws my hand across his mouth and I feel his teeth slick on my fingers. I nod my head to tell him I'm all right.

In the night I wake to find him tugging at me and I push him away. He turns on the light. He looks frightened. "You were crying out," he says. "Like you were hurt."

"What did I say?" I finger my mouth. It's dry. My jaw feels achy. My leg numb, as often happens. I take a deep breath and jiggle it until the sensation comes back, first in pins and needles.

"Your father. You were crying, 'Daddy.' I couldn't make out the rest." He's looking at me in that way again, watching for my pain. "What was it?"

It was my dream, the one I had as a child. I'd wake up screaming because my leg was gone, the right one, the good one. Someone had sawn it off in the night, because I felt nothing there except an unbearable coldness. The door would open and I'd see my father dart toward me, lit up in his underwear by the hallway chandelier. He'd throw back the covers and slap my leg, rubbing and slapping until it stung and I screamed, "No Daddy! This one, the right one!" because it was the left he was slapping; always he went for the left, no matter how I cried. "Daddy," I finally sobbed, relieved because it was the left one after all and the numbness had passed, from the sting of his slaps.

"Now get up," he would order, yanking me out of bed, into the air, onto my spindly mismatched legs. I cried out again, because of the pummelling at my heart, the stomping of boots inside my chest that wouldn't stop. I pounded back to make it stop. He grabbed my thrashing hand, my right, and put it to my throat; the left he brought to his throat, clamping my fingers around the trunk of it. It was almost still, like the pulse of the ocean, and I was on the shore watching its surface. "See?" was all he said, and it was true, my heart was in a lull. The stomping, the pounding heart belonged to somebody else, to the dream, just like my right leg which I thought had been sawn off.

My father would march me around the bed, stepping high, swinging the arm that wasn't propping me up. Round and round my room: *ichi ni, ichi ni,* one two, one two, he made me chant with him until the blood was looping from my right leg to my left, my heart was beating like my own and I ached from exhaustion. Then he let me fall back into bed and sleep through the morning, missing school.

"Miyo." David is shaking me, not letting me sleep. "Tell me what it was."

I open my eyes. "Just a dream."

"Does he hurt you?"

"My father?" I shake my head and giggle. It's the dream's exhaustion and David's accusation all at once.

I've never laughed in bed, not in my own, and I've never been in anyone else's. It's the most luxurious mixed-up sensation, laughing in this bed under these strange-coloured sheets; the pulsing between my legs. "No, no," I tell him. David stares, not quite believing. Instantly the laughter empties; the pleasure drains from me. "How could you say that?" Only my father would do all those things for me, silently, like a good soldier. I throw off David's hands and the covers and run into the hall. What drips down my leg feels red, feels like blood.

"Miyo, I'm sorry, " David calls, following me down the hall to the bathroom door.

The overhead light is bright, lighting up everything. I close the door and bring my face close to the mirror. It looks different, sloppy, my mouth that has been kissed for the first time. I watch myself cup my breast, the one that had no chance to blossom. I do what I haven't done in years, not since high school, those hours hiding in a cubicle waiting for the flush of toilets, the slam of doors, the squeak of the taps, the place emptied out, and my own breathing. I stand on tiptoe and put one hand over the dent in my temple, what David says hardly shows; with the other I cover the hollow under my breast. My game of if-only, of peek-a-boo-I-see-you, and the you in the mirror is not especially pretty or ugly, but is whole and healthy and not so different from any other girl, from that waitress who smiles at herself in the café. Alone in the school washroom, I'd mouth words I could barely say aloud out in the hall, limping past a boy with curls like David's; simple hellos and chatter and smiles that were tossed up all around me, casual, to the sky.

David starts knocking, softly at first. There is a slow stream down my inner thigh, like the tip of a finger drawing a line—of blood, because I can feel the spot it comes from inside me, where I've been cut loose. But when I look it's colourless, like glue, translucent, wormy traces.

"Miyo," David calls from the other side, "I didn't mean to upset you." I hear his hand sliding on the door.

"I know." How can I explain that there was only him, always, to comfort me or hurt me, to keep me alive? I think of my father at home, that I haven't called to say I won't be home, that he shouldn't wait up, not now or ever again.

"I love you, Miyo," David says. What my mother might have cooed to me, had she lived and made everything different. I touch my inside thigh, I smell the goo on my fingertips and put them to my mouth with a terrible craving. I lean into the door that separates my body from David's. "Miyo," he whispers, still there, still waiting for me on the other side. He taps again with his knuckles, those long slender fingers like people huddling.

At the edge of the drapes sunlight bleeds in, and as David sleeps I examine the portraits on his night table: a woman who is a younger, softer him, with three little daughters, pale flowers in a garden. An old man, as old as my father, with white hair, tall and thin like David, stooped, his eyes not like David's at all, but large and glistening with a story in a glance.

The light bleeds out and I sleep. Days are lost, but inside the room and inside the bed everything is saved, my new possessions. David brings food in and we eat out of each other's mouths, another new thing for mine. My tongue foraging under his, our teeth clinking. He plants his mouth on my belly and I feel his smile tickling as it spreads, the slippery hardness of his teeth, his saliva. I start to giggle, my stomach rising; he sucks and bites and makes me giggle more, I can't stop, I'm hysterical. This feeling of drowning in these sheets; I love the sound of the screeching laughter that comes from my new mouth.

Finally the smells that come back at me, his and mine, are overwhelming. I start to see a darkening pattern in the stains on the too warm, too limp sheets, and as I lie under him our bodies are sprawling stains too. He likes to hook his chin over my right shoulder when he holds me; already he's formed his habits. I wonder what mine are. He starts to mumble with his face buried in the pillow, so I don't quite hear or see him, I only feel his penis stirring in me. He lifts his face slightly from the pillow to peer at me. His face is different, fearful, as if, for the first time, he can't find the words.

"The way you sounded," he says. "I just want to be sure."

"It was a dream!" I shout. I shove him off me and when his penis slips out, I feel emptied and panicked. I hear the counting, my daddy holding me up, keeping me alive, saving me.

"But the photograph," David says, still quiet. On the pillow beside me there's his spit, his teeth marks. "The uniform. Do you know what those men did?"

"He was just a boy," I say, my shout died down. David pulls me to him and I remember my black pouch that was never recovered, still dangling off the subway car, undetected. I imagine it going on and on, one station to the next through the city, and inside, the details of my life I'd have liked to keep to myself.

"Miyo, don't go," David groans the next morning as he tries to pull me back into bed.

"I'll be back." I give him a smile. I won't let him drive me; I'll take the subway.

"Don't go," he says again. "Stay here." I haven't heard him like this before, quite so foolish and plaintive. He helps me dress, kissing each part before it's tucked away. For a moment, my breast in his hand that is sweaty and holding tight, I sense him measuring how strong he is by how weak I am, and I feel like a rabbit's foot, with tiny breakable bones he can finger beneath the fur.

When I get there, the street is quiet; it's a Sunday morning. It's that sunny quiet that makes my footsteps clear and crisp, without the echo that comes at night when the sky closes shut.

I knock first but there's no answer. The drapes are open, the living room is in disarray. I hear the radio buzzing, untuned. The lights are on, giving the sunlight that streams in an unnatural glow. I bring out my key and open the door.

Inside, I pick up the photograph from its place on the cabinet. I look at my mother first, as I always have—at her beautiful young face, her full breasts that weren't passed on to me. Somehow I know she is fourteen here. He might be eighteen, maybe nineteen, barely more than a boy in a schoolyard. For the first time I look closely at his uniform, what David saw. The jacket is creased at the shoulders—a little caved in, as if he was slight for his age, sickly even. His face is so thin and small I don't recognize him as my father at all. At the bottom of the photograph—what I've never noticed, or recalled noticing—is the date, 1943, seared in white.

I hear my father's slow footsteps coming down the stairs. In a moment he's in front of me, standing there, undemanding, his face still and expressionless: a silent soldier. Not like the young man in the photograph smiling at his lovely friend, those weapons at his belt decorations to impress her. I realize then that I can't ever picture my father as a boy in a far-off land; only as a man, not young or old, but strong, when he carried me up the steps of my school a mile and a half down the road.

TWO

IN THE WEEKS before her father died, Miyo was sleeping deeply and long, as if each night were winter solstice. She rarely woke in darkness while David slept—as she had before, when things were new—to grope for the mattress edge, a reassuring comfort from the years in her single bed. It could all seem strange and stifling and intoxicating. By morning, she had slipped back into his arms. She was growing more and more used to it, the touching, the stickiness of flesh on flesh; the fleeting sensations of heat and cold, of another heartbeat passing from his body to hers, as if in halves. The feelings of excitement became familiar, though no less changeable.

She now knew David's morning habits by heart: how he shed his pyjamas and folded them with care while standing naked and oblivious by the window before stepping into his briefs; how he put on his socks before his pants, left then right, pulled to just under his knees. There went the swish of his pants sliding off the hanger, the friendly clink of his belt buckle; the cluck of his tongue when he checked himself in the mirror—noises of daily life with him.

This morning, the bed dipped with his weight. "Love you," he whispered, not the first time. His lips hovered over her eyelids; she could read the words there branded with his breath. He was waiting. She could only giggle sheepishly.

But before leaving the bed, he smoothed her hair away from her face, exposing the slight dip the size of a quarter at her temple; the gesture grown into a new habit. He smoothed the hair over and over until Miyo opened her eyes and sat up. He tugged her hair just a bit too hard. It didn't hurt but she winced, and his hands flew off. He looked at them; they were to blame. "I'm hurting you," he finally said, more to himself. Maybe he was making sure that she, in her silence, belonged to him, and that things could be this simple and certain—her hair under his palms in this room in which they both slept; that his half of "love you" was enough to last to the end of the day, when they would be back at home, together.

Many times she was on the brink of telling him that she loved him too. The words were in her mouth, her heart gaping and, between her legs, the pulsing, ready for him. Hadn't he changed everything? She could laugh at her desire, even coax and nurse it, because the ache would no longer have to burn on, unfillable. Yet a part of her hung back, alone. Was it a corner of her heart, her mind? Was it that she'd waited for so long, and grown used to that space between herself and what she craved?

The night she moved in with him, they went to the café that had become their place. They sat alongside the mirrored wall, at their table. David confided his tales of past love, what new lovers do; how things would be as good but better—different from all that had come before. She confessed that she had no offering in return—only a child's past with her father—but told his reflection, unable to look him in the eye. As if he hadn't guessed the first time he saw her. In the glass his eyes looked shimmery and sad, but exhilarated. "Don't be sorry," he said.

"Don't go," she said now, to his back, as he stood up to get his shirt from the closet. "The early worm," he said brightly. She knew he was smiling at his own little joke. He insisted on leaving before her, on her making her own way to work: as much a discipline for him as for her. Still, she couldn't shake the feeling of losing him each day to the outside world. The clients who waited twenty minutes apart in ruled columns in his appointment calendar—who were they all? He'd sat her in the seat they sat in, two inches lower than his across a wide teak desk. The tall window with the city fanning out behind him. *Don't go*, she thought, echoing his words to her not so long ago, when neither was certain she'd come back. She pulled him back down and to her and quickly, with the ease of knowing where things belong, unzipped his pants and tried to push his limp penis inside her.

"No, Miyo, no." He was laughing but she couldn't help hearing his first "no" to her. The first time she'd acted without waiting for him. He slipped away but then he came back and sank onto the bed; she caught his penis in her mouth, and almost instantly it was sprung. It didn't quite feel natural yet, and the taste was too salty or musty for morning—a taste she hadn't yet found a word for—but she didn't mind at all.

Finally he pulled her up, and was tasting his own mustiness in her mouth. *You do love me,* she thought.

Work, like everything else, was the same but different. The lone smoking squatter had disappeared. She experienced a twinge of guilt for the empathy she no longer felt for that figure who'd crouched in the canyon between buildings, glimpsed only by her, or so it seemed. Maybe it was just the fallish weather, the recent creeping cold in the air, that had sent him into hiding.

She picked up the phone to call David. The other line lit up just as she was dialing. It had to be David, calling at the same exact moment. Because so many of her thoughts and feelings were now connected to him—one for one, like his fingers stretched out and his moist palm held to hers. Nothing was too inconsequential to be shared. Wasn't this love?

But when she picked up, before hello, there was the tug of another connectedness. The voice sounded odd because it had been so long, and because they'd rarely spoken by phone. It was far away and small.

"Daddy," she said, shrinking to a little girl again, smaller than his small. "How are you?" Even that sounded too grown-up.

He cleared his throat. "Good, good," he answered. "You?"

"I'm fine too, Daddy." She heard herself: *Daddy, Daddy,* echoing in that empty house. Then silence, nothing more to be said.

"I'll come after work, okay Daddy?" she said finally.

"Good, good," he said again, saying that much more than usual, and it worried her. The line clicked loudly when he hung up, but she stayed on, hearing herself breathe over the dial tone, wondering how she had ever gotten away.

Even in the dark the houses were familiar, shaped or painted like the people inside, their names or something about them. Had she expected them to change, or expected herself to have forgotten them, after only a few months away? She wanted to feel that years had passed. She wanted to feel she would've never come back. She wanted a marker of change in herself: something as simple as a stick in the ground that had once dwarfed her, that she could now tower over. But there was the house of the boy who gave homemade valentines to the pretty girls with its coral-pink door: Timmy Doyle, remembered for the white doilies he mounted with red hearts. Cindy Chase had lived in the house with the mottled stone front, and taunted Miyo down the block with her festering hands chafed with eczema, held high in the air. Miyo had no fear of oozing cankers, only of being caught, the two facing each other's disfigurement.

Now she crossed the intersection where the telephone repairman was electrocuted one afternoon while everyone was at work or school. She used to linger there, trying to imagine when no trace remained and only the news on TV told them such a thing had happened in their neighbourhood. The same with the house whose furnace exploded in the night. In class the next day, Johnny Gabley told of rushing out in his pyjamas just as fire trucks roared to the scene. Yet the house looked the same from the outside, intact.

They were all grown up and gone, though their aging parents might remain. There was the house with the gnarled pine in front, stunted, its branches twisting around themselves instead of reaching skyward. The white stones around the base sparkled in the street light, but candy wrappers, bottle shards and dead pine needles had collected there too. The house was dark. A Japanese couple had lived there with their son, younger than her. As a boy he'd been sullen; she'd seen him pee on the stones under the tree, not knowing she was there watching—or maybe because she was. His parents were both stocky and short and walked the neighbourhood after dark, as if consigned to it. Miyo's father shunned them when they passed with their timid glances and tentative smiles. Once they came to the door, but he refused to answer. *I'm not one of them,* he said, and she peeked out the window after they'd left. As a child, she'd seen a few other Japanese faces in the neighbourhood— though she couldn't always tell if they weren't Chinese or Korean, except if she heard a snippet of their talk and recognized the accent.

They disappeared one by one, those families, moved to the new suburbs, to one-storey or split-level bungalows with space they could afford. She was envious sometimes of their escape, and missed seeing their faces on the street. When she was alone and still young they smiled kindly, as if the smile wasn't just for her but entrusted for her father, and it felt like charity or, worse, pity. She found herself watchful, crossing the street when she saw them coming.

But that had been long ago; surely she was bolder these days. Standing at the door—her father's, her own

until recently—Miyo was afraid that he wouldn't open it
to her, that she'd become one of the *them* he wasn't a part
of. She didn't dare use her key, which by now felt old and
extra, like a useless baby tooth. When he opened the
door he looked aged, and angry that she'd knocked and
not simply walked in as if nothing were different.

The place was messy as never before. There were
piles of things in each corner of the room, the mess in
some kind of regimented order known only to himself, a
schema, what the inside of his head might look like. She
shuddered.

"He looking after you?"

Miyo studied her father, trying to make out why he
seemed suddenly old. "Is he?" he prodded. She stifled a
sour laugh at the irony, the sadness of it all. She began
picking up things here and there, straightening yellowed
newspapers into a neat pile. He was watching, seeing
that her limp had lessened, that she was stronger without him. There was a smell about him, like vinegar. It
was on the shirt she made him take off as she gathered
laundry to load into the machine downstairs. It was difficult seeing the slowness of his movements, and his
sunken chest, which she hadn't glimpsed in years; it
might've gotten worse since she'd left. Could it have
been that long?

Upstairs, she went to strip the bed; the sheets were
twisted and wrung, half pulled to the floor as if antici-
pating her. When she came down, he was still sitting
where she had left him on the couch, without his shirt.

"Have you eaten, Daddy?" Stupidly, she hadn't thought
to bring food. He'd always done the shopping, kept the
freezer full with portioned meals he prepared ahead of

time. But now the freezer was empty, bearded with frost. She peered into the ice trays dusted with breadcrumbs.

Her father shook his head and let himself be cared for, for the moment at least. He'd let her see that it was he who needed her this time. Hastily she took out cereal for him, all she could find, added some milk that smelled all right and brought it to the living room. He pushed it aside angrily, pointing with his thick fingers. "In there," he shouted, "in there!" Because food was to be eaten properly, at the kitchen table, as always.

He ate amid the din of the washing machine rising from the basement. The spoon seemed too big for his mouth, which trembled, open and waiting for it—had she never noticed before? The house was suddenly filled with that morning sound, what she used to wake to in broad, streaming sunlight, what helped her up out of bed with its purposeful rhythm. She felt better but nauseated too, hearing the chug-chug rise out of the dark, dank basement when it was night. Her new-found strength sickened her, as did the squeal of the chair legs when she rose abruptly, finding that she could not stay a moment longer.

Swept inside the revolving doors of the subway station, Miyo fell against a cool tiled wall to catch her breath. Only then did she remember David. She hadn't told him she was going. He would have searched, waited for her and searched more, wondering how he could have missed her. It was nearly eight o'clock. She thought of calling but instead rushed down to the trains. She went to the last car, as she would have if she'd kept their date, knowing that by now he would've given up and gone home. In a way, she was relieved to have missed him. It made her nervous meeting up on the subway, instead of at home. He'd made it into a little game, testing the fate that had brought them together.

She hadn't understood that the first time, months ago in September, when he'd called her at work at the end of the day. "Wait on the southbound platform at six o'clock. Let two trains go by, then get on the one that comes after," he'd instructed. She'd giggled at him sounding so mysterious. They'd synchronized their watches and he had hung up before she could say anything more. She'd hurried to the station and waited for the third train to come. She got on, crushed and carried by the rush-hour crowd. He'd never said which car to get on, how or when they'd meet. Miyo remembered the sensations of being inside that crowded car: the ceiling fans swirling air that was too warm for fall; no seats, just faces pressed in close. And then the train stalled between stations. She wanted only space and coolness, and leaned against the door with her cheek to the glass; on the other side a grizzled dead end faced her, the wall of the tunnel. Her side had begun to ache, her stomach was empty; she cursed David's stupid game. She wanted off.

Tonight the train was empty and cold as it pulled into St. Andrew station, near David's office. The platform was empty too and she felt relieved. She wanted the ride to go on: no one waiting for her, no one for her to await. For the first time, she contemplated a life alone with some relish: to neither need nor be needed; to not love in desperation.

When she had tried to meet him that time in September, this platform had been lined with commuters waiting to get onto the already packed train. She'd tried to get out but, before she could, the doors had shut. A kindly man had smiled and shrugged his shoulders as if to say, *Tough luck,* and the train had surged ahead. Miyo pictured herself as she'd been that evening: exhausted by the crowds, as overwhelmed as on her first time in the subway, when she'd been helped by David. She'd watched station after station left behind, and the passengers who'd reached the platform too late. But David could never be late; he was always where he said he would be. Intention means nothing, he often said.

And all of a sudden he'd appeared, rushing up alongside the train. The whistle squealed, the doors began to close and he flung his arm between them, all in a second—his one arm and leg planted inside, his other half, swinging a briefcase, stuck outside. She almost shrieked, almost laughed. The conductor bellowed and the doors opened and he pulled himself in. He faltered as the train jerked and started, but steadied himself. There was David: red-faced, askew, rumpled David among the drab and sullen commuters. She watched him scour the crowd for her, waiting for him to find her—her own test of fate. His eyes were a little desperate. Not the calm, collected David she knew.

When he found her, he bounded up, tripping over briefcases, feet, jostling other passengers. "I found you!" he said, like a boy winning at hide-and-seek. He pulled her close. Under his coat, he was sweating. She felt the damp heat, his heart thudding and her own catching up. "Hello, you." His voice was shaky, his breathing quick and shallow. They rode south around the loop that night, passed their stop and crossed back over at Bloor, wordlessly hand in hand. When their stop came the second time, David lifted her over the gap before the doors shut. He held her waist tight. That was when she finally understood the game. She understood that he'd wanted to feel what she felt: the peril of her lameness, and the relief.

But now, tonight, he wasn't coming. Now she was arriving into the station—their station—on an empty train without him. She glanced down as she stepped out. The gap looked bigger than she remembered. This wide, David had shown her, with his hands precisely parted. He'd made her practice with her lame leg, putting chalk marks on concrete in the park across from his apartment, applauding when she crossed the finish line. The gap was dark and wide and deep, and a slender soul, lame or not, could slip down into it, beyond rescue.

"I'm sorry," she said when she came in. Three hours late—he'd been ready to call her father. He'd picked up the phone and dropped it more than once. He'd contemplated the police.

"Where were you?" He tried to sound casual.

"I'm sorry," she repeated. "Were you waiting long?" There was a hint of something new, of guile, defensiveness.

"It's all right," he said. He smiled but she'd gone into the kitchen and was checking the refrigerator for something to cook. She hadn't noticed the frying pan on the stove or the pungent garlic in the air. "I figured I'd missed you and came home," he called out.

"I checked every train," he added under his breath. He didn't mean for Miyo to hear, but she did. "I'm so sorry,

David," she said, at his side now, where she belonged. She hugged him. Her coat was still on, that cherry-red coat that had first caught his eye. He saw himself on the platform, exhausted and panting as another train left the station, and no red coat, no Miyo. "I was afraid that you—"

"He's old," she blurted, loosening her embrace. She sank down onto the couch. "He's lonely."

"Did he say that?" Of course her father wouldn't. That was how he'd kept her close all these years. Never saying what she wanted to hear. She shook her head.

"How did he look?"

She shrugged, to mean all right, or not so good.

"He needs a hobby." He knew he was sounding like a social worker. "He needs—"

"Hobby," she repeated. "Sounds like a pet." David looked at her. She got up and went to the mirror in the hall and studied herself. "I was his hobby."

It was the first bit of sarcasm he'd heard from her. He'd tasted the fear, the melancholy, the loneliness on her lips, but all that was sweet, never quite bitter. She hardly looked at herself ever. No makeup, a quick brush through her hair in the morning, a dab of colourless lipstick, nothing more. That was why the coat, the red, had been so surprising. "Your father bought this?" David asked. He brushed his palms across her shoulders and the coat's strained seams.

She nodded. "It used to be so pretty."

He phoned her at work the next afternoon and was told she'd called in sick. He came home to find her as he had left her, in bed, eyes wide open to the ceiling.

"I'm all right," she said, sitting up abruptly. Her breath was rank, her mouth slick when he kissed her. She pulled away, covering her face. "I'm sorry," she blurted and scrambled to the bathroom. She slammed the door when he came near. When he knocked and called out, the shower came on, full blast. But when the telephone rang, Miyo swung open the door, wet and dripping, with raised red welts over her breasts where she'd scrubbed herself. She had that condition, a skin sensitivity. It didn't hurt, she'd assured him the first time they made love by day, but it unsettled him to see her marked by his touch, as if he'd been brutal. The ringing stopped, then started up again immediately.

"Don't answer," she said. "Please." He guessed that it might be her father, that she truly was afraid of him, as he'd always suspected.

"What is it?" he asked, but she merely stood there in a puddle, tilted in a way that had endeared her to him. It wasn't coyness. He loved that she was vulnerable with each step, her body faithfully tethered to her heart. Though to her it was her body's constant betrayal.

Finally the ringing stopped. She drew him near and buried her face in his shoulder. He felt the dampness of her skin, and her breath tickling his ear. "I can't go back there." He felt the words reverberate from his own chest. She tugged his head back to look into his eyes. "He doesn't hurt me," she said, "that's not why." She pinched the skin at the back of his neck.

He nodded to say that he understood and he believed her.

"I can't go back." She burrowed into his shoulder again. "He'll want me to stay."

"I know," was all he could say.

The ringing started again, and she pulled him into the bathroom and shut the door. The shower was still running, raining down on the porcelain tub, drowning out the telephone. "You'll catch cold," he said, reaching for a towel to wrap around her. Before he knew it, he was pulled under the shower; Miyo was suddenly giggling, hysterical and his suit was clinging to him like a half-moulted second skin. "You're crazy," he said.

They sat on the floor eating sardines, in Disney T-shirts his mother had given him. She was Sleepy and he was Doc. His jacket and pants lay in a pool beside them. He didn't mind; an old girlfriend had bought them years before and he'd outgrown the style. The two of them laughed at it: a clown suit, funnier without the clown in it.

It was the middle of the night when the phone rang again. That was when he noticed the red light throbbing on the answering machine in the dark. He'd forgotten to check; later he'd play the messages left at intervals during the day, each the same but more urgent. The odour of sardines overwhelmed him when he switched on the light, as if he had to see to smell. He picked up the receiver before Miyo could stop him. "No, no," she murmured, sliding under the covers, pulling them over her head.

A woman's voice came on—"Miyoko!" it demanded and repeated; nothing else. He held the phone away, repelled; he'd never imagined her name as a sound so shrill. Still, he coaxed her out and put the receiver in her hand, to her ear.

"It's not him," he mouthed.

Moments later, when he'd put the phone back in its place, Miyo retreated under the thin floral sheet again, and he let his fingers climb the ladder of her spine, over rustling pink orchids, as she curled into a ball.

"He doesn't hear you," Setsuko said. Then again, louder: "He doesn't hear you."

It was because she kept calling, *Daddy, Daddy*, to wake him. Setsuko tried to pull her back from the bed but Miyo only edged closer to her father, straining to recognize his face, so shrunken and slack, as if beaten back to the bone by a strong wind. It was blank, too, missing a vital feature. It was his eyes that seemed gone, because they were closed and sunken in his face. There was a tube at his nose. She tried again: "Daddy!" He was just a mound, though there was a slight but steady rise and fall.

"Miyoko!" Setsuko said, the name that she'd always called her, that Miyo hated. She.clamped her elbow and pulled her back from the bed but Miyo resisted. "The doctor says he won't wake up," Setsuko said finally, and let go. Her voice was less harsh than on the phone.

Miyo leaned down to her father's ear. His skin draped in folds around it, suddenly cavernous, mysterious. She didn't quite know what to say. "Please, Daddy," she whispered after a moment. His eyes seemed about to flutter open at any instant, as if to say, "I'm your father, it's what I do!"—as he had before, except exhaustedly this time, because there was nothing more to be done.

David drew her away and she didn't resist. "He lied," she whispered into his ear, smooth and pale. "He lied," she repeated more loudly when they stepped out into the hall from the maze of white tents, sighing blipping machines and human groans. David's moist hand was groping at her mouth now, his eyes desperate as they had been on the subway, and his lips were saying, *Shush.* "Lied!" she said when his hand slipped away. It came back, that sweaty nervous animal hand, and she would swallow it whole. He jerked it away and there was a spot of red on his finger, growing.

"It's all right," he was saying. "It's nothing." She went with him back the way they had come, where the walls were yellow and it was busy and bustling but quiet. Slow and quiet down the hall, past the rooms on either side. Nurses gliding in and out around them, patients creeping close to the walls trailing their IVs, families huddled inside darkened doorways. They stared out of the dimness when she and David passed. She tasted blood on her lip. *No one will look after you like I do,* Daddy had always said, like a promise, or a threat.

They stepped out to waning daylight, a waft of smoke where workers clustered, and sallow patients in wheelchairs planted by the entrance.

"We'll come back," said David.

They went back to his apartment and he promised to wake her in an hour. When she opened her eyes, it was dark. David was slumped in the chair beside her, very still, his breathing barely perceptible. His sleep seemed so peace-filled; could her father's be like that too? The room was a jumble of shapes she barely recognized. It wasn't her home; she no longer had one. She felt numb, as if she didn't know herself. She wasn't Miyo; she wasn't Miyoko either.

It was through the wall between her bedroom and her father's that Miyo had often heard Setsuko call her that.

Miyo had pushed her bed right up to that wall. Not until late would her father answer Setsuko, when he thought Miyo was asleep. He always thought that if she didn't cry out, she was sleeping. *Miyoko is strong. She should be more on her own.* That much she had heard in English from Setsuko, prodding her father. Her name fashioned into a little lady's, more grown-up than she felt. Almost overnight the pain in her leg worsened, as if she'd willed it, then spidered up her side to her temple. She begged to stay home from school. Only her father could make it better, rubbing and kneading; only he knew how, and slowly he did. But the night before she was to go back, he and Setsuko went out, leaving her for just a bit, she was promised. It was a summer night, with the windows flung open, the red sun sinking in her room. She cried at being left behind until the next-door neighbours heard. She didn't answer when they knocked, then pounded at the door. Then the police arrived, a car and an ambulance, with sirens, the scream and the flashing red light winding down. A small crowd gathered on the driveway, some of them the neighbourhood Japanese who would soon vanish into the suburbs, having never been invited into their home.

Did they leave you by yourself? the sad-eyed policeman asked. There were laws against leaving an eight-year-old child alone. Her father and Setsuko soon arrived but Setsuko left by herself. The policeman questioned her father as though he were stupid or cruel or a criminal and, watching, Miyo tried hard to believe it, to keep from feeling bad.

David now sat up abruptly, as if wakened by her thoughts. "Tell me about Setsuko," she heard him say.

He flicked on the light. Instantly the table appeared, too close at her knees, too sharp at its corners; the chairs they sat in, their colours sickly to her in puce, mud, rust. Miyo wanted to say, *She's no one*, but Setsuko was once more someone.

"She was his girlfriend." David's shrivelled suit lay abandoned and damp on the floor, not really a suit any more. "She went away one night and never came back."

"What did you do, scare her off?" David was grinning, trying to be light.

But it was Setsuko's monstrous shoes that came into her head. She'd glimpsed them on the hospital-room floor hours ago; and years before, in the hall when Miyo came home from school, first on Fridays, then every day of the week. They were so wide that Miyo could fit her two feet into one, yet they teetered on a heel the size of her middle finger. Then, after that evening when the police came, they were gone.

"Yes," Miyo said, "I did scare her away."

As they walked through the hospital, the sky outside the windows had begun to lighten to a soft but unpretty grey that dulled the bright yellow walls of the corridor. It was almost four in the morning—the most desolate and wakeful time, David had once called it. Miyo had insisted on coming now, even if they were made to wait. It was the hour for lonely souls, which they were no longer, because they'd found one another. It was true that she'd wake at exactly 4:05 for nights on end, even as a child. That was when she'd hear the sounds through the wall, of her father with Setsuko—noises mingled with words she later realized were the Japanese her father never spoke by day, never in front of her. Only with Setsuko.

At reception, they said he'd been moved out of ICU. "Is that good?" Miyo asked David. He only shrugged, reaching for her arm, catching up.

"Don't run," he said.

She stopped at the doorway. "He might hear you," he said. "He might understand if there's something you want to say." He clasped her hand in his two. "He might feel it when you touch him."

"I never touch him," she said, but already David was leading her in.

Setsuko was there waiting, in a pink blouse that somehow looked familiar. Not from hours ago, but maybe years, though it couldn't be. "He asked for you," she blurted, and stood up. "He went, 'Miyoko, Miyoko.' Like that." Her large hand fussed near her mouth as her voice trailed off.

"You said he wouldn't wake up. The doctor, you said." Miyo felt her shoulders being squeezed, to quell her as before. She caught the warm smell that was David. Her heart was beating a little harder, faster.

The tube at her father's nose was gone. Maybe that was good. She hunched close to him, wondering where to rest her hand, where to touch, that he might feel; what to say that he might hear. There was a whistle when he breathed out, a faint tooting from his nostrils.

Setsuko sat back down in the chair by the window. She seemed on the verge of a smile. "Miyoko, Miyoko," she repeated.

"He never called me that."

"Be a good young lady, Miyoko," Setsuko murmured. "For your father, before he goes."

"What if he's not ready?" Miyo felt for his hand through the covers. She could feel the bumps of its bones, like a little carcass. His lips were thinned, curling under his teeth. She tipped a glass to them but the water only trickled down his chin. The whistle seemed to grow louder, then higher until it was pitchless, a wheeze, like someone drowning in air. "He can't breathe." Miyo said. "He needs the oxygen." She flailed around for David, who'd stepped back from her. "Doesn't he?" He only shook his head.

Setsuko stood up for an instant and wobbled on her heels, then slumped back down. "He said something else." She began to mumble. "He said, 'Tell Miyo, endure the unendurable.' That was his message to you." She looked to Miyo. "Nothing for Hana," she wailed, then stopped herself. "He forgets her."

Miyo waved her away. She'd never seen Setsuko like this, making no sense. "He needs air, he needs oxygen."

"He wanted it like this," Setsuko said. "He wants to go." She let herself sob in spurts, her face scrunching up, then smoothing out, as if she couldn't quite grasp and hold onto her grief. She clutched a stub of a pencil in one hand and a napkin crushed in the other. The coral polish on her nails was like the inside of seashells. "He said some other things. I wrote them down so you'll know what was in his mind at the end. You think you remember but you forget."

"No!" Miyo fumbled for the buzzer, her eyes not leaving her father. The rise and fall of his chest was barely there. "Call the doctor!" She looked to David; he stepped closer but didn't touch her. She dropped onto the bed and lay down alongside her father. Her body felt gross and heavy and heaving on the bed beside his, shrunken, still and almost soundless.

Setsuko read from the crumpled napkin. "I did not disgrace them, Setsu-san. I don't want to die but I will."

David touched Miyo's back. She sat up. Her father looked the way David had looked to her a short while ago: a soft swelling shape in the dark, before he woke up and turned on the light to make everything harsh and known.

"He wanted it like this so I told the doctor," Setsuko was saying and suddenly Miyo heard. "I don't understand. I'm his daughter," she said, feeling the button on the red coat she'd never taken off. "It's what I say." She was crying for him. *Don't leave me, don't!* rang in her head. But she couldn't look at him, she couldn't make him stay. "I'm his daughter," she cried, her eyes too full and stinging. She couldn't see him, or anything.

"Yes," Setsuko said, as she stood up dropping her hands, quiet and defiant. "But I'm his wife."

THREE

OUTSIDE BY THE DOORSTEP, someone had left a pot of white flowers wrapped in green foil. There was no card. A neighbour, maybe, who'd read of her father's death in the newspaper; the elderly couple down the street.

The few plants her father kept in the kitchen and living room had bowed and shrivelled at their tips even as frail new shoots sprouted. The hardy cactus that needed little water had withered too. Miyo hadn't wanted to come to the house but Setsuko had insisted. There were items to be thrown out, packed up, decisions to be made. Dust was everywhere. The house smelled old, of its own slough, having been closed up, unaired. Nothing of herself left behind. Setsuko threw back the drapes and opened some windows. It seemed wrong, her father dead only two weeks, but the air felt fresh.

Upstairs in her father's bedroom, Setsuko had stripped the bed down to the mattress. It sagged on the side next to the night table, where an old crossword puzzle from the newspaper lay. The carpet was worn at the spot where her father would've rested his feet on rising or retiring; there was a faint track to the closet, where the doors were thrown open and empty hangers dangled like unused instruments.

"Come. Sit," Setsuko said as she sat down herself on the edge of the bed. Miyo slunk to the floor. It felt wrong to sit on the bed where her father had lain alone those nights after Miyo had left him. It felt wrong to sit there beside Setsuko now that he was gone. It was the first time she'd been in her father's bedroom since she was a girl. Even then, she'd only stood at its threshold or, lying in her own bed next door when Setsuko was still in their lives, imagined what was happening inside.

Setsuko held a cardboard box in her lap. It was an old blue jewellery-store box that might have once held a gift, a porcelain bowl or two wine glasses. She held it possessively, close to her belly. "I found this in your father's closet," she said. She cracked it only partway open, as if something inside might escape, and carefully drew out a yellowed envelope. She held out a snapshot of herself with Miyo's father. Setsuko looked young, unrecognizably plain, fresh-faced with little makeup; not the way Miyo remembered her at all. She wore a plain powder-blue dress that her father might have picked out; blue was his favourite colour. She was clutching a bouquet of white chrysanthemums. He wore his grey Sunday suit, which they had just packed up with his other clothes and sent off to the Salvation Army. He had that young, early-morning, open-road look. He was smiling. It all flashed in Miyo's head—an impression from years back, a hidden something in spite of the rare broken-out smile: her father slipping out and returning late on a school night, which he seldom did even if he'd been out with Setsuko, in that suit he never wore. Without checking on Miyo, disappearing into his bedroom early. The closed door.

"I made him marry me," Setsuko declared, leaning down to her on the floor, close enough for Miyo to see the tears that refused to spill from her eyes. "But you see, Miyoko, he wanted to. He wanted me to push him, even if we couldn't be together. Do you understand?"

Instead of waiting for an answer, Setsuko slipped another picture out of the box and said, "This is Hanako. My Hanako. And your father's."

Maybe she had always known, because she felt no shock; she didn't know what she felt.

It was a Japanese girl in a navy-blue school uniform, hands clutching at pleats of her skirt at each side. Miyo noticed the legs, how straight and sturdy they were. She couldn't judge the face, if there was something recognizable in it. It wasn't exactly a pretty face, but it might have been, had the girl been smiling.

"Hana means flower," Setsuko said, and gazed at the picture lovingly. The girl looked healthy, strong; almost too robust for the name. "She was born when you were nine. After your father and I separated. For a long time I was jealous of you. Not for me, but for my Hana. Isn't that silly, to be jealous of a child?"

The first clear memories that Miyo had were from when she was eight. It was then that she'd brought the police to the house with her crying. Before that seemed blank or broken up. And it was when she turned eight, she was sure, that she could first begin to measure her own flaws and the cost of them with paining precision.

All without knowing that she had a yardstick to hold herself to: a sister.

There were more things in the box, letters maybe, more evidence that this person Hana existed. Miyo waited for Setsuko to show her more but she didn't. The two of them sat staring at the schoolgirl in the picture. Miyo eyed the box and the tips and edges of things poking out: a scrap with Japanese written on it, and a bit of red yarn spilling out as if from a knitting box. When Setsuko pushed the lid back down, Miyo was somehow relieved. It was not her box, and if her father had intended for her to see what was inside, he would have shown her. Already she was overwhelmed by the secrets he had left behind to be told by others. But this Hana was a person, living and breathing, linked to her, not simply some boxed memento.

"When will she come?" Miyo asked, unblinking. "When will I meet her?"

"Come here?" Setsuko said, incredulous. "No, no. She'll never come. You must go there with me, to Tokyo. That's what your father wanted."

David seemed panicked at first when she told him, as if it were his news, his half-sister, instead of her own. "I can't leave work, not now," he said. Miyo thought to protest, to beg him to come, but didn't. "Maybe if we wait for the summer," he told her. He looked at her across his desk, as she sat in his visitor's chair at his office.

"No, no," he said, watching her closely. "Summer is too late."

It was still there, the connecting thought for thought between them. As if sensing that too, David reached for both Miyo's hands and stood her up. She felt the moist pressure of his palms on hers. "Go meet your sister, Hana," he said.

At the airport, Setsuko stood some way off while Miyo and David parted. It was a late-night flight and the place was half empty. So little needed to be spoken. Miyo clung to him and thought she'd cry, but didn't. With a light smile, he cupped his hand behind his ear to tell her to call, but he needn't have; he knew that too. She pressed herself close to him one last time, as if to imprint his body on hers, then watched him disappear through the sliding doors into the night.

It was the dreaded hour of lonely souls, ten after four in the morning, when Miyo awoke. She had to remind herself of where she was, the strange bed, why David wasn't beside her; of the endless plane ride, her first; the strange sensation of being suspended impossibly high above the earth; the ghostly clouds at her window that she imagined walking on and falling through. Was it the time change—this side of the world revolved ahead—or was she reconvening with the sleepless of the world after only one day without David?

At the window, she watched the dark slowly lighten to the colour of ash over the jumbled rooftops; the sky was singed. She tried not to think of David. He would've been up all night, she knew; if she called, he'd pick up in barely a ring. He was missing her as much as she him; or more, because he was the one left behind. Setsuko wouldn't let her call from the house, promising to take her to a phone where the rates were cheap. It seemed a punishment, or callous thrift. She wanted simply to hear David's voice, and to hear her own with his.

His night, she realized, was just beginning to fall. She was one day ahead of him. They were out of step, no longer twinned.

The house was half empty, everything low to the ground, or not high enough. She bumped things with her knees and elbows and head. For the first time, she felt big. The sliding doors of paper and wood were light as air but laden with a musty scent. It was an old house, mostly wood; cool in the night, when she'd heard every sound outside, footsteps marching into her ear, but the thick, musty bedding Setsuko had left for her kept her warm and soothed her aches.

"It used to be a shack," Setsuko told her. That was right after the war, when thousands of repatriated Japanese came streaming in from all over Asia, some even born and raised there; some came from the United States or from Canada like Setsuko, seeing Japan for the first time. There were crippled soldiers, homeless families, maimed victims of air raids sleeping two or three to one mat. "This is Shitamachi," Setsuko told her. "The Lower City. You know, the wrong side of the tracks." This was where the barrack zones had been set up after the surrender, where shacks and tents had sprung up overnight. The whole area had been levelled by the firebombings; wood and paper houses gone up like kindling.

"Your father built this before I knew him," she said, "for him and your mother." He'd fixed it up little by little until they left for Canada. That was the father she knew: never to be, or long remain, one of the helpless;

he would work with what he was given, however scant, and carry on. For wasn't that how he'd managed to raise her?

A relative of Setsuko had lived in the house for the past few years and, as it deteriorated, had hammered on sheets of corrugated steel siding and fibreglass to keep it standing. Setsuko had stayed with him on her visits until, one day, he disappeared after quitting his lowly bank job. There were no traces of him in the house: no old snapshots, no shirts dangling in closets, no knick-knacks on windowsills. He'd left his belongings to scavengers. A year ago, a neighbour had spotted him sleeping on the street by the flophouses for itinerant labourers in nearby San'ya. "Nothing but men there," Setsuko warned. "Dirty old men who drink and gamble."

On the way to the subway station, Setsuko led Miyo across a long bridge that arched over a railway yard, blackened, deserted. They stopped to gaze out. Cables cut the sky, strung to sooty posts and signal-lights sticking up like rusted instruments. The yard was ugly and spread in all directions. Miyo glimpsed a pattern in the tracks and ties, the entangled spines of some creature; a prehistoric boneyard.

"Do you know what they call this bridge?" asked Setsuko. "Namidabashi. The Bridge of Tears. Back in the time of the samurai, criminals waved goodbye to their families before they were executed down there and left on the Street of Bones." She pointed behind them in another direction. "This is where I first came to in Japan"—she sighed heavily—"and here I am again."

"Then why did you come at all?" Miyo asked bluntly, unmoved. She couldn't help herself. Setsuko had cared so little for her those years ago, that much she remembered. She recalled her father telling her that Setsuko had been orphaned in the internment camp. He'd asked her to be kind, even when Setsuko was not. There were so few things he'd asked of her.

"We had no choice. Canada didn't want us." Setsuko seemed lost for a moment, a short, stocky, older woman in her ridiculous high heels on the Bridge of Tears. "Japan wasn't any better. We had to hide our Canadian accents and pretend we were born here."

"But you left your daughter here," Miyo said. *An orphan like you,* she almost said. She felt the pity and bitterness pool in the pit of her stomach, and at the same time, the wonder float up at everything half-known or utterly new before her: her father had become a husband, and a father to someone else, and never told her. Now it was too late.

Why too late? Miyo could hear David saying, puzzled, then determined. *Too late for what?* She'd be like one of his pathetic clients seated in the lowered visitor chair, gazing up to him. Too late for life to have been different. *Your flesh and blood,* he'd called Hana. One known fact.

Setsuko was unriled. "Why did I leave my Hana-chan? I thought you understood." A look crept over her features, knowing, then accusatory, and then it vanished, or maybe Miyo had imagined it. Setsuko strode off quickly. "Hurry up," she called back. "Hana will be waiting to meet her sister."

The subway was crowded but inside the cars people stood very still, nothing touching, with eyes closed or downcast; some read from books held in the palm of a hand. It calmed Miyo, this privacy at the heart of a crowd. A small boy slipped off his shoes to climb up on the plush red seat and watch a building go by, curved and buttressed like the hull of a huge sailing ship. She and Setsuko rode in the first car at the very front, next to the glassed-in compartment where the driver rode. Each time they pulled out of a station, one white-gloved hand curled into a loose fist, then pointed a finger to the tracks ahead. A salute, empty and for no one, yet he kept it up, station after station, aimed at the next destination. His cap was tipped low over his forehead. All she saw was his neck, very pale, and his hair a blue-black bruise on it; an impulse to touch that white neck flickered through her, a brief repellent yearning.

At Shibuya station, the two of them stepped out onto a tile patterned with irises marking where people patiently queued to get on. The station was high above ground, and workers could be seen in adjacent buildings and, between huge crossed beams, in the swarming street below. They followed the signs for the Hachiko exit, down the stairs and down the escalator, through the turnstiles, until they came out to a vast square, every corner of it dotted with black-haired heads. On all sides of an intersection people waited. Cars swished past, quiet and smooth as if on carpet. High above were giant screens with a girl's face pulsating in checkers, and layered singing voices lagging a split second behind her lips. The face shimmered with diamond facets, fleetingly lifelike but like nothing human. The girl would move in tiny spasms, then melt. *I have never seen, I have never seen,* sang the voices, coming down like mist.

In front of her, Miyo saw the back of a man who could've been her father—his size, his walk; his darkened neck; the whorl of black and grey at his flat crown. The spectacle of this man in the crowd fascinated her; in seconds she lost sight of him and a feeling of utter aloneness overtook her. Here, so far from the home she'd shared with her father, she was missing him more intensely than ever.

The lights changed and everyone moved in unison, all crossing at once, at the same pace. Miyo was carried by the tide even as she swayed backward, unable to keep up, churning up her own undertow: a convulsion at everything new. "Stay close," Setsuko said, and pulled her away from the crowd into one corner of the square where Miyo could steady herself and try to catch her breath. Cigarette smoke walled them in, and people sat on curved benches with their trilling cellphones, or milled around a small statue. This was better, things scaled to human size, though the smoke was nauseating.

"This is Hachiko," Setsuko said. "If you get lost, always wait here." She passed her hand over the granite head of a dog seated atop a pedestal. "Hachiko greets his master here every night until one night the master doesn't come home. He's been called off to war and he never comes back. But Hachiko waits, night after night, until he starves to death." She watched Miyo for a reaction. "Stupid dog," she snorted. "Waits and waits, like me and Hana." She tugged at Miyo again, just as Miyo reached out to touch the dog's lifeless stone eyes. "It's easy to get lost here. Everybody looks the same, right?"

With that, so much more of Setsuko came back to Miyo: the odd things she said, tinged bitter and petty for no reason; what Miyo had known to dislike as a child. The small items taken from her without her father knowing, or her knowing why; she remembered a box of pretty crayons, a favourite book, *Patricia's Secret*. Miyo shook off Setsuko's grip but followed after her.

They turned onto a quiet side street that wound down into a warren of narrow paths. It was as if a door had closed behind them in a roofless house, leaving party guests behind. The ground was swept clean, the houses sat side by side, little set-down boxes with walls not of paper but paper-thin; occasionally one came to life with a sneeze or a cough echoing from one side or the other. The unfamiliarity of it all filled her with regret. If only her father had brought her here himself, walked her down this laneway, showed her this place that had been his home for a time. If only he had not hoarded his secrets. He could have told her things to make it less alien and more her home too. Given her a word for those deep patches on the sky, the blue roofs she'd seen from the plane as they landed; translated a sign on the street from the Japanese she had never heard him speak beyond counting. Those two meagre, infantile words, *ichi ni*, were all he'd given her; they spoke of everything and maybe nothing between them.

Beside her, Setsuko walked on in silence. Crows soon appeared, ominously black and massive against the now bleached sky. They cawed and perched on the tops of walls, dispersed as Setsuko and Miyo approached, then gathered again not far off. They were larger than any crows Miyo had seen at home; fleshier and oily black; their beaks hooked more menacingly. Every so often Setsuko would briskly walk ahead, remember Miyo and turn to wait.

The neighbourhood gradually changed, street by street, house by house becoming less pristine, less neatly boxed. They were cramped crookedly up against low-rise apartment buildings, white but sooty at their base, with iron railings spidering the sides. Soon she and Setsuko were climbing a staircase that rattled under their weight. It led to a flimsy door, one in a row that resembled the back exits of seedy motels she'd seen on highway service roads back home.

Setsuko rang the bell, and as they waited, Miyo smoothed her hair and checked herself; the middle button on her coat was missing. Setsuko rang and rang. "I talked to Hana last night," she finally said, all her weight anxiously pitched forward as she pressed the bell. "She said she'd be here."

The street echoed with stray sounds. "Hana-chan, Hana-chan," Setsuko murmured under her breath, beckoning as if to some skittish stray animal. Then words in Japanese, incomprehensible, her mouth slack. For that instant, Setsuko was transformed into someone vulnerable; someone who loved and whom Miyo's father could've loved.

Setsuko began knocking on the door, lightly at first, then pounding. "She said she'd be here," she repeated, then stopped, staring at Miyo as she had on that bridge. "What is it?"

Miyo could only finger the nub of red thread on her coat where the button had come off. Her hand was wet, she realized, and her eyes. Her cheeks went instantly hot with shame; the tears did nothing to cool them. "Why didn't he tell me?" she finally asked.

Setsuko looked as if she didn't want to say at first. "You don't know?" she asked.

Miyo shook her head. "Why didn't he come to see her?"

There was the look again, an accusation, unmistakeable and without sympathy. Setsuko cleared her throat. "He would never leave you behind. Not for anybody, not for even a minute."

When the door opened, it was a boy there squinting drowsily behind a long curtain of hair. His robe was parted to reveal his chest, smooth and hairless; his hands were blindly tying a bow in front. He'd been sleeping. A smell wafted out of the apartment, warm, of something just done. Cookies, rice, something.

Setsuko swept past him. "Hana-chan!" she shouted through the place, though it was clear that Hana either was long gone or had yet to arrive. Setsuko rifled through papers and clothing scattered on the floor as if hoping to find her among them.

"Speak English," Setsuko said when the boy muttered something. She pointed to Miyo. "*Sansei desu. Canada-jin desu. Gaijin-desu.*" It was what Setsuko had explained to the airline hostesses, customs officers, porters, puzzled because Miyo couldn't understand them: a third-generation Canadian, Japanese too far back. A foreigner. "Hana taught him some English but he's too lazy to speak it."

When he turned languidly toward Miyo she saw he wasn't a boy at all. It was the puffiness of his flesh on his chest, his cheeks, even the hand reaching out, that was deceptive: smooth as a child's, but strong and broad. "I am Ryu," he said. It was a complex sound she didn't try to repeat. "You are Hana's sister?"

"Half-sister," Setsuko said before Miyo could say.

Ryu shut the door behind them and the smell filled Miyo's nostrils: buttery, musty, yeasty; bodily. The scent of the two of them. On the floor in the dark was a futon with two pillows and bedding hunched over it like a cave, or a shell he'd just emerged from. A rectangle of light from a single window fell on the far side of it like a phantom doorway.

"She did not come home last night," he said. The words lolled one into the next, lazy-sounding, careless.

"You should have called me." Setsuko threw down an unopened envelope she'd been scrutinizing.

Ryu shrugged, refusing to be burdened. "She will come when she wants," he said, a touch defiant, possessive. He slipped behind them and shone a lamp onto the wall. "It is almost finished," he announced. A sprawling form was painted there, pink and doleful, its shadow swimming onto the ceiling, a creature outgrown its cage. Miyo nearly stumbled into pots of pink paint and pink-tipped brushes strewn on the floor.

"What is it?" she asked.

"Sakura," Ryu said, "cherry blossom."

"My Hana is an artist," Setsuko said with some pride. "Sa-ku-ra, sa-ku-ra," she half hummed. "Didn't your father sing you the cherry blossom song?"

Miyo shook her head. The mural was like nothing she had seen before. Weird, beautiful, intricate, grotesque, all at once, and more so as she drew closer. Someone's dream or nightmare, whimsy or trauma. Giant stamens sprouted from the blossom's centre like monsters mutated by a cosmic ray. On the tips of the stamens perched passport-sized cut-outs of blurred faces, old photographs of young Japanese soldiers. The faces looked exotic, from another time and place where people were smaller and swarthier; another species of adult-children.

"She painted this yesterday," Ryu said. He pointed to airplanes like oversized bees hovering above the flower. On the sides of the planes were small flower insignias.

"They crash into the enemy ship." Ryu made an explosion inside his cheeks and his eyes brightened. "It's like a blossom in the sky. They want to bloom again in Yasukuni Shrine."

"They were kami, they were divine. They sacrificed for Japan and the emperor," Setsuko said.

"They should not have to die."

"You believe whatever Hana tells you." Setsuko climbed up the stepladder to study the faces. "Where's Mas? Why doesn't she respect her father's sacrifice?"

"Why," Miyo broke in, "would my father be there?"

Setsuko cast Ryu a warning glance, then gazed down at Miyo distantly, with pity. "He never told anybody. Only me."

"Told what?" The one person Miyo had always thought she knew, and knew better than anyone else could, even Setsuko, was her father. She'd never doubted this. Now everything had changed.

The photo on the dining-room table flickered in her head: the boy who had become her father, a face unwritten on, too skinny for his uniform, the hand on the side of his rifle and bayonet. Safely fenced inside the schoolyard with his pretty friend, his future wife, Miyo's mother. "He never went to war," Miyo said. "It was just practice, he told me." She couldn't recall precisely when he'd told her that, or the words he'd used, but she knew that was what had been meant.

Setsuko climbed down a step and met her gaze. "Miyoko," she said, "your father did go to war. It was his duty and he did it."

His duty—something David had once asked Miyo about. Miyo shook her head. She knew her father; he'd keep silent but never would he lie. Not her father. "No, he didn't," she said simply.

"He was back in Canada. He let his pride go. He was too humble."

"Hana says he had his war crime. He did a bad thing," Ryu said, pausing to watch Miyo. Before Miyo could speak, Setsuko shot back in Japanese and swatted his arm. She glared fiercely.

"That's ridiculous," Miyo said. An echo sounded in her head of David's questions about her father, the brutality he suspected him of; of her anger at David for thinking such a thing. It wasn't a war crime he'd suspected; it was Miyo he'd been worried for. She'd laughed and pushed him away. She felt a pain flicker down her side now, a silent alarm.

"Hana says all Japanese has war crime." Ryu poked a thumb to his own puffy chest then pointed to Miyo. "Me. She." He looked at Setsuko. "You. Hana's father also."

"How can that be?" Miyo laughed, but her voice was strung too taut.

"Bad things happen because nobody tries to stop. Hana says."

Setsuko sighed. "Hana says, Hana says. Hana only wants to hate her father because he never came." She stepped off the ladder and leaned tiredly against the wall. "Where is she?"

"Hana will come when she wants," Ryu said and turned away.

Behind Setsuko, the petals curled menacingly like a flytrap. On the tip of one stamen, a photo, too crisp and sharp to be as old as the others, caught Miyo's eye. It was Hana as a girl, the same picture Setsuko had drawn from her father's box. Miyo recognized the look of sullen indifference as if it were directed at her, even shrunken down and artfully weathered to match the other pictures.

They stayed until the rectangle of light near the futon faded to nothing; outside it was completely dark. Setsuko bristled at everything, anything that was not Hana on the telephone or at the door. "This is just like her," she said.

They left Ryu sitting beneath the mural, and took a taxi back. In the kitchen, in the dark, Setsuko sat herself by the phone and waited. A package had come from David; his handwriting, the sight of his even, straight-backed letters forming Miyo's name, filled her with longing. He must have sent it off before she'd left Toronto. *Just you-o and Miyo,* she could hear him say, his silly good-night joke. It had never felt truer to her than now, alone with only herself to rely on, the sister she'd travelled this far to meet forgetting, or worse, shunning her.

She slipped out and walked up to the pay phone on the main street, empty except for cars whizzing into the night. She dialed but there was no answer. She checked her watch; David would be on his way to work, stepping out of their apartment building, passing the mansions with their wide windows onto airy unused rooms. Maybe he was stepping onto the train at his station—their station—Rosedale, where the spring wind might be breezing through the open-air stop. He might be squinting at a flash of morning sun, thinking of her or not. She almost called back to leave a message, but he would know from the hang-up that it was her. What could she say to convey how alone she felt, how odd this place was to her, how harrowing and at moments, she could admit, delightful; how much she missed him, how estranged from her father she felt, not just in death but in the life he'd lived as a Japanese and possibly as a soldier, and never shared with her. The fact of it disturbed her as much as knowing that he'd never brought himself to tell her, and that he'd lied.

Miyo stood under a neon-lit sign and tore open David's package. It was a silver toonie-sized disk that sprang open: a compass, little more than a toy, a Chinatown novelty, with a needle quivering from zones of black to red. Still, it worked, pointing south toward the railway yard they'd crossed this morning. There was no note. She clamped it shut, warming it in her palm as she walked back to the house.

When she came in, Setsuko was standing by the door, waiting in the dim kitchen, eager and bright, eyes sparking from the beam of the street lamps outside the window. "She called. She says to meet her at Yasukuni Shrine tomorrow." Then the brightness died in her eyes;

she held up her hands to fend off Miyo's questions. "You talk to Hana."

Miyo lay wakeful through the night, hearing footsteps just outside, and stray cats scrabbling and mewing. She kept David's compass by her pillow, the silver gleaming when she tilted it. When it popped open, she felt the needle quivering nervously inside her. She missed David's body around hers; she missed the first glide of his penis into her, showing her the way. Yasukuni could be a beautiful or horrifying place. From what Setsuko and Ryu had said, and the way they'd said it, Yasukuni was a hallowed site where men believed they could be reincarnated in the petals of a flower. Had her father believed too?

In the morning they rode the Tozai subway line to the Kudanshita station. After her fitful sleep, she felt a chill and a nervous exhaustion that left her unnaturally alert to her surroundings. On the train she thought she glimpsed familiar trackside roads, houses, trees, then lost them like swirls in the sand. But out on the street the names of places and things in general had begun to assume a known look and feel; patterns were showing themselves in the way things worked, how people moved. No one ate or even sipped a coffee on the street—or if they did, they would stand facing a wall, so close they almost touched it with their noses, and they'd be quick, cloaking themselves in plain sight. She felt invisible and liked it; no one looked at her; no one looked at anyone else.

They came out to an expansive winding avenue, sized only for the cars that sped past. They walked toward a grey steel gateway that towered above trees just ahead: two smokestacks bridged by two across the top, like elaborate goalposts. A torii, Setsuko called it; the tallest in the world. How many could there be? They passed under it, along a wide gravel path, then looked back. "They took it down near the end of the war when Japan was losing," Setsuko said, "when they needed steel. They rebuilt it during the occupation." It framed the sunless sky, rendering the space beyond it infinite and emptied and doomed, as if everyone had fled. The air was cool and arid and unspring-like.

They passed a huge statue of some regal samurai who'd sacrificed himself for his emperor. Soon they arrived at a gate with heavy wooden doors. Giggling schoolgirls scurried up and huddled in front, holding still barely long enough for a passerby to snap their picture. Their skittishness irked Setsuko, their short skirts with swinging pleats. "Look at that," she muttered, pointing to white socks pushed down into folds too thick, too adult, pooling around bony ankles. Miyo followed her to a large altar, where Setsuko set down the heavy shopping bag she'd been carrying. Miyo reached to take it from her but she yanked it away. "You're too weak," she snapped, holding it close. Miyo remembered Setsuko's quick anger, rearing up in minor telltale incidents, at Miyo's mere presence.

Setsuko reached up to a heavy rope and clanged the bell. She clapped her hands twice and bowed three times, blank-faced. The echoes felt hollow, pure sound tunnelling through air.

"Did you call your friend?"

"I tried."

"You can call from the house tonight," Setsuko said. "I know what it's like to wait, not knowing." The softened tone, the unexpected concern: that had to be for David, not for Miyo.

They sat down on a nearby bench. "I'll stay with you until Hana comes." Setsuko tucked the bag under her knees. On the front was a pretty ring of pink roses and, through it, the name Takashimaya, the big department store visible on the street and on bags in the crooks of countless arms. She relented and opened the bag briefly for Miyo to see a box wrapped in white. "It's Masao," she said. "I told him he'd see Yasukuni again."

Miyo went cold. "My father?" Inside was his urn, the burnished metal surface icy and smooth, and his ashes and bits of bones, unsettled, not yet allowed to rest. She was trembling and could not stop. Setsuko had traipsed through the city with her father's urn bumping against strangers, on the subway, in the street, clunking it onto pavement. Could he possibly feel that, somewhere?

"He's supposed to be with my mother," Miyo said as calmly as she could. "That's what he wanted. We agreed we'd put him there when we got back."

"He belongs in Japan. He wants to be with others who believed." Setsuko's face had quickly hardened. "I want his spirit to rest here. But they say it's only for the war dead, the kami who died in battle." She shook her head warily. "They take anyone here, petty officers who caught the flu, even war criminals. Masa was ready to die in battle. Why can't they take him?" She gripped the bag tighter, clamping it between her knees. "He served, he sacrificed."

Miyo would not leave her father here, far from her

mother, that hovering unchanging shadow over their lives. What of her spirit waiting, without him? At home she would tend the grave, bring flowers, just as her father had. Sunday afternoons he had tilled the soil while Miyo squatted on a corner of the stone bearing her mother's name, *Beloved Wife and Mother, 1929 to 1970.* He'd send her back to the car when it got too cold and late; he left potted white chrysanthemums even in winter, to yellow and wither in the snow.

Setsuko was watching a flock of doves strut beneath a tree with countless bits of paper tied to its branches; cooing bubbled up from their round bodies. "Do you like that tree?" she murmured absently. It was bare except for the paper and budding tips of green and pinpricks of pink. "It's paradise here, don't you think? The only place in all of Tokyo where the white doves come. Everywhere else are the ugly crows, hundreds of them. So dirty and big." She sighed. "Masao would be at peace in this place."

"It's not right," Miyo finally blurted, but Setsuko sprang up. "Ah, there she is." Across the grounds a figure was talking with an elderly man; a red kerchief garishly tied at his neck flashed against the dull sky. "Who is she talking to? She looks healthy at least. You go. She doesn't want to see me." Miyo watched Setsuko walk briskly back the way they had come in, past the shuttered kiosks that were now open with their wares out for browsing schoolgirls. She passed through the large wooden gates with the shopping bag swinging gently at her side.

The doves flew up at Miyo's face as she threaded her way uncertainly toward the figure, who'd now turned her back to the man. She looked less stocky than in the pictures; grown taller without adding on flesh. When they came face to face, Miyo was shorter, her nose to Hana's mouth—a sweet Cupid's-bow mouth, a pretty mouth. All of her prettier than in the pictures. She broke into a wide smile that showed crooked front teeth, one nestled half behind the other. "Ne-san!" Miyo heard, "sister!" as arms were flung about her and held her so close she felt their bones touch; her heart, beating hard, or maybe it was Hana's, seemed to rack them both. A familiar scent rose; it was the smell from the apartment, that yeasty unwashed odour.

"Pigeons," Hana said, pretending to kick at them as they walked. She threw seeds in their path and lurched downward to pat one with her palm. It scurried off. "Poor pigeons. They'll never fly far."

"Don't they carry diseases?" Miyo asked. She'd heard of people suffering fevers of the brain.

Hana laughed with her head thrown back. It wasn't the way the smartly dressed women in the shops and the schoolgirls on the street tittered, with hands hiding their mouths, heads down. "They're pets," she said. "Poor pet pigeons. You see how good my English is? This is what I learned at international high school."

"I don't speak Japanese," Miyo told her sheepishly.

"Nobody understands us Japanese anyway. They think we speak in silence." Hana laughed again and kicked her foot up, just missing a strutting bird. "Everybody calls them doves, peace doves. They put out special feed the crows don't like, it makes them sick. You can buy some from the machine." She gestured to a metal dispenser under a tree.

"Setsuko sits by that tree every time she comes," Hana said. "She is waiting for it to bloom, so one day she will meet up with our father's spirit. Did she tell you that?"

"Yes," said Miyo. "She misses him."

"Poor butterfly." Hana laughed and flapped her long, thin arms. "Do you know the story of the butterfly who always waits for her man?"

"Madame Butterfly."

"That is Setsuko." Hana looked over at Miyo, unnerving her. "Why do you stare?"

Miyo reddened. But she had glimpsed something—was it the dainty mouth, or the smile it couldn't contain, the darting glance that beguiled until it came back? In her father, she'd taken that furtive glance for his way of being on guard for her.

"Ne-san, you're so serious. Do you know that, big sister?" she teased. "Does it sound strange to be called that?" Hana ran a finger under her chin. "Do you tickle here?" Miyo reared back at being touched, stumbling.

"I forgot, forgive me ne-san." Hana looked down at Miyo's weak limb. "Setsuko told me. But I can tell you're strong. Maybe stronger than me." Hana stopped and holding her torso rigid and tall, took Miyo's hand, guiding it under her blouse to just below her ribcage. It was hollow and almost fleshless; Miyo felt Hana's aorta pumping down there, far from the heart. "Stand up straight!" she commanded. "Why do you do this?" Hana hunched her body over.

"I don't know," Miyo stammered, shrinking and resisting at the same time. Could it be true, at least partly? Did she do this to herself? Her leg was quivering; she'd almost forgotten.

"We're the same, you and I. We'll be the same white bones in the end." Hana circled her, heedless of the pigeons fluttering by her feet. Some flapped up around them and into the air; the schoolgirls were crying out, gleeful, pointing up. "I believe that. Do you?" Before Miyo could reply, Hana had grasped her from behind, cupped her chin and pulled up, pushed down her shoulders, prying the top from the bottom, opening the spaces between vertebrae. Her touch was ungentle and brief, and that commingled bodily scent almost pungent as she stood so near. "Stand up straight," she repeated. Her voice became as soft as it could without being a whisper, as gentle as Miyo had ever imagined her mother's might be. "Try, even if it hurts."

Her father had never asked that of her. He made her march when that was the only thing to do. If she gave in, he picked her up, always; he never pushed.

"What did he say," she asked, "before he died?" She'd turned her pretty face away but Miyo caught every word, even as the pigeons' wings beat perilously close. "Did he say my name, ne-san?"

"Yes," Miyo said after a moment, wishing it were true. If only he'd left Hana something. "Yes, he said your name."

"What else?"

Another moment passed. "He said to endure the unendurable."

Hana murmured a phrase—the same, it seemed, in Japanese—then threw back her head and forced a laugh. She stomped the ground like a cranky child and the pigeons scattered; a few crows swooped darkly among them. "He said that? It's funny, ne-san. You don't know how funny it is." Her eyes rolled up to the sky and the flapping birds. "Sometimes, this place, it makes me sick," she groaned. Behind her, the man with the red kerchief at his neck was walking toward them. Hana half-twirled, saw the man, then grabbed Miyo's hand and led her away quickly, toward the wooden gates.

FOUR

HELTER-SKELTER, Hana led her through a noisy winding street cluttered with shops and concessions. "Wait," Miyo panted, but Hana dragged her on with an iron grip and her legs somehow kept up, one then the other under her; she didn't look down. Schoolgirls with their plaid skirts hiked up to barely cover their crotches stood in gaggles in front of CD shops, giggling into their cellphones. Familiar pop tunes warbled in Japanese filled Miyo's ears, then were gone, and she yearned for home, David; simply to hear English around her.

"Hana, please!" Miyo said, and brought herself to a standstill. Hana paused, then doubled back. "I'm sorry, ne-san, I forget." She smoothed Miyo's hair and clipped back each side with pink plastic hearts she'd taken from one of the store displays. "No, please," Miyo protested; her face felt too bare, unprotected. Her hand flew up but Hana pushed it away gently and pulled her along again. A shopkeeper wailed after them as they ducked into a laneway, then into a junky cosmetic store. Miyo was giddy, her breath fast, her heart fast; she felt alive—

almost too alive to bear. It was like the subway game with David.

She skittered after Hana past rows of skin lotions, tonics, creams under gaudy lights; boxes with pictures of glamorous blondes. White Essence, one was called; Pure White said another, and White Light, another. Hana dipped her finger into little pots of powders; pinks like Hana's paints in her apartment, the pinks of the giant flower. Down another aisle were all kinds of contraptions. "To curl eyelashes," Hana said, and picked up another—"To make fold in eyelid." On that box was a girl who didn't quite look Japanese, with enlarged sleepy eyes.

"Close," Hana ordered. Miyo felt her eyelid pulled and patted. Hana held up a mirror. One eye was propped open looking startled with its lid creased. On the other side, her plain self blinked under a hooded lid. "Silly Japanese girls want to look pure and white." Carefully Hana peeled the strip from Miyo's eye. "You see, we don't want to look how we look, we don't want to be who we are. We don't want to say what we've done."

Hana studied her hard. "Pretty, pretty, just as you are," she murmured, and for a moment Miyo believed it might be true.

At the apartment, Miyo fell exhaustedly onto the futon in that cave that belonged to Hana and Ryu, and slept. She dreamt of her father, for the first time since he had died. She'd come to pack her things from the house, to move them to David's, and her father had already taped up box after box. He gave a look of disgust when he saw she'd come alone, without David. He made a sound, too—not a word—of disgust, meant to say, *He doesn't even help you.* She didn't tell him that she'd made David stay home so she could come alone, so her father could have that much: the satisfaction of knowing no one could ever take his place, and the worry.

He'd even folded up her underwear, as if she were still that little girl to be protected, the crotch safely cradled at the centre, buried beneath the folds. He made her wait on the porch as he hauled out the boxes, warding her off, even as he winced setting the heavier ones down. There were so many, soon piled high as a wall on the driveway, and on one side of it a taxi driver waited with his arm draped lazily over the car seat, the radio fading in and out, the trunk lid up, back doors open.

Her father picked up a stick broken off the big birch tree. He shook it at her. *Go now,* he shouted. It was she he was chasing off instead of taunting schoolboys. *Daddy, it's me, it's me,* she was crying, all the while shielding herself from his stick. She opened her eyes to a silent room, not her own in her father's house nor hers with David, all the brightness of the afternoon streaming in through the one window.

Hana was there, miraculously, lying beside her in the shadows. "I cried for him too," she seemed to say, distant and removed, as if her tears had been shed by someone else a long time ago.

Before Miyo could think to reply, Hana touched her shoulder. "Do not be sorry for me. Do not be sorry for him either." Her fingers traced Miyo's neck up to her jaw, her cheek, and to her temple, lingering in the hollow there. "The same white bones," she murmured, and

Miyo lay back, languoring in the comfort of being touched. The dream of her father slipped away. He was gone; all, whatever need be, forgiven.

Under her she felt the worn-in velvet and grit of the sheet, and there was that smell, now on her own skin. She tried to conjure David for herself, for just this instant, their bed, their scents as they lay together after making love; when she could sense each precise spot where their bodies touched, even the faintest wisp of contact. She would map out a starry constellation of those places on the ceiling in the dark while David slept. The irresistible sensation at each point on her body she could not deny herself, not even for her father. She never knew if it was a constellation of light in darkness she was glimpsing, or of darkness inside light.

Hana's voice came back: "You think you know him because you lived with him. But I know him better." She slid closer; Miyo felt the chill of her breath in her ear. "He was a bad man."

Miyo recoiled, confused. Did she mean David? But no, it was her father—their father. "You're wrong," she declared, and buried her head; everything went dark and muffled. Her father had been a good man. He didn't speak his tenderness. He did things, and without her having to ask, ever.

"I understand, ne-san," Hana said soothingly. "It is okay."

But Miyo moved away, her head still buried. She heard Hana's soft laughter, then: "Don't be so serious, ne-san." Hana's fingers poked through the bedding and curled under Miyo's chin. "Everyone has bad and good inside. Even you."

When Miyo sat up, she found the sunlight had changed; the rectangle had faded but there was a golden cloud floating through the room, and in it Hana's head was slightly thrown back, the ragged outline of her hair in relief, and her low, delicate profile. "You like my art, don't you?" The giant cherry blossom drooped from the wall, wanly brought to life by the afternoon light.

"Yes," Miyo said. But it was exquisite and hideous, and frightening for having come from Hana's head and hand.

"I don't make a picture to look pretty. I make it ugly also, so people will pay attention. So it will make them think about things they don't want to."

The soldiers' faces were not visible from where the two of them lay. But they'd remained vividly in Miyo's head since she'd first glimpsed them, the tiny moon-faces of boys in caps.

"Sometimes I can almost hear their voices," Hana said. "But all they can say is, 'See you in Yasukuni.' Secretly they are afraid of dying. They want their mothers."

"But they might not die," Miyo said, as if the story had not been lived out nearly sixty years ago; as if she could will every one to be saved. Anything else was unimaginable.

"Do you not understand tokkotai? Kamikaze?" Hana stared at her squarely. "If they survive they fail. They live in shame. They must die honourably for their families and the emperor and for Japan." She rose from the futon and stood very close to the flower, her hand resting protectively on one photograph. She was thin but sinewy in only her underpants, veins roping down her arms and calves, breasts small and tight to her chest like an athlete's; they barely hung or moved when she moved.

"This one is Hajime," Hana said, fingering the portrait of a sleek-faced boy. "He must sink ships and then die." Miyo went to stand beside her, but Hana flopped back on the futon and curled into a ball in the lowered, dusty light. The gold in it was almost gone.

Miyo searched farther along the wall through the cluster of faces until she came to the one different from the rest; the one Setsuko had happened on the day before. "Why is your picture here?"

Hana coiled herself tighter, her knees to her breasts; even her toes curled under. "I don't know," she said. "They are so lonely and sad. I keep them company." Her arms flailed out as she rolled upright onto her knees. "Stay with me, ne-san," she implored, and grasped Miyo's arm.

"I should go," Miyo stammered. She felt panicked at being drawn in so irresistibly, at the warm clamp on her arm as she stood barefoot in only her slip, scanning the floor for her skirt and blouse. "Setsuko is expecting me. She might be worried."

Hana let Miyo's arm drop. "She doesn't care," she said coldly, turning away. "She only cares for herself and our father." She turned back, pleading, "Don't you know that, ne-san?" She slid under the covers again and peeked out coyly. "Why don't you stay? Call your friend in Canada."

"My friend?"

"Don't you have a special friend who misses you? He is waiting to know you are okay, ne?" she teased. The room had again darkened, but Miyo could feel Hana's desperate smile through the dimness. "Stay with me, sister, please."

♥

Once Miyo heard the familiar rhythm of rings tunnelling across half the globe to David, she was overtaken by longing, winded and choked by desire for him. She let it ring twice, then hung up, then dialed again, their code when they wanted to shut out the rest of the world. Her fingers were trembling, her voice too when she answered his hello. She didn't know what to say; it was absurd being reduced to a mere voice, a breath in and out on either end of a receiver.

"Miyo," he said. "Are you all right?" She longed to see him and touch him and smell him.

"Yes, yes."

"Did you—?"

"Hana's here with me now. She's sleeping."

"You're all right?"

"Yes."

"I didn't hear from you."

"I couldn't call. I tried."

"Miss you," he said. She let that sit between them, the two words that fit together exactly as she and David did, his hands on her from collarbone to the spot he liked to call her mound of Venus. He wasn't measuring her to some ideal or someone he'd been with before, but to himself: his right hand's span, how many it took to climb down her. His penis, he said, fit perfectly in her vagina, just tightly enough that she could hold him there, clenched inside.

"Me too," she finally said, and popped open the toy compass retrieved from her coat pocket. The needle was curiously still, even as she jiggled it in her palm.

"Did you get—?"

"I have it with me now."

"So you don't lose your way back."

Miyo silently shook her head. "I know," she said, "I won't," and gently hung up.

The street was listlessly alive with neon colours blinking, music blaring from blackened doorways; people shuffling by, less purposeful than by day. Drunken salarymen in too-tight suits roamed in packs, leering at girls who squatted by the windows of darkened shops. Under neon, the girls' too-tanned faces flashed like marigolds lit from within, spider-lashed eyes at the centre. They smoked furiously, butting cigarettes on the ground between their ankles. "I might have been one of them," Hana said as they turned down a laneway to the side entrance of one club, "but Ryu saved me."

They'd taken a taxi here to meet Ryu, to the Kabuki-cho side of Shinjuku. At the end of the laneway, Miyo glimpsed an elderly woman pass on a bicycle; up between the buildings into the inky sky, all the noise and neon fell away. She thought of her mother, what she might have become had she stayed here, and what Miyo herself might be, if at all.

From a long lit bar inside the club, Hana grabbed two glasses aglow with lime liquid, and led Miyo into a space brimming with frenetic bodies and streaks of orange and pink that flared and died. The music boomed like an engine inside her. She gulped down the liquid and it burned her throat. She stumbled after Hana into the undulating crowd.

In one dim corner on a raised platform, a skinny bespectacled boy leaned intently over a pair of turntables, headphones looping his neck, record in his hands. He dropped the record onto the turntable, swished it around, then raised a spindly arm into the air like a salute. There was a growl and a rising screech above a thudding beat. The crowd turned toward the boy and a hundred arms flew up. "He's our emperor!" Hana called out, laughing as she flapped her arms and green from her glass spilled down her sleeve. "DJ Atomic," she shouted near Miyo's ear. "He can make them do anything."

The music hiccupped back into a fast, hard rhythm and the arms slipped into their own chaotic movements; Hana inched deeper in, clutching Miyo's hand. They were jabbed and bumped, and a girl's blissful face swam past; a ribbon of orange flew after her. They were so young, their bodies careless; how in the world did that feel? Instead the music constricted Miyo, her throat and chest; maybe it was the smoke and the heat but her body was heavy, anchored, her leg like lead.

The music sped up and slowed, and each time Miyo felt a click-click in her heart, a changing of gears. Around them the crowd flailed and contorted. "See how their bodies obey?" Hana said. She bent down and cuffed something to Miyo's ankles, then to her wrists: orange and pink glow-sticks. Hana pulled her in close, whispered, "You let go too," then pushed off, giving a little wave as she disappeared. Miyo called after her but could not hear herself; she was falling but could not fall because of the bodies around her, tight up against her, then lapping away in waves, and suddenly she was flung with centrifugal force and she saw her feet and her arms, the ends of her fanned out into arcs of sherbet light. She was the ride, as before, on the subway, but better, faster, arcing the darkness. There was no rescue; she was dancing.

When she came to a standstill, Miyo glimpsed Hana poised momentarily on the raised platform before she let herself drop into the crowd, her back and neck perilously arched, a giddy upside-down smile quickly obliterated. Hana's torso was caught by a gaggle of hands; the rest of her spilled into blackness. Miyo stumbled to her knees on the floor; she groped through the jungle of legs and feet. Powerful arms at last hauled her up and stood her upright. It was Ryu, and there was Hana opposite her, gleaming with sweat; there was a faint grid of blood at her temple; her eyes were wildly bright even as she let her head drop onto his shoulder. "You see, ne-san? Ryu always saves me."

Outside, the air had grown balmy and the darkness was breaking up into particles of early dawn; it felt as though they were gliding through the night's residue. The music was gone but it had left a hollowness in Miyo's ears. There was only a remote tremor under her body from the taxi's engine. A cloud-white doily hovered before her on the driver's headrest, behind his swarthy neck. It had to be the drink; she felt dizzy and nauseated, relieved to be out of the club. But she had danced! She had to tell David.

Ryu was speaking rapidly in Japanese, angrily.

"No, not home yet," Hana shot back. "We have to feed the cats. They're alone and hungry." She closed her eyes. "Speak English so Miyo can understand." Hana's head was cradled in Ryu's lap, her body sprawled across him and Miyo in the back seat of the taxi. A damp heat rose off her. Her face and hair were slick with sweat though cool air streamed in the open window; a faint feverish smile played on her lips. "Did you see Miyo dance?"

Ryu kept shaking his head, and said, "Saké is no good." Hana murmured into Ryu's lap, "No good, no good."

The taxi let them off on a curved stretch of a deserted avenue that rimmed the nest of highways leading out of the city. The sun and the moon both dangled hazily in the sky. Hamarikyu Garden, a sign said in front of a high stone wall. The gate was closed. Ryu slung his bag behind him and climbed up over it. Once inside, he unlatched a side gate and let Hana and Miyo in.

It was a large empty garden, a faded, lifeless green that went on into a horizon with no skyscraper in sight; instead there were crabbed shadows of skeletal trees. It wasn't at all like the Japanese gardens Miyo had seen on calendars. It wasn't even like the gardens in High Park in spring, with a natural sprawl of leaves and blossoms, and pert rows of marigolds and petunias and low-lying shrubs. They walked on in silence, Ryu in front, glancing back furtively at Hana straggling behind Miyo. Finally they arrived at a pond whose surface was too stagnant and filmy to show its bottom or reflect the sky.

"Soon," Hana murmured, staring across the water at the sparse lawn they'd crossed, and the bare trees with their fluted green tips. "Two weeks. It will all be different." She cast a plaintive glance at Ryu. "Won't it?"

"You have to finish," he said.

"Finish what?" Miyo asked, but no one answered. Already, everything was different; some things had ended and others begun.

Just then, a soft something furled around her ankle; she let out a cry. It was a cat, a stray, and suddenly there were a dozen of them circling and darting in closer and out again. They'd all lost their tails or large tufts of fur. They looked restless and wild with hunger, their patchy coats filthy, their tiny faces a little savage. Still, Miyo reached out to one, the one who'd come close, but Hana slapped her outstretched hand. "Dirty!" she exclaimed, then gave a nod to Ryu, who unslung his bag and brought out tins of cat food, opened them and set them down.

"Poor dirty things," Hana said, the disdain in her voice touched with pity. Just as one ventured near, she stomped her foot and sent it scurrying. It came back an instant later, pushing its head in hungrily beside the others devouring the food. "Nobody cares for them."

"They are like the salarymen who lost their jobs. They have nowhere to go," Ryu said.

They walked around the pond and crossed over to a dock on the Sumida River, where they boarded a small ferry on its first run of the morning. Here and there, Miyo glimpsed people emerging from cardboard-box structures erected along the concrete walkways that walled in the river. She even spied shoes sitting neatly outside their flapped openings. "So many with no home," Ryu told her, "the police cannot chase them away."

The ferry passed under an airy spiderweb of a bridge and in front of a gleaming silver globe. To the right, a tower flashed the letter F, on and off. "Hana says it means forever," Ryu said, and sighed as he stared off in the opposite direction.

Miyo stretched out both her legs on the bench and gazed at them without flinching. She arched her neck back and cast her eyes to the sky, to the lifting grey of early morning. The letter blinked at her, receding into the distance: *F for free,* she thought.

An open-mouthed cry broke the air, a hungering cry as close to human as animal. It was one of the cats, small and ravaged like the others, emerging from inside Hana's coat as she slept on the seat behind Miyo. It leapt down and scrambled to the front of the boat, disappearing into the captain's wheelhouse.

Ryu closed the blinds on the one small window in the room, obliterating the rectangle of brightly blown morning light they'd arrived home to. He laid out bedding for Miyo in a far corner. Hana crawled into her and Ryu's cave and drowsily beckoned. "Miyo, come sleep with us. Don't be alone."

Miyo wanted only to sleep, to savour the lingering sensation of dancing, flinging her arms and legs into the air for split seconds at a time, the music and her own heartbeat telling her when. When David had made her try to dance, he'd held her very close to make her move with his body, his heartbeat; she'd stumbled all over him.

"You can see Ryu use his new device." Hana laughed and dragged a small, low table behind her as she crept across the room.

"It was not to be serious," Ryu said, disappearing into the bathroom.

"They gave it to him at the heya, at the sumo stable," Hana said. "Did he tell you he wants to be a sumo rikishi? But he's too skinny."

"Futabayama was not big," Ryu called out.

"Because there was no food to eat during the war. They were all skinny then," Hana said. "Futabayama was his hero. So handsome. He was blind in one eye, but no one knew until after he died. That was before Ryu was even born." Hana stood over Miyo as she lay in bed, then leaned down to plant the table over her torso, two wooden legs on either side of her. Slowly Hana lowered herself down on top, eyes locked on Miyo's, balancing her own torso on the table.

"This is for big yokozuna champions. They are so big that if they lie down on their wife, they will crush her," she said. "They must lift up their big bellies and rest them here because they hang like aprons over a little penis." She laughed, burying her head into Miyo's shoulder, her mouth breathing a hot circle on her arm. "But Ryu will never be a sumo champion. He is skinny with a big penis."

Ryu slipped into bed and hid himself under the covers.

"He's shy," Hana said. "But it's true." She got up and flew across the room and dove under the covers with Ryu. They giggled hysterically; Miyo could make out Ryu's laughter, veering high, breathless and staccato. The covers heaved and rolled. Miyo could not stop herself from watching that rhythmical mound at the other side of the room, nor from holding her breath, listening to their sounds. Every so often, she made out the tip or edge of Hana's voice, a sweet, sharp sliver. Finding Hana had almost been like what love at first sight must be: an immediate, thrilling connection of flesh and blood. It changed everything. Those unlikely stories of separated siblings, brothers and sisters falling deeply, irrevocably in love, then choosing a life together after a childhood apart, now seemed entirely believable.

Miyo held and squeezed herself, her legs with no one between, the table pinning her; she tried to conjure David, his penis that fit her so perfectly. The compass was in her coat pocket, the needle quivering and stilled; David wishing her back home with him. She finally brought her hands out to rest on the table, its cool and smooth wood. There was a picture taped to the surface, an old black-and-white postcard of a man in an elaborate loincloth of brocade, his hair slicked back and knotted on the top of his head. It must be the great Futabayama, the sumo wrestler, Miyo realized, because he looked majestic but thin, and because of what she imagined to be his laconic half-blind gaze.

She woke what seemed hours later to find Hana, her eyes wide and locked, prone beside her. "Ne-san," she asked, "what was he really like, our father?" As if hoping to be convinced against herself.

"He was a good man," Miyo said, "a good father."

"Are you sure, ne-san?"

"Yes."

"He was a pilot in the Imperial Army. Did you know that?"

Miyo shook her head. She told Hana what she had told Setsuko and Ryu, about the boy soldier who never went to war.

"It s' true, ne-san. He was conscripted from the university in 1943. Japan was losing then. Even students had to fight."

It could only be a stranger Hana was speaking of, a stranger in a foreign land far away, long ago, who had never truly existed. It must all be a mistake, a bigger mistake than she'd first imagined, wrong in a more complicated way; Hana's father might not be Miyo's father; they might not be sisters after all. Mistaken identities.

"No," Miyo said; it seemed to be all she could say. She remembered the train rides she and her father had taken together. "He couldn't have been a pilot. He never flew anywhere. He only took me on trains."

Hana lay in silence until Miyo reached out to her, and then she slid away. "Hana?" The name felt awkward on Miyo's lips; from the moment they had met, she'd never pronounced it quite right, as a Japanese would.

"I will tell you two bad things our father did," Hana said, suddenly very present, very alive in the room. "I wrote him one hundred letters but nothing came back." She held something and slid it onto the table beside Futabayama's picture. It was a wooden pencil case with flowers painted on it. It looked homely sitting there, as if the hand that had crafted it still rested on it. It looked familiar. "Setsuko told me it was from him, but I don't think so. She sent it."

Miyo let her go on. There was nothing to say to make up.

"What does it matter now?" She started to shiver; she had no gown on. Miyo moved to cover her but the table trapped her. Hana rolled herself into a ball on the bare floor, then poked her head up. "Did he do things with you? Did he take you to special places?"

There was one place outside the neighbourhood, one besides school and all the doctors' offices, the hospitals, church; it was the zoo inside High Park, just the two of them on a Saturday afternoon—once in the fall, maybe twice in spring and summer. There were llamas with large glistening eyes, the slow blink and fan of their long curled eyelashes, the smell of them. Bison. Peacocks' cries. She saw in her mind a big tall maple tree a way off, other children running and jumping into piled-up leaves. She had always feared they'd hurt themselves on something lurking within.

"Nowhere special." Miyo's throat felt scorched from the lie. "Tell me the second bad thing."

Hana stretched out on her back, her body offered up to the air, her mound of Venus to the afternoon light, to the soiled stuccoed ceiling; she lay motionless, whatever pain she felt mysteriously opaque. When she finally spoke, her lips barely moved. "He never came to tell me he was sorry."

Midday light leaked through the blinds and woke Miyo an hour later. Across the room, the cave rose and fell the tiniest bit; Ryu was still sleeping. The light flickered across the mural making the flower appear to vibrate. Beneath it, Hana was kneeling silently, naked still, among small flat bundles of red yarn. Her hands worked furiously. Abruptly they ceased; she gazed up, murmured something, broke off the yarn with her teeth, then started to wind again. Sensing her wakefulness, she turned to Miyo. "Help me, ne-san," she said, as if unable to stop herself. She pointed to one of the tiny pictures sprouting from the stamen above her head and said, "For Hajime I need one hundred more."

Miyo knelt by her side as Hana placed the end of red yarn in one of her hands, squeezed together two fingers on the other. Tautly she wrapped the yarn around them till they were ready to burst at the tips. "Like this," she said under her breath. "Think a different thought for each stitch, as if you are a different girl each time you make a stitch, wishing Hajime luck in his mission."

"Who is Hajime?"

Hana barely looked up. "He is just one of the hundred million."

"But why him?"

Hana smiled. "Because I like his face, ne-san. It's yasashi. Gentle. One thousand schoolgirls each sewed a tiny bundle of red on his white sash that he tied around his belly." Hana scooped up an armful of the flat bundles, bright red suns in the leaked light that momentarily blotted her face. "Wish him a glorious death," she said, releasing the bundles. They scattered across the room like toys those stray cats might frolic with.

Hana stood and leaned face first into the wall, her nose to the blossom. "Hajime is told to endure, but there is nothing left to endure." Her head dangled back in that way that was now familiar. "Did you know the emperor had a little voice like a girl?"

"No," Miyo said; it didn't matter. She wanted those words explained, what Setsuko said her father had uttered before he died: *Endure the unendurable.* So grand and final, and so unlike her father. But Hana was intently gathering the bundles she'd just scattered. She carried them into the next room and before she shut the door behind her, she turned back. "Keep going, ne-san. One hundred more for Hajime."

Miyo wound and wound, mesmerized by the circular movements of her own hands. She waited for Hana to emerge but the daylight waned and she dozed off again.

When she woke, there was red yarn everywhere: underfoot, unravelled in her bed, in her hands, and cluttering the open doorway to the room Hana had disappeared into. Ryu was in bed, asleep, alone; Hana nowhere in sight. Miyo got up and walked past the cherry blossom; now it seemed to cower in the shadows, ungainly, with its pinks a little sickly and sorry. She nearly slipped on one of the red bundles as she came into the room. In the dimness she vaguely recognized her father's eyes, his photograph from long ago blown up large, covering the whole wall, youthful and bright before either she or Hana was born. But when she flicked on the light, the rest of his face did not appear. Instead the picture's black and white dispersed into grey dust marked only by red yarn clotted like blood. It studded his cheek, a nostril, his chin, his forehead, in rows past the edges of the photograph itself, erupting from the walls of the room on two sides.

On a table were clippings from newspapers, magazines, photocopies from books methodically arranged in piles, each layers thick. An old photo on top caught her eye: Rising Sun flags in the sky and, before them, rows of people, mouths agape, arms raised like those teenagers in the club. Three photocopied pictures were pinned to an alcove wall. In the first, schoolgirls waved flower branches at a small airplane, its propeller awhirl. Their faces were turned away, and you saw only the wing-like jut of shoulder blades under their uniforms, white sailor-collars at their necks, grazed by their sleek dark hair.

In the second picture there were six young soldiers, with flower branches like tails at their sides, the blossoms still thick and blooming, and curling at their necks with animal muscularity. The boys' faces were fading away, blanched like albinos, their heads bound in white sashes floating amid the cloud-light sky like disembodied ghosts; lower down, their uniformed torsos materialized in detail: belt buckle, pockets, buttons, rifle strap, creases where the body strained the fabric, only to darken down the thighs and round their calves, boots sunk into marshy blackness at their feet.

The third was a photocopy of a recent photograph, a group portrait, each face scribbled on with Hana's writing. They were all women, all Japanese, all Setsuko's age or older; some prosperous and well dressed, others drab and shabby. Hana was there too; hers the only face unmarked. She was leaning solicitously toward the person beside her, an elderly woman in a kimono. Hana had written a name and a phone number over each face in pencil; at the picture's margins were lists of more things, places, addresses, phone numbers, half in Japanese, half in English, with dates to match: 1939, 1943, 1945 and so on.

She nearly missed the one man in the bottom corner of the picture, shrinking from the frame. Miyo instantly recognized the face and the scarf distinctively knotted at his neck: it had to be red, worn by the same man she'd seen with Hana at Yasukuni Shrine. In fact, the photo had to have been taken at the shrine; there were the wide gravel walkway and massive wooden gate behind them.

Beneath the table at her feet were trays and trays holding spools of thread and yarn, mostly red. There was a relentless order to the room: all elements in grids, in rows; Hana's busy, restless mind laid bare; its blueprint in red.

Half hidden by the trays of spools, low to the floor under the table, was a small checkerboard of smaller photos pinned to the wall: portraits like ones taken in grade school, no different from the tiny pictures of the kamikaze pasted to Hana's blossom. Miyo had to crawl under the table to see; they were pictures of herself as a little girl, growing bigger, crooked, gawky and more sullen year by year. She couldn't help but see the melancholy, unnatural for a child. There were dates intimately scribbled on the wall in pencil above the pictures, ages. Twinned to them in rows below were pictures of Hana herself, each at the same age. All along Hana had known of her, and Miyo had known nothing. She scrambled out from under the table, and banged her head.

Miyo reached out to touch one of the bundles—a hari, Hana had called it—an oversized stitch on her father's face. She forced herself to cup its fullness in her hand, against the revulsion she felt. It was thick and swollen, unexpectedly alive in the way it filled her palm. She tugged at it gently but it resisted, not like paper or even cloth but like flesh, with give. The yarn was sutured into their father's jaw so tight and even, so carefully; it was a clenching fist that would not let go. "Hana," Miyo found herself muttering, and she could not help noticing the pitch and tone of her own voice: the protective worry of an older sister.

Ryu appeared at the doorway, a sheet wrapped around him. "Hana is gone," he said.

FIVE

MIYO'S LEG WAS ACHING by the time she arrived at Setsuko's house. She'd run almost all the way from the subway, along the busy avenue and down the winding street.

"You can't go yet," she panted, panicked to find Setsuko's bags by the door, packed, her ready to leave the next morning.

"Ryu will find her," Setsuko said carelessly. "He knows her places." She clattered plates onto the dish rack and flung a washcloth into the sink.

"Hana likes for me to suffer the way she did, without her mommy and daddy." She looked tired and shrunken, shuffling across the cramped kitchen in flowered slippers. "I should suffer," she said without rancour. "It's only fair."

"I won't go."

"You'll be on your own then," Setsuko said with a cold eye. "Who will look out for you?"

"Hana will," Miyo said without thinking.

Setsuko laughed harshly. "Ryu can look after both of you. He always finds Hana." Her laughter melted to a rueful smile. "She wants to be found, don't you see?"

In her pocket, Miyo felt the taut bundle of red yarn in her palm and recalled the same yarn spilling out of the box from her father's closet.

"She was angry that I left her," Setsuko said. She looked almost clownish with her bright pink lipstick and smudged pencilled brows, more clutter on her creased face. At this minute, precisely not the woman Miyo could imagine her father loving. "Hana wet the bed every night after I went, just like a dog. She pried the heads off the dolls I gave her."

A gnawing ache crept up Miyo's side; a returning pain. It was the thought of those long hours spent alone and wakeful, needlessly; the sparkless twosome of only her and her father, lonely when it could have been so different. "Then why did you leave her?"

"I wanted her to grow up a Japanese," Setsuko declared. "Better than you," she spat. "You never would have accepted her anyway."

"Yes I would've." Miyo clenched the yarn in a fist. She wanted Hana; she loved Hana.

"You were a selfish child, Miyoko-san. You kept your father all to yourself. You wouldn't even share your toys with Hana."

"But I didn't know!"

"Inside, you knew." Setsuko tapped a finger to her head. "You were smart enough."

"No," Miyo said steadily, "no, no." It couldn't be, for how could her father have given in to a child? How could a child be held responsible?

"Children can be cruel," Setsuko said, as if countering her thoughts. "All those dolls I bought her. Hana-chan gave them funny voices. No heads, just voices that squeaked." She sank into a chair and stared at her feet, swinging them gently. "She wasn't an ordinary child. She was an artist, even then. You can't expect to understand them."

"She thinks you don't care."

Setsuko snorted. "You see? It's no use." She got up, shooing Miyo away like one other nuisance.

Miyo held out her hand with the wad of red yarn in it. "I saw . . . in that room, on the wall." Her hand flew to her face as she remembered the picture of her father, his flesh pierced and poked; she was chilled by her own touch. She could not describe what she'd seen.

"You can't expect to understand them," Setsuko repeated.

"Hana says my father, our father did bad things. Is it true?"

"Your father was foolish, that's what. All his life he sacrificed. For Japan, for you. Even for me."

"But not for Hana?"

Setsuko plucked the red yarn from Miyo's hand. "He was your father. You knew him."

The man she didn't know was the young one in the old photograph that had sat on the table in their dining room for as long as she could remember. The man with the unlined open road of a face, and the girl beside him with the tender, glittering eyes. She was the one Miyo had always studied: the slender calves, the dimpled hand; the loveliness; the mystery had always been how Miyo could have come from such loveliness. But the uniformed man in the picture had never quite seemed to be her father.

"What did he do?"

Setsuko sat calmly, folding her flowered, slippered feet neatly under her chair, falling so short of that lovely image of Miyo's mother, or of herself as the demure widow of a war veteran. "He was a lieutenant in the Imperial forces," she told Miyo.

The uniform he wore, the peaked cap, the buttons, the collar, the insignia—he was just like one of those very young men bedecked in blossoms in Hana's picture. A rifle and a sword were at his belt.

He was a soldier in wartime.

"Did he kill people?" she asked.

"He flew a plane over the ocean," Setsuko said. "The enemy came with their big guns and ships to destroy Japan. He was trying to save it. He was trying to save everyone." She began to fidget, her feet breaking into a restless tap under her chair, her hands dancing around her face. She leaned in close to Miyo and gripped her arm so tightly that it hurt. "His only crime was that he survived. Is that so bad?"

"No," Miyo found herself saying, utterly confused but relieved and grateful; "No, it's not."

"His spirit deserves to rest." Setsuko sighed and let go of Miyo's arm. "He'll rest now that he's home. I go to Yasukuni tomorrow and try once more." She patted her thighs and stood up. "Then I go back to my home. I belong in Canada." She glanced at the spot on Miyo's arm where she'd held it, as if a trace might remain. "Just like you. You're kimin too. A throwaway from Japan like me. Pack your bags and you leave with me tomorrow."

❤

Another package from David had arrived while she was gone. Miyo began to unpeel its thorough cross-hatching of tape at each end, then stopped. She could leave it sitting on her bed, so tightly sealed that it demanded nothing more. There was her name printed in his precise hand, instantly familiar except that he'd reversed the order of her first and last name according to Japanese convention: *Mori Miyo*. It rang false to her; inauthentic. It irked her, his having to master every detail; it was her first time feeling that. She tore off the end of the envelope and a smaller plain envelope slipped out. On it, he'd written their names:

It was the way he liked to see them, together in the simplest equation. There was a letter inside. *Come home soon*, it said on the first white sheet. A pink plastic, clover-shaped whistle fell out too, another Chinatown novelty item. Miyo unfolded the second sheet.

It was a map he'd sketched of the Toronto subway. On it he'd marked three X's as Where We Met, Home, and Where We Said Goodbye. Beside the last X, he'd drawn an airplane. On another page he'd taped a subway token and a quarter for the telephone. She unstuck them both and set them aside, along with the pink whistle.

In the kitchen she heard Setsuko fussing with her luggage, unzipping and zipping to retrieve things she needed for the night. Miyo paced the room, then lay down, holding David's letter and the map he'd drawn for her, which appeared so spare compared to the dense subway network of Tokyo that she was now learning to navigate. Within a mere few days their worlds were veering farther apart than ever, and the fact of their chance meeting on a platform seemed more remote and unfathomable here, where the subways were a maze and each person was an atom, silent and untouchable. She did feel untouchable, alone with herself, and estranged from her father and everything new she was learning about him. She was wide awake from having stayed up and slept in, the night turned to day just as when she'd first arrived, and she was no longer certain where home was.

When the phone rang, it was late, the house dark and silent; even the street outside was quiet. Miyo ran into the kitchen. It was Ryu.

"Hana says to call her at this number tomorrow," he said, and read it out twice while she scribbled it down.

"Where is she?"

"She won't say but it is south, I can tell from the number," he said after a moment. "Not too far. Maybe on tip of Shikoku."

"Is she all right?"

"Yes, I think."

Setsuko appeared in the doorway in her nightgown, plain-faced in the dimness.

"Hana always comes home," Ryu said, and yawned exhaustedly.

"Go to sleep." Miyo pictured him childishly rubbing his eyes with balled fists, overgrown and overburdened.

Setsuko was shaking her head, muttering in the dark: *No good, no good.*

"No, I wait for Hana," Ryu said.

When Miyo hung up, Setsuko was gone from the doorway. On the counter, across the dark kitchen, she glimpsed the shopping bag with the wreath of roses, and her father's urn inside.

Miyo couldn't wait until morning to call. It was just after midnight when she slipped back to the kitchen past Setsuko's room; Setsuko was in a deep sleep. Miyo recognized the sound from nights years back, when Setsuko had stayed with her father and Miyo had lain by the wall separating their rooms, helpless to break the rhythm of her own wakeful breathing twinned to that slow heavy drone.

A man answered in rapid Japanese. She felt foolish reciting the line she'd memorized from her phrase book. There was a click, then two long rings, then "Moshi moshi." That greeting that sounded like baby-talk. It was Hana. Miyo listened for an instant; was the voice happy or sad, or something worse?

"Ne-san? Is it you?" Hana whispered hopefully into the phone. Maybe Setsuko was right after all; Hana wanted to be found.

"Yes, it's me," Miyo said.

"Ne-san, I knew you would call."

"Where are you?"

"I'm in Akiyoshi-dai," she said, "with my friends."

Miyo felt a prickle of jealousy, her first, that Hana should leave her for others. "Where is that?"

"It's in the mountains, not so far."

"You left," Miyo said, "you didn't tell me. . . ." Her eyes filled. What if she'd been leaving with Setsuko tomorrow? When would they have seen one another again? Where?

"Ne-san," Hana said, as if there were only the two of them in the world. "You know I have to do my work, don't you?"

"Yes," Miyo answered. "I know." She did know that what she had seen in Hana's room disturbed her for a reason; that it was beyond her yet to understand.

"I have to finish before sakura time," Hana went on. "When the cherry trees bloom. It may come early because the weather is too warm."

"Are you coming back?"

"Of course." Hana laughed lightly. "Wait for me at my place tomorrow morning. Ryu will leave the key for you."

"Won't he be there?"

"He'll be back at the heya. At the sumo stable. Didn't he tell you? It's his last chance."

"Setsuko is leaving—" Miyo started to say.

"Tell Setsuko goodbye." There was noise in the background, voices, things being moved. "You promise to be there tomorrow, ne-san?"

"Yes."

"Goodbye." The noises behind her grew louder before she hung up.

Miyo carefully replaced the receiver and crept out to the hall. Setsuko was there, startling her. Her face was scrubbed clean, the clutter cleared; her eyes were recessed and remote, her lips curling under, half-swallowed.

"Hana said to say goodbye," Miyo told her. "You were right, she's fine."

"Goodbye," Setsuko echoed, almost as a question. She headed down the hall a way before turning back to Miyo. "I didn't know your mother, but I saw her one time in Toronto after the war. There weren't many Japanese in the city in those days. I was very young then. I saw her from far away, with your father. Of course, I didn't know him then." She lingered a second more. "She was pretty," she said, and walked back to her room.

Miyo packed what she could carry in a small bag and went out at dawn, careful not to wake Setsuko. She took her father's urn. She could never leave him behind. He belonged beside her mother, where even Setsuko pictured him in her memory—not with those ghosts of soldiers on Hana's mural who seemed as alone in life as in death. Her father belonged in the cemetery by the grave he'd tended himself, near the pots of white chrysanthemums placed, winter through summer, at her mother's headstone.

She had to stop frequently to rest and stretch out and rub her leg, and when she did she glanced nervously down the deserted avenue, expecting Setsuko's briskly bobbing figure to appear at any instant. She reached the subway station just as it was opening for the day. She took a seat on the last car, for luck, thinking of David and the last time they'd played their game. How could she have been irritated with him? David, who in the end had urged her to come for Hana, who had only wanted for her what she was afraid to want for herself? She watched the stations appear out of the tunnelling distance, one by one, checking them against the sequence that Ryu had written down for her, waiting for the stop where she had to transfer to another line. At each station more sleepy-eyed salarymen pressed in, with their bent heads and palm-sized pocketbooks, and the car grew more crowded. These men seemed a world away from the leering salarymen in Kabuki-cho, and that night seemed distant, though only two days had gone by. For the moment, at least, she felt safe. Soon she would be with Hana.

Across the aisle, on the floor, she glimpsed a pair of tiny black patent-leather shoes, a child's, unscuffed yet holding the shape of the child's feet. Miyo peered up through the forest of men to a woman in a pink suit with her little girl perched on the seat in stockinged feet, at the window, watching the scarred concrete swish past. Miyo had worn shoes like that when her father took her to church once a year to mark the day her mother had died; it was two days after her own birthday. The church was a dark place where the light came down from high up, through falling dust, and the seats were hard and made her ache, and her father would slip out partway through, then come back near the end. The minister spoke in a strange way, as if his tongue were rolled up to the back of his throat. He'd read a list of names, and when he announced her mother's, her father would get up and go to the front with the others. He'd come back flushed and sweaty and carry her outside.

After was when he'd take her to High Park and the zoo. He'd cast off his jacket and tie, even if it was a cool spring. They never lingered long by the animals. The yaks and bison were homely to him, massive and still; their matted pelts smelled and flies buzzed over them as they cast their slow, indifferent, sidelong glance. He liked the peacocks, especially when the sun shone through their plumage. But he didn't like to see their ragged, soiled feathers when they strutted close to the wire fence. He'd say to Miyo, *Don't you get dirty now.* He didn't like her shoes to lose their shine or, worse, get scuffed.

Finally the train emerged from the tunnel and there was the jumble of the city again, its jagged pieces puzzling together, the sunlight needling its way in here and there. The little girl was as rapt and quiet as when she had been watching the concrete wall slide past.

The train suddenly jerked and slowed, and the salarymen swayed to the right, then to the left, amid a screech. Miyo reached under her seat where she'd tucked her bags, and her hand dipped into the shopping bag to feel the urn. When she glanced up, a man was watching her with a faint smile; he studied everyone around him in turn. Why hadn't she noticed him before? His head sailed above the other commuters. It shocked her how familiar he looked: his paleness, his height. She opened her mouth almost by instinct, like a lost child exclaiming to a found parent. He was lanky, his fair hair drained of colour, his features so distinct and angular on his face; or maybe it only seemed so here, now. David might be just like that man, just as shocking and familiar to her at this moment; just as conspicuous: her David.

The train came to a full stop; the little girl fell forward into her mother's arms with a cry. Several seconds, a minute passed and the car came alive with chatter into cellphones, with ringing and shuffling and rustling of packages. Out the windows on either side of the car was pocked concrete. She was stuck and no one was coming for her. An elderly man was now sitting beside her; someone must've given up the seat to him. What she could glimpse of his face was wizened; thick, cropped, very white hair sprang from his head. His legs were crossed and on his feet were raised wooden thongs— geta, they were called—and white cotton socks like mittens, with a section for the big toe instead of the thumb. He held a newspaper at his knee, folded in quarters. It was an English-language paper, *The Daily Yomiuri.* Slowly the train began to inch forward.

Miyo watched the old man's hand hover over the page, then methodically begin to cross out words and phrases with a black pen. She watched him, mesmerized—a censor at work, his face expressionless and unreadable. By now the car had returned to a fast clip, slipping into tunnels and out to open air. *Everything will be fine,* she told herself, clutching the slip of paper Ryu had given her. Her station would be coming next. Soon she'd see Hana. Soon.

Again the train lurched to a halt. The old man clamped her wrist to steady himself, so tightly she felt the bones of his fingers. He exclaimed in Japanese as the lights flickered off then on. In that flash she saw his face, fearful and convulsed, his tiny eyes wincing. "Are you all right?" she asked, just as an announcement came over the PA system. The man released her wrist, muttered and cast her a wounded glance and got to his feet. The car doors opened and Miyo followed him out of the train, through a second set of sliding doors, and onto the platform. The station looked different from others she'd been in. The tracks were blocked off by a high barrier wall all the way along the platform's edge.

She found herself standing between the old man and the tall man she'd taken to be American, maybe an athlete because of the Adidas bag slung over his shoulder. "Poor guy doesn't understand English," he said, smiling. "He never reads that paper." Miyo saw the paper in the old man's hand; the page was blackened, every word, every line, every column; there were even lines crossed through faces in the photograph.

The tall American saw her looking and made a loop with his finger near his head. "You're not from here, are you?"

Miyo shook her head.

"Then you don't know." He made a wider circle with his finger, to mean *all this*. "It's the economy. The express line used to be bad, now it's happening everywhere. People are getting desperate." He laughed nervously and shifted from foot to foot. They were large feet, long and narrow. "That's why these go up." He reached out a lanky arm to tap the barrier. "But they find a way to climb over."

"You mean somebody jumped?"

He nodded. "Happens all the time."

"Did he survive? Did we stop in time?"

The man, she realized when she looked up, was more a boy, only slightly older than Ryu. He'd gone a little pale. "I don't think so, ma'am."

As Miyo made her way along the street to Hana's apartment, she felt the burden of her body and the bags she carried, her father's urn, more than before. Was one of the jolts she'd felt on the train its own resistance to stopping, or the impact of that body cast before it?

She reached the apartment and knocked and knocked on the door but no one answered; it was just past rush hour and the neighbourhood seemed newly quiet, as if everyone had just left. Hana hadn't told her where Ryu would leave the key. Miyo searched around the door but there was no ledge the key could rest on. The iron-rail landing was empty of any flowerpots where it might have been hidden. She sank down on the rickety steps with her bags. She was thirsty and very tired but there was nothing to do but wait. An hour went by and, warmed by the morning sun, she leaned her head on her bag, looped the shopping bag over the crook of her arm and drifted off. She woke once with a start; her skin was prickling. She felt a dream slipping away, in which she had been running, chasing after something or someone, maybe Hana, deep into a warren of streets—but no, that wasn't it.

She was back in the park with her father. She wanted Hana to be there with them, she wished it and willed it, but Hana did not appear. There was no Hana back then, when she was four. Miyo was in kindergarten for the first time, with the teacher, Miss Whitten, at the piano, and they were snowflakes flying up and falling down. Miyo could not get back up; she could only fall down, and there she was on the ground, a fallen melting snowflake, while the others flew up to the sky. And then she was back in the park with her father, and the air was filled with falling white flakes—not snow but blossoms—not white but a faint pink. It was windy and the hill was steep, and the blossoms flew all the way down to Grenadier Pond. *Up, up*, she wanted to say, tugging at her father's hand, *make me fly up*, but he wasn't paying attention. All down the hillside, the trees became half-bare as the blossoms were carried off by the wind. Miyo and her father stopped at a large boulder; a metal plaque was mounted on its side. *This Japanese cherry tree someiyoshino prunus yedoensis matsum one of 2000 presented to the citizens of Toronto by the citizens of Metropolitan Tokyo. Planted on Wednesday, April 1ˢᵗ, 1959.* She hadn't been born yet.

Her father plucked a single blossom from the air. *See how it's different?* Across the road, on the opposite side of the parking lot, the trees looked crabbed and darkly stained, like jam. He drew an outline of the cherry blossom in the air for her. It was delicate and plain; she could count the petals: *one two three four five.*

Hana means flower, Setsuko had said. Hana was falling. *See you in Yasukuni,* she'd promised, before she fell into the blackness of the dancing crowd.

Miyo was jerked to a halt once again. She wasn't on the train, there was the blue sky; she was waiting for Hana. Below, through the railing, she glimpsed the top of a head, a man's; a Japanese man rattling the stairs as he climbed. Hana was right, she thought vaguely as she struggled to stand up; it was too warm. Too warm for spring. She was out of breath and sweating as if she'd been running; had she been running in her dream after all?

Miyo watched the sleek black head bobbing; the man was quick, graceful. When he pivoted on the landing, his face startled her: the skin taut to the bones, each feature angular, feral.

He spoke in rapid Japanese. Miyo stammered to explain herself: *Doozo yo roshiku . . . how do you do . . .* and

gave an awkward bow of her head. She was dizzy from
having risen too quickly, the blood draining from her
brain, another something the doctors had always warned
her against. She gripped the railing; it burned in her
palm, heated by the sun.

"Stay there," he said and sprang up the remaining
steps. He thrust a handkerchief into her hands. It was
deep navy, like midnight after this pure sunny day, dotted with rosebuds. Everyone here carried kerchiefs to
dab a cheek or forehead. He opened the door to Hana's
place—unlocked all along—and disappeared inside.
Seconds later, he emerged with a glass of water, and a
cushion which he slipped under her as she sat back
down. He dipped his fingertips into the glass and
pressed them to her wrist, three fingers side by side,
then made her drink. The water was sweet and his fingers were cool.

"I've been waiting for Hana," she explained.

"I need to see her too." He sighed. "I'm Hana's friend.
My name is Rinzo." His English was fluent, vaguely
British-sounding, but his name was utterly exotic. "You
are Hana's sister from Canada. Miyo-san." He smiled
briefly. His eyes were like a bird's—lidless, wakeful,
hardly seeming to blink at all.

"Come inside." He helped her to her feet. She could
smell him; under his black suit like crumpled paper he
was perspiring. He led her inside to Hana and Ryu's
futon, then went back out. He returned with her bags
and a can of juice from a vending machine on the street.
He opened it and put it in her hands. "Drink this."

She took a gulp and shoved it away, it was too sweet.
Instantly her temples were pounding. "Where is Hana?"

she asked, and this time heard the unravelling end of her voice, the hint of hysteria. He must hear it too.

"She's in Akiyoshi-dai. Didn't she tell you?"

Miyo glimpsed her things on the floor by the door, the Takashimaya bag already a little tattered, her small carry all with barely a change of clothes. "What is that place?"

"A retreat."

"How do I get there?"

"Hana will come to you. She always does," he said, echoing Ryu.

"How can you be sure?"

"Money," he said, with another fleeting smile. "She needs money. I sell her art." Rinzo took off his jacket and hung it on the knob of the closed door to Hana's studio. The countless wads of red yarn that had been scattered through the apartment, even in their beds, now all behind that door.

"There are people who want to buy. Germans. They pay well, though you wouldn't know from this place."

"Germans?"

"They would like to remind themselves they aren't the only ones who did atrocious things in the war."

What Miyo had seen inside that room flashed in her mind, the red yarn furiously stitched to their father's young face. "Hana thinks our father committed some cruelty," she said. She knew her father better than anyone. Now she understood Hana too. "She wants to think he's cruel," she went on, her voice growing louder. "But it's because he abandoned her. That's why she has to believe. He was a good man all his life."

She was heaving now, her left side seizing up as if an unsnappable thread were being pulled through it to convulse it. She was wheezing, her breath a thick rope in her chest. Rinzo eased her back onto the futon; she was trembling.

He put a finger to her lips and said, "I wasn't speaking of your father, whoever he may be, whatever he may have done." His finger stayed firmly pressed to her lips, forcing her to slow her breathing. Gradually she grew still.

He was leaning over her, and to see him this close, this keenly, overwhelmed her. It was like viewing some creature telescopically, so the smallest, slightest movement loomed powerfully. His finger pressed so deeply that her teeth dug into her lip.

Before she could help it, she'd bitten the tip of his finger. She touched her tongue to the tip and let it go.

"I'm sorry," she said, though she wasn't. She wasn't embarrassed, and she wondered at that. But he'd provoked it, even if he had been trying to help her.

There was no blood but he frowned playfully over the wounded finger, looking more plaintive than he meant to. She gave back his handkerchief and he shaped a little sling for the limp finger. When he dangled and wriggled it before her like a forlorn puppet, she felt an inexplicable pang of pity and endearment. It was a relief to laugh, and she was reminded of lying in this room with Hana close to her. Rinzo laughed too, a practised laugh, but Miyo liked his face like this: a little pulled and scrunched and less exquisite.

She'd hardly seen laughing people here, except for teenagers, who seemed to make a show of it. People looked busy, preoccupied, sometimes lonely, with no time to ponder their loneliness. Or maybe it was her own isolation, her own loneliness she was seeing.

She let herself settle deeper into the futon. "Close your eyes," he said, but they were already shut. His finger had tasted of soap and blood; its surface was rough, and with her tongue she'd felt the swirled imprint of its tip.

"Does it hurt?" he asked. She felt his fingers sink into her below her breast, pinpointing the pain in the hollow there; then into her hip, by her buttock, where it ached from carrying the bags and walking too quickly and hard, trying to keep up with the crowd.

"Here? Here?" Her eyes flew open to find him watching her closely with his own alert, unblinking gaze. He'd found the exact places, the ones that David had discovered and would tenderly kiss. She thought to push him away—this was ridiculous, obscene, his hands on her, not David's—but she didn't.

"Hana told me about you," he said.

Was that how he knew? His fingers probed expertly, unshyly, almost like a doctor's but not quite; or almost like the hands of the one Japanese man her father had let into their house long, long ago, when the pain had gotten worse. He'd let the man try, pressing his fingers into her almost like this. The pain had deepened in a way that was good, but only for the moment. Her father had still been taking her to all kinds of doctors then; they hadn't yet given up.

She swallowed a cry when he rooted out an especially tender spot.

"Here," he declared.

"No," she insisted, but recoiled a little in spite of herself. Instantly he lifted his hands from her.

"You're an odd girl," he said. He was still close; he hadn't moved away.

"More than Hana?" she had to ask. He didn't answer.

She wasn't intimidated by him any longer, or by the churnings of her body. He'd felt her; he knew now what she was, what lurked underneath her blouse. He'd felt her nooks and crannies, a few of them at least, and still he stayed.

She couldn't help thinking of David and herself collapsed on the subway platform at rush hour, all the city milling around them, the passengers staring. Afterwards, everything had changed. Someone desiring her had been so new, so special. It hadn't mattered so much how or why. He'd been her refuge, right from the start. Could it be that that was just what he'd wanted, what had made him desire her?

"Hana is with her friends at Akiyoshi-dai." Rinzo's voice was close to her, and low in the throat. The way it said "friends" hinted at disdain. The sound of the place's name implied a purpose she couldn't guess, though she'd heard it and said it herself more than once.

"What is she doing there?" she started to ask, but his finger was at her lips, then in her mouth when she opened it wide, sliding along her gums, then farther in, until she felt its tip graze the back of her throat.

She twisted toward him and away. "What if she comes home?" she murmured.

"Hana never comes during the day," he said, but his hands stopped. "She only comes home at night."

"Is he with her?"

He shrugged, perplexed.

"Ryu. He lives here with Hana."

"Nobody is here except Hana, and only at night," he said. "She hates the light." His profile was a smooth, polished slope, those bird-eyes seemingly incised with some fine instrument. "Hana can only work at night. When the work is finished, she says it screams in pain at the morning light. She likes that."

Miyo did not tell him that she'd been here with Hana in daylight, that Ryu had been here too, though it was true that she'd woken in the night to find Hana at work with her red yarn.

Rinzo's two perfect hands eased under her blouse and over her breasts; one hand partly cupped the air over the sunken spot, and travelled down the scar.

She felt light, too light, as if she'd drift away, his hands sliding down and away, off her. She wanted him on her, and felt the familiar, painful wet gaping of her vagina for the first time since she'd left David, and for the first time not for David. She reached for Rinzo's white sleeve and his chest where the shirt opened up. She almost called his name, but didn't.

He rolled onto her, his lips to her ear. He weighed less than David; his skin was soft; the hair was coarser but sparse; there were other differences. Then he stopped, struck. "Hibakusha?" he whispered. She didn't know the word. It sounded exotic the way he said it; like a taboo. She raised her eyes and there were his again, ever alert, watchful, and she felt the way he must see her, the dread and wonder.

"Your mother?" he asked.

"Your mother was in Hiroshima?" he said again when she didn't reply. He pronounced it slowly and deliberately, so there was no mistaking. "Nagasaki?"

She understood what he must take her for. She'd seen pictures, hideous ones; she'd read of deformities that might persist through generations. But she'd never thought of her mother or herself. For how could she imagine such a flash in the sky, and what they called black rain pouring down? She'd never thought to ask her father.

"No," she said, and pushed him off her, repelled, relieved, confused. No, no. She waited for him to leave.

But he didn't. He raised one arm, with hairs scattered as if from dropped seeds, up in the air, and slowly he wrote the characters for her name—a mystery drawn in air, but she could see it. "Mi-yo," he said.

The sound of her own name conjured a woman's voice, the memory of hearing it and wishing it might be her mother's. Whose finger was it writing on her palm, the tickle? Was it a memory that had somehow survived, or the memory of a memory she'd made for herself?

"Beautiful night," Miyo declared, with something like pride, and irony. "That's what my name means."

"Yes," he answered, as if it all made sense. Despite her denial, for him the pieces had fallen into place, and his hand dropped down into her hair, *her pretty hair,* he called it, though she wondered how it could be special or prettier than any woman's here.

SIX

BEHIND THE CLOSED DOOR, inside Hana's studio, the telephone was ringing.

"Don't answer," Rinzo said. He went on turning the pages of his book for Miyo, wearing a pristine white cotton glove.

"What if it's her?" Miyo said, about to rise. Rinzo took her hand and passed it over a succession of clouds in watercolour, each contained and symmetrical, not like the mercurial sprawl of clouds in an everyday sky. They were only photographs but she was not to touch. She felt like a healer, or diviner.

"It's never Hana who calls."

"What if something's happened to her?" She scrambled to her feet and started toward the closed door.

"Don't answer," Rinzo said again, and pulled her back to his side. "It's only the kamikaze." He gave his fleeting mirage of a smile.

"The kamikaze?"

"Look at this." He turned to the centre of the book, where a blast of light and shadow billowed up into a thunderous roiling cloud frozen in a burnished sky.

Beneath the photograph it said *Mushroom Cloud #05,
Hiroshima, Japan. August 6, 1945.* His gloved finger
traced the cloud's fiery stem to its blooming cap.
Instinctively Miyo glanced at Hana's mural, the monstrous pink blossom on the wall.

"What do you think?" He watched her, still holding
onto her wrist, testing her. At last the phone went quiet.

"It's beautiful," she said. She dared to touch the surface of the page with the hand he was holding, and he
didn't resist. The page was smooth and cool.

"All gone without a trace," he said. "No trees, no
buildings, no people." He turned the page to *Mushroom
Cloud #06,* to *Mushroom Cloud #07* and so on.

"The artist said that if we find beauty in this scene, it
is more awful than we imagined." He let go of her wrist
and closed the book. He peeled off the glove and lay
back, his face receding into a mysteriously dappled light.
She could not quite grasp, in this instant, that she was
in this foreign place, that her father was dead and that
the sickliness within her might be traced to the beauty
she saw in this painting.

She touched Rinzo's cheek, following its curve with
her finger just as he had traced the cloud in the book.
"Then why does he make it so beautiful?" she asked.
She slipped her hand down to his waist close to the
band of his pants, where the hair was wiry and dense
and slightly moist. She watched his face for signs but it
remained unchanged, and quickly she withdrew her
hand, shamed, embarrassed.

"It will always be beautiful," he told her, and caught
her hand in his. "Beautiful and terrible, and distant.
When it comes close enough, it will be too late."

♥

"Who is the kamikaze?" she asked. "Why is he calling Hana?"

"He's her friend," Rinzo said. "Hana has many friends."

He was showing her a drawing he'd carefully taken from a folder. It was done on a scrap of sketching paper, like a child's doodle. A misshapen circle, a misshapen yellow sun burnt red at its rim, X'ed over with black strokes that began thick and strong, then grew faint, as if the artist had become weak or discouraged or disgusted.

"It reminds me of Hana," Miyo said.

"It is Hana's." Rinzo opened the door to the studio and turned on the light. Red everywhere, no less disturbing than in her memory, and there was her father, the old black-and-white photograph faint as dust beneath the red bundles.

"There are one thousand stitches on this wall," Rinzo declared with a sweep of his arm, "like the sennin-baris, the one-thousand-stitch belts that schoolgirls gave to soldiers when they went off to fight. Each stitch made by a different hand."

One thousand stitches meant the same wish wished a thousand ways. That was why Hana had asked Miyo to think a unique thought with each length of yarn she wound: for every soldier, a thousand girls' wishes.

"What was the wish?" Miyo asked.

"Success in destroying the enemy," Rinzo said, "and glorious life or glorious death."

"Why wish for death?"

"It is an honour as a member of the emperor's Special Attack Forces."

"Kamikaze."

He nodded, that elusive smile flitting at his lips' corners. "Like Hana's men." He glanced through the doorway to the cherry-blossom mural and those pictures resting on the tips of stamens.

"All dead?" asked Miyo.

"In the line of duty, long long ago."

"What about the kamikaze? The one who called?"

"There are no more kamikazes. All dead," he echoed. "He's some lowly old soldier Hana feels sorry for." He started to laugh, too hard. "Maybe he was a coward, or someone smart enough to weasel his way out."

He passed his hand over the neatly stacked photographs and briefly held up the one she'd seen before; "With their glorious cherry blossoms, ready to die," he remarked absently, and went on shuffling through the stack. He paused at a photograph of a rectangle of cloth spread out before a frail, bent figure. "Poor woman. That's all that was left of her son." There was a large circle in the middle of the sheet with writing down either side of it, faded and unreadable.

"What is it?"

"It's a Hinomaru. The boy wrapped his country's flag around his belly for his final mission, inscribed with his family's farewell messages." Across the top were two large characters, black and thick as worms. Rinzo slowly read one character: "'must,'" then the next: "'sink.' Of course, most of them never hit their targets," he added. "Foolish woman. I have no sympathy for her selfless mother's heart that was supposedly so unique to Japan. So selfless that she gave up her son in the name of the emperor."

"But how could a mother . . .?" Miyo could not imagine how you could give a child over to certain death: your own or anyone else's. She could not imagine war.

"No one dares speak of this today. Only Hana and a few others. Everyone would rather forget."

He reached out to finger Miyo's hair. "So fine for Japanese hair," he said with a capricious air. "Hana is growing her hair for her new work. Did she ask for some of yours?"

It was then that Miyo noticed the coarse girlish braids on the sheet, tacked down at their curled ends, which made up the strokes of the written characters; she saw the brownish stains here and there on the cloth, not made by design, not quite as faint as the rising sun at the centre.

"No, she didn't, she wouldn't," she stuttered, flinching, and pulled away from the photograph, away from him.

He was silent for a moment; cast a sheepish glance up, all the more pitiful on his face. "No," he said solemnly, "of course she wouldn't."

From Hana's table Miyo picked up another photograph, this one a large portrait of a handsome, smiling man in a Japanese army uniform. He looked Japanese but there was something exotic about him; the shallow softness of his face seemed at odds with the sharpness of his features.

"That is Kusuru Ryo," Rinzo said. "Hana keeps it because he reminds her of me." Miyo saw no similarity; there was no softness in Rinzo's face, and nothing of the other man's guileless smile. "Only because his father was a Japanese diplomat, like mine, and his mother was

American, like mine. He was Ken to his friends at Harvard. I was Richard." He bowed with a mock flourish. "But my mother was Japanese American, a nisei like your father." He gave her a meaningful glance. "Kusuru-san fought for Japan, and died right before the surrender."

Miyo set down the photograph with the others. "All dead," she murmured.

"Hana says Kusuru Ryo had a divided heart, like mine, between here and there. Maybe that's true. But her own heart . . . ." He paused. "I-chi-o-ku gyo-ku-sai," he pronounced slowly. "It is shattered like a beautiful jewel. Like Japan's one hundred million hearts."

Rinzo closed the door as they stepped out of the studio. He slid his book back into its jacket, and wrapped it with as much care as when he'd brought it out. He took hold of her wrist again, with three fingers carefully spaced side by side. He shushed her when she started to speak. He held her other wrist, also with three fingers, feeling and listening. "You're better now," he said.

"I studied Chinese medicine for a short time in Beijing," he explained, "but gave it up. It was beyond me how one could perceive from the outside what a body experiences from within." He put his own wrist in her hand, positioning her three fingers. "Now you're touching me. Look at me and listen, smell if you like, ask me anything. Tell me, am I floating or sunken? Withering or blooming?"

All she sensed was the wilful beat of his pulse, and the smell of him, an indescribable mingling of cologne and sweat under the tips of her fingers, growing warm and moist. She shrugged and let go.

"It's all right. We're all withering." He buttoned the immaculate cuffs of his white shirt.

"Soon it will be cherry-blossom season," he said, with a hint of sarcasm. "Hana must be with her friends, the ladies, preparing. For them it's the saddest season of all when the cherry blossoms begin to bloom, because eventually they must die." He made a dramatic gesture and the clownish frown, and stood up to look at Hana's painting. "That's what makes them exquisite." He brushed his hand across the wall, just as he had the pictures in the book, lingering on one petal that hung down, ready to be shed.

"Hana shares their melancholy," he said. "All the widows who lost their husbands so young, dying for the emperor. It makes her sadness bearable, the ache beautiful. The rest of the seasons bring mere distraction and emptiness, an ugly emptiness, here." He pointed to his stomach. "This is where Japanese feel pain. You feel it here," he said almost bitterly, patting his chest: an accusation, a retribution; as if she was so very different from him or complicit.

It seemed unbearably sad to Miyo that she might never feel what Hana felt.

"Hana said you only just found out you had a sister." He paused and watched. "Hana always knew you existed."

All along, Hana had known that their father had chosen between them; even as a child. Setsuko had made sure, sending pictures of Miyo over the years that Hana had catalogued and arranged along with ones of herself.

"Yes." There was no way to even their losses. She would have to live with that fact.

"She blamed you," Rinzo said. "She would have had a father if not for you."

They both stopped to hear the words echo. "Instead she has the widows." He sighed. "That's where you'll always find her."

She wanted him to say more but he'd turned his face away from her, into shadow.

Miyo understood: *he loves her*. She may have understood this in the very first moment when he'd come up the steps toward her. That was why she'd felt such an intimacy, had let a stranger touch her; it was because of Hana. *He loves her but can't have her*. Hana couldn't belong to anyone: not to Rinzo, to Setsuko, to Ryu, and not to Miyo herself.

Miyo sat alone inside Hana's red room. Rinzo was long gone. He'd left her his handkerchief and promised to call if he heard from Hana. But he didn't expect to. She'd simply arrive home one night soon enough, maybe even tonight. He'd told Miyo nothing more about Hana's widowed friends and their mysterious preparations. She sorted through the clippings and photographs on the table: countless images of smoke ruffling the sky over blackened heaps in a pocked ocean; or of young officers waving, smiling, raising tiny cups to one another on an airfield, Rising Sun sashes tied round their heads.

She scrutinized the names and phone numbers tacked to the wall, futile as it seemed; she recognized none of them—why would she?

She thought of calling Ryu but had no number; she'd assumed he'd be here.

There on the wall, beside the names and numbers, were her own telltale misshapen head and body as an infant, an adolescent, then as a young woman. Below, twinned to hers, Hana at about the same ages. It was unmistakeably Hana, ever strong and straight.

Miyo wasn't used to seeing pictures of herself. She was a tree with sickly roots, that was what Miss Whitten had told her in kindergarten. Her tree would never be quite as tall, quite as thickly branched as the others. Miss Whitten would touch her chin and give her a look that seemed to say, *Poor, poor child.*

Where was the half that she and Hana shared? Hana must have wondered that when she placed their pictures together on the same wall with their father. Miyo gazed up, and even through Hana's red piercings she saw the open road she'd always seen, the unlined youthful face, but also the deep furrow already formed at the brow, and the eyes that were angry and darkened, smothered by some inward fury.

"He never fit in," Setsuko had told her one night. "Nowhere. He was sure the nisei didn't like him because he had fought for the Japanese, but they didn't have anything against him. He wasn't in the internment camps back home, and he wasn't a repat in Japan. In Japan he saw all the Japanese pouring in from Taiwan, China, the Philippines, Malaya, all those dirty places that got dirtier after the Japanese left. He wasn't one of them either," Setsuko had said, shaking her head.

"We've got no use for them," Miyo's father would say about the Japanese in the neighbourhood. He'd barely say hello. But it was Miyo keeping them away too, not playing out on the street, not able to join in with the others.

There was Hana sitting in this darkened apartment day and night, stitching and winding her yarn, then mysteriously disappearing for days at a time. Out of the jumble of photographs left on the table, Hana peered up at Miyo from among rows of elderly women. Their faces were pallid and drawn, solemn, folded up into old age, receding into themselves. Hana's face was bright, brittle and faceted; refusing to be dimmed. There she stood beside the woman in the kimono, while others sat below with hands folded, faces placid and ever-believing.

She recognized Yasukuni Shrine in another photo, the bare-branched trees she'd seen with Setsuko here trimmed with white blossoms, the sky bleached whiter, the stark grounds she'd walked in flocked with people, with families, toddlers feeding pigeons, men standing in peaked caps. It was the place where she could imagine the afterlife being lived, if anywhere; not heaven but a kind of paradise, a perpetual day when you were in your Sunday best, though nothing was out of the ordinary; your cares perched so lightly on your shoulders that they were hardly there.

It would be a day you thought and wished would never end, and yet just another day, or a small part of one. Something like when she was little and her father picked her up from school and they drove in the car: that short, silent ride home. It was when things came cleanly end to end; the time and place where there was no dread of what was to come, no regret for what had gone before.

She found a sheet of paper with English printed beside the Japanese, so neatly and uniformly that the page looked dotted with a kind of code to be further deciphered. Across the top it simply said *A Song,* and alongside the words were musical notes, a do-re-mi melody. She tried to hum it; it sounded like a singalong for children:

You and I are Cherry Blossom comrades
Blooming in the same garden of our squadron.
Knowing that cherry blossoms soon must fall,
Let us fall bravely for our country.

Though we may fall one by one,
Let us return to Yasukuni Shrine
And meet again as blossoms in the same garden.

The words sounded wishful, in a childish sort of way, but eerily from another world. Had her father yearned to return to Yasukuni, as Setsuko said? Would he have fallen bravely for this country, chosen it, never living out his life as he had with her? She gazed up again, searching for some clue in that young face, some sign she'd never detected in all those years of him being her father, of hearing barely two words of Japanese pass his lips. Had he sung this song? Had he believed?

There was Rinzo's jacket, folded as he'd left it. On top of it sat his business card, carefully placed. She picked up the jacket, knowing that he'd guessed she'd do just this: touch it and hold it, smell it. She studied the card, one side Japanese, the other English. It said his name, an address in Shibuya and a telephone number. He wanted her to call, if only to push her away, push her down, because of Hana. She was right to see the cruelty in him from the first moment, and then to feel distant and sorry for him.

In the red room, Miyo picked up the telephone, the card held by its sharp edges between her fingers. She set it down. The red light flashed repeatedly on the answering machine. One, two, three messages.

The phone rang, startlingly; it could only be him daring her, because she'd been so close to calling, and because they'd become toggled together through Hana. She pictured him at the other end, in a spare, elegant apartment, long white walls adorned with works of art, in his crisp white shirt, the phone held to his massive head. *Pick up,* he was telling her, those cut-out eyes glaring as if he could will it, will everything except Hana.

She reached for the receiver but the ringing ceased, the machine clicked. It whirred and clicked again, beeped, and the tape started to play. Someone was retrieving the messages. She picked up and it was Ryu, startled to find her there. "Meet me at Le Rendezvous," he said. It was a café on Omotesando, not far from the apartment.

From Ryu's directions she found the café easily, on a wide avenue lined with expensive shops and towering trees. It was late afternoon but the streets were busy as ever—no busier now, at what she supposed was near rush hour, than earlier in the day. She sat at a table outside, just as he'd told her to. She'd arrived early; she was learning to pace herself, to find her own rhythm through the streets and the crowds.

"Bonjour mademoiselle. Café crème?" the waiter asked as he slid a tray over his fingertips. She asked for a glass

of water. It was odd, these sounds from this waiter's face, the authentic accent, the wicker chair she was sitting on, looking onto the wide avenue. And how did she, with her Canadian English, seem to others—the few people she'd spoken to, at the stores, when she bought a newspaper at the concession stand?

"They think that something is wrong with you, that you're slow" was what Rinzo had said. "They know you're Japanese. They see it in your face. But you can't speak. What do you tell them?" She'd recited the words from her phrase book, telling them she was a foreign-born Japanese, a visitor from Canada. "Then they wonder why your papa or whoever left and why you come back now," he'd said, casual, brutal. Setsuko had been disdainful too, disgusted at her father not teaching her Japanese.

"I never tell them anything," Rinzo had said. "I'm just another salaryman on the street."

What she craved at this moment was hot green tea, acrid and thickly clouded—what she'd now, here, acquired a taste for, for its cleansing bitterness. But this was not the place for it. Here, each and every thing had its place.

The air was cool. It was three-thirty, already late in the day. It was that hour of golden light she missed, that sadly waning light she had sat in after work, waiting, in the days before David, for her father to pick her up. She was still trying to find that quality of light here. The sun seemed to drop abruptly from the sky; on the trains she'd pass through a tunnel and come out to find it gone. She'd have to catch the golden light slanting across the sky in early morning.

A voice came back to her from the tape on Hana's machine; it was deep and gruff, manly, the way some older men spoke here. But it was also commanding, menacing. Or maybe she only imagined that, since she couldn't comprehend the language, couldn't read its noises. She'd snatched up the phone when the messages started rewinding, not knowing who would be retrieving them at the other end. But it had been Ryu, Ryu's sweet boyish voice. He was checking Hana's messages for clues, worried too because she hadn't yet returned. This time he didn't say, *she'll come home, she always comes home,* as before.

When she spotted him on the street she was flooded with relief, more than she'd expected: the homeyness of him, his solid body, the thick curtain of hair. She had no one now, with Hana vanished and Setsuko about to leave; no one but him. His clothes were rumpled from being slept in. She couldn't help noticing how tired he looked, his eyes puffy, like a teary, cranky child. He was young after all: not more than eighteen.

"Setsuko called too," he told her as he sat himself down opposite her. He was suddenly cool and diffident as when they'd first met, daring her to prove herself. "She says you're leaving soon."

"I'm staying," she told him, furious at Setsuko. She'd abandoned Hana before and she was doing it again for her own selfish reasons. Miyo shivered.

Ryu reached under the table and cupped each of her knees, her cold knees, in his warm, dry hands. Somehow he knew. "That's good," he said, his voice cracking like a boy's; he was alone too. "A man will come to meet us."

"A man?"

"Someone Hana has been talking to for her work."

"About my father?" He didn't answer. "Is it the kamikaze?" she asked.

Ryu laughed, and she laughed too, without knowing why. "That's what we call someone who is crazy," he said.

"Rinzo called him the kamikaze. Someone who was calling. He wouldn't let me answer."

"Rinzo? What were you doing with him?" Ryu was angry. He snatched his palms from her knees and instantly they were chilled, bare.

"I was waiting for Hana and he let me in," she said. The heat rose in her cheeks. She looked down, hiding her face like those silent, weary workers on the crowded subway, keeping their cares to themselves.

"He sells Hana's art. He makes money for her." Miyo didn't know why she was defending Rinzo. Out of shame for letting him touch her, or to provoke Ryu; she didn't know which.

"He keeps most of it for himself," Ryu said bitterly. "Don't listen to him. He wants you to think things."

"He said Hana might be with the widows," she told him, though she didn't believe it. She waited but nothing came. Ryu only snorted.

"He does care about her," she whispered, half to herself.

They sat in silence until the waiter came and Ryu ordered tea for both of them; they served it here after all. He knew what comforted her.

"Hana likes to sit at night when the street lights come on," Ryu said, suddenly animated. It was Hana bringing him out, up to the surface. She could do that even when she was absent. "She likes to watch people go by, kissing and hugging, trying to be natural, like American teenagers." He laughed again, draping his arm over the empty chair, missing Hana. "She thinks it's funny. She says, 'I'm too old for that.'"

Miyo looked out on the avenue too, seeing girls curl their slender bodies like kittens' tails round their boyfriends even as they tottered on high stilt shoes: their hair bleached ginger, their lips glowy white. Ryu was younger than most of them. It was endearing the way he recounted what Hana had said as if he were the wise old soul. His hand crept back over her knee. "Better?" His skin had that youthful resilience; everything would bead off it, even his own turmoil. It was sad to think how he would change. He couldn't be sweet Ryu forever.

"Rinzo is not good," he said, almost regretfully. "I try to tell her that he is angry because she won't love him back."

"When she called, where was she?" Miyo asked, impatient from things she hadn't wanted to hear.

He shrugged. "She wouldn't let me come." Miyo's heart fell when she heard that. It was foolish, but something of herself seemed diminished by his feeling for Hana.

"When did you last see her?"

He dropped his head. Just then, the waiter came and placed a croissant in front of him and he came to life, eagerly biting into it like a boy going from one thing to the next. She squeezed his shoulder, half in affection, half in impatience. "Tell me where," she said, more sternly than she meant to.

He began to cry a little, but stopped as soon as he started. She almost expected him to wipe his face with the backs of both hands, the way little children do, but he didn't; he just left the tears. She had an impulse to reach out to touch them, maybe to convince herself that they were real, maybe just to feel his face under her fingers—as David had done with her when they first met. But she held her hands in her lap.

"I'm sorry," she said.

"I haven't eaten all day," he said, munching on the croissant again. "Hana sent me back to the sumo stable but I followed her. She went into Shinjuku station. I couldn't find her." He smiled messily. "I have to find her before it's too late."

"Too late for what?"

"I think she is planning something."

"What do you mean?"

"One time she was arrested at Yasukuni when the prime minister came there. They let her go, but next time they won't. I think this time will be trouble."

Miyo looked out onto the avenue, wishing Hana would suddenly appear. She recalled the crowd at Shibuya when she'd first arrived with Setsuko, the spectacle of those thousands of black heads; she imagined the people she'd marched among gathered together, on and on for miles, their heads becoming pinpricks; Hana was somewhere among the twelve million of Tokyo.

They sat until it grew dark and the lights came on. Miyo drank cup after cup of tea, until its cleansing taste turned acrid and the fine grit of its residue filmed her teeth and shrivelled her throat. In the bathroom she found to her dismay a Japanese-style toilet; she had to squat over the porcelain basin with her underwear pushed down her thighs. Her leg quivered as the pee streamed crookedly from her, and its pungency rose.

As she made her way back to Ryu, she spotted the man in the crowd, approaching the café. It had to be him, the kamikaze, just as Rinzo had said. It was the kerchief at his neck, now puffed as an ascot, that told her so—the red kerchief he'd worn at Yasukuni Shrine. Instead of his soldier's uniform he wore a dark blue suit like any salaryman. It was the same man that she and Setsuko had glimpsed talking to Hana, that Hana had then fled from, Miyo in tow; the man in the photograph pinned to Hana's studio wall. There was a certain stiffness in the way he held himself; the brittle, bony angle of his shoulders made him seem both youthful and aged, with a soldier's self-discipline inbred.

Ryu stood up and waved. "He said he'd wear red," he whispered to Miyo.

The song came to her then, that bit of tuneless melody she had tried to hum in Hana's room, but there were the words, dotting her head as they'd dotted the page beneath the undecipherable characters: *Let us return to Yasukuni Shrine and meet again as blossoms in the same garden.*

SEVEN

THE MAN BOWED DEEPLY, red kerchief fluttering at his neck. He held out a soiled, dog-eared card to Miyo. "Call me Buddy," he said.

Koji "Buddy" Kuroda, she read, in friendly old-fashioned type, nothing in Japanese.

"Don't use these too often." He chuckled and leaned forward, clamping womanish hands between his knees. Miyo had to stop herself from recoiling. "Surprised you, didn't I? I'm a little out of practice." He glanced nervously from side to side and lowered his voice. "Nobody knows I speak English." He winked and smiled; that made him both guileless and grotesque to her, but she could not help thinking of her father with his secrets.

Slowly he untied the kerchief, uncovering a long thin neck, the skin creped over nuts and bolts of tissue and bone.

"We're looking for Hana. Do you know where she is?" Miyo said. She was surprised at how demanding she could be for someone else: her flesh and blood, as David had said.

Buddy babbled to Ryu in Japanese and Miyo nearly grabbed his shabby sleeve in frustration. "Was it you calling? Are you the kamikaze?" she asked.

Everything stilled: Buddy, Ryu; a young couple embracing on the avenue shifted their eyes away. She'd used the word for crazy people too loudly. Kamikazes didn't exist any longer, Ryu had said, not today, not real ones; only the silent blue-suited salarymen who worked themselves to death. But even they came back alive, eyes shot with blood, drunken and devastated by midnight. Maybe there had never been any kamikazes at all.

Buddy laughed until his eyes shone. "I am not kamikaze," he said after a moment, full of rue; as if it were something you were born into and stayed forever. "Sometimes I wish I was."

"Why?" Miyo asked.

His eyes turned dull. "Because then I'd be a kami. I'd be a god. I'd be getting ready to bloom in Yasukuni right about now. Everyone would come to visit and say, 'How good it is to see him again!' Even my wife."

This man wanted to be one of those tiny faces glued to Hana's wall. He was one who believed.

"If I'd left Manchuria and gone to Tokyo, like that girl's daddy, I would have been picked."

Buddy was dabbing his face with the ridiculous kerchief, though there were no tears, no sweat. Miyo's fingers easily circled his wrist. "Whose daddy?"

He was disturbed by her touching him. "That girl's daddy. Kamikaze. I told her so."

Miyo's breath quickened: her father one of those doomed moon-faces? A cherry-blossom comrade, as the song said?

Buddy drew back from her nervously. "She wanted to know."

"That's not possible. He was Hana's father and mine too. He lived in Canada." Miyo laughed with glass bits dancing in her throat. He hadn't crashed like the rest of them in the song. He had gone home; he had lived, he was her father even after her mother was gone. That was the proof. All kamikazes died; it was what they did. "He lived," she said.

"Yes, it's so." Buddy shook his head sadly on its wilting stem. "He lived. He failed. Hana knows."

Her father one of those young men in Hana's pictures, with their cherry-blossom branches draped around their necks like funeral wreaths? Poor Hana. She must have pored over stacks and stacks of photographs searching for him. But she would not have found him.

"He flew a plane, that's all," Miyo said. Even Setsuko had said so. She could not have been mistaken.

"Your father served, just like I did, only I wasn't tokkotai, Special Attack Forces. I was not kamikaze. But I sacrificed. He didn't," Buddy said. "They say I did bad things." He stared at Miyo, at once sheepish and proud. He drew out his kerchief again. He spread it across his lap as a magician would, smoothing the edges with his palms. "You think you know the way it is? What do you know?" He draped the kerchief over his fist, raised it in the air, then tucked it into his breast pocket. His face drooped in long folds.

"I served five years in prison like the kangaroo court decreed. I paid my debt for doing what anybody would've done, for following orders. I'm wiped clean." He held up his hands like a defiant child who's played in mud or eaten chocolate. To Miyo he seemed nothing more than a stupid man not smart enough to go home where he belonged—to Canada, as her father had.

Finally Buddy rose, waddling back, crablike. "Your daddy's story is the same as mine but different," he said, still holding the chair under him, gazing up with empty eyes. He released the chair, bowed and walked away, dabbing his forehead with his kerchief. Quickly he was lost in the sea of salarymen.

Miyo scribbled a message on a napkin for Ryu when he went to the washroom, and waded into the crowd, slowly at first, then faster. The red kerchief flashed up ahead, a mute siren.

"Hey!" she called. She didn't dare call him Buddy. She called again; no one turned. "Hana!" she cried impulsively, and a head swivelled round. There he was, thin and hunched, the skeletal trace of his body in his suit showing like bones under skin. She thought of her father pounded down to his core at the end, his arms suddenly shrivelling. Buddy threaded his way toward her, ceding to the oncoming crowd. When he stood before her with those floating eyes, red spilling from his breast pocket, it frightened her to know that she could conjure him with Hana's name.

He urged her aside, his outstretched hand pointed down, digging into air—she'd come to understand the rudeness here of an upturned, beckoning palm. Their reflection was cast in storefront glass over garments dangling from a rack, pleated and iridescent, afloat like tropical fish. She glanced twice to see that it was her there, hovering over Buddy. Sixty years ago he would've been a gangly youth, not long past puberty, in an ill-fitting uniform like the one her father wore in the photograph at home.

"You want to know about your daddy, right? Like little sister did."

Miyo could only nod.

Buddy led her to the basement level of a department store, down aisles of food displays, past uniformed women offering samples on toothpicks. The displays stretched in all directions, and smells wafted from block to block, though she couldn't link the sweet or salty or savoury aroma to the look of things; she didn't recognize them. She did take a square of chocolate from a girl, a deep black-brown; it was mud in her mouth that wouldn't melt. She spat it into a tissue and tucked it into her pocket.

They sat at a pristine counter where an array of blenders churned in front of them in different colours, each labelled in Japanese. Shoppers lined up, drank and left. Buddy ordered a cloudy green drink for her, and pink for himself.

"Warabi—fiddlehead," he said. He talked like her father, words were flotsam in an ocean. *Bad things.* "Try," he urged. She drank. The taste was bitter but refreshing; it washed the dark wax from her tongue. "Mine is sakura. Cherry blossom." He smiled and held out his glass; she wasn't sure if he'd chosen it deliberately, but Miyo pushed it away.

"I told the story to your little sister. I can't say all of it again. I'm an old man." He kept his smile.

Miyo sighed impatiently. "But I don't know where she is." She pronounced each word slowly and loudly to make him understand.

He sat very still; the smile vanished. "Don't talk like I'm stupid," he said. "Your sister's been in the mountains with my wife and the other ladies. You'll find them tomorrow afternoon, at this place—" and he carelessly tossed a card onto the counter. "Now go. Your friend's waiting." With that, he turned his back to her and noisily sucked up the last of his drink with his straw. As she walked away toward the cluttered aisles, scanning for an exit, she heard him once more—"Your daddy wasted his luck"—but she didn't look back.

Buddy wanted to tell the girl his story. He saw that she could be trusted to keep his secrets, she'd sit like a key in a lock. He hadn't felt sure of the other one, Hana, but it was too late, and what did it matter now? He'd kept them too long, his secrets; they were worthless as wooden coins.

He was even ready to tell this girl about her father and the old days, but women could never wait. Only Kiku had waited for him, back when he served his time, and every day of their married life. Except for these few days every year at cherry-blossom time, when she left him to be with the other ladies, and to be with Hajime, at least in spirit, at Yasukuni Shrine. But she called him every day faithfully, told him where she was, what she and the ladies were doing. This time, for the first time, she'd asked him to come to one of their gatherings.

Something about the first girl, Hana, reminded him of Mas, though it had been sixty years since they'd last seen each other in Manchuria, or Manchukuo, as they used to call it. Something about the mouth, the hard thin line of the top lip and the too generous lower one that tried to make up for the other. She was skittish with him, ready to jump on him one minute, and running from him the next. She exhausted him: fingers on the table, and feet under it, thrumming; eyes hooked onto his, unwilling to let go until she got everything she wanted. So he had told her, from the beginning, about him and Mas in Manchukuo.

It was paradise. Where else would you see a white man carrying a yellow skibby's bags, or the skibby telling him what floor he wanted in a hotel elevator? And they were all nikkei—no matter where you came from, where you were born, you were just as good as Japanese from Japan. World-class citizens with streetcars to ride, roomy, reserved for Japanese only. You were a man one time in your life. Back home, *yellow skibby* someone once called him on the street. It was forever one ugly name or another, even in the neighbourhood around Powell Street. Yellow skibby stuck, no escaping it.

Before he set foot there, he saw it on a map: Dairen, southern gateway to Manchukuo. To Asia for Asians! He still remembered the shape of it, and traced it now with a wet finger on the white countertop—a glistening organ, disappearing as it was formed. Dairen at the mouth; Mukden at the heart; Hsinking, the north end of the railway, as far as the Super Express Asia would take you. All six thousand miles of it. All these places gone or called something else now, the whole of it laid waste.

From the train, the houses leading up to Hsinking looked like California bungalows, sunny through big front windows, through clouds spun faint as spiderwebs, dry heat held under deep porches. Though he'd never been to California. Walking along the wide main street

in Dairen among the bob-haired girls gave him such a
sunny feeling inside and out.

Akogare no Manshu. Yearned-for Manchuria, they
called it. It was 1938, when the Empire of Manchukuo
was still ruled by the Japanese Kwantung Army. The
mystery of the place: the brightly coloured rooftops, the
raying avenues; the white boys who toted his bag—
White Russians, Poles, Germans, Italians; the shiny
buttons on his Imperial Army uniform the first time he
wore it.

"Akogare no Manshu" was the title of the essay he'd
written when he was just a boy, green as could be, back
in Vancouver.

The pictures he'd first seen of Dairen and Harbin.
The rapt faces in them, in front of ancient buildings
with oddly curled roofs. What his cousins who'd been
there wrote in letters about these places, what articles
they'd clipped from the Los Angeles daily said. It was
paradise of the kingly way, they wrote, where harmony
reigned among five races. At Dairen Port you could spot
Chinese, Koreans, Russians, Germans, Jews, even some
Americans, Brits, French, Italians, Poles—surely more
than just five—pouring off the ships, milling around the
pier. And soon enough there'd be five million Japanese
or more, riding on top. Not like the Koreans, who let
themselves be beaten, or the Chinese, who slunk along,
coolies or thieves.

Buddy would sit at his desk, final year at Vancouver
Japanese Language School, two blocks from Oppenheimer Park, watching his own hand setting each character in its square like a jewel on a crown. The teacher's
clap-clap of her palms when time was up—how hollow

it sounded by the end of a drab day, a tinny, unkingly echo that dogged him out onto the cramped street.

It was a contest. They were to write on the subject of "Manchuria: The New Asia." The teacher brought in a book on Manchuria that showed pictures of big new trains speeding through a huge open land, and workers in the fields, side by side, and the Japanese apart and above, and graphs that showed the production of crops climbing and climbing. It was their very own New World.

For the first time, the words had come to him in Japanese. The English wasn't passing into his head first, his lips pursed to stall it between stammers. It was a sign. *Boku wa, ningen desu. Canada-jin desu ma . . .* and so on. The English came after instead, when he'd sat down after reading his essay in front of the class, and Mitzy, Mitsuko H. for Hiraki, was told to stand up and translate for him. He was Koji back then: Koji K. for Kuroda. *I am a human being. I am a Canadian but my face says I am Japanese, and I am held down. I yearn to stand up as a Japanese. I yearn for Manchuria, where I can stand up and not be held down. I will make my way in the new land of Manchuria as a proud Japanese.* Mitzy read it like a wind-up toy winding down, no swell of pride; that girl was puny with no dreams, couldn't see past her window. She was nowhere now, he was sure—maybe long gone without ever having seen Japan.

He'd been embarrassed at first, hearing *my face says*: himself in her girly voice. She stumbled over the last part with the difficult words; Buddy had copied it straight from a newspaper his cousin had sent. *There is a new era of racial equality in the new land of opportunity.* The words themselves swelled, without her and without him. The teacher was impressed; he got his first A.

He'd folded the paper inside an envelope when his sisters were out, secretly kissed it for luck and counted out his pennies to buy a stamp. Two last pennies he found on the basement floor, where he'd been kicked and thrown by his father the day before, for keeping change from buying eggs. *My father was a mean man* was one thing he told his wife years later. *A mean man.* When he was thirteen, he saw his father strike the Indian asleep in the backyard bushes with a steel pipe. That was all he confessed to, by way of explaining himself to his wife—his own meanness, which was no different from that of the next man in uniform, except that he'd paid the price of five years exacted by the kangaroo court.

All those years before, across the ocean, when Manchukuo and Japan were yearned for, not yet glimpsed, he'd folded that piece of paper encasing his words, fold upon fold, because the Japanese expect neatness and precision, even from a boy. They must have noticed how fine his characters were, mounted inside the squares, showing that he was a smart, upright young man of morals, faith, loyalty. He could do that better than anyone, even now, with unsteady hands and no one to write to.

They gave him a prize. A study tour of yearned-for Manchuria. It was 1938 and he was sixteen, seventeen.

He looked at his hands now, old hands—the pucker on your knuckles spoke your age even if your face didn't—smart hands; cleverer than the rest of him. His wife knew. He'd never let a word of English pass his lips to her. He was Koji-san to her. For years he was convinced

that he'd fooled her, that she never knew Japanese wasn't
his first tongue.

Back in Manchukuo, Buddy noticed Mas right off.
Mas stuck out just as he did, having been born in
Canada. The rest were Yanks. They were Japanese all
right, but different for being second-generation
American. More cocky, Stars and Stripes, the bees'
knees; smiles all around. Slim, Skin, Johnny, Kaz, those
were some of them. They gathered outside the station
at Mukden in late winter, the horizon appearing scruffy
and stark, the landlocked heart of Manchukuo;
obscured by smoke left behind by the train, the clump
of buildings, some peaked and curved in that different-
shaped way; the city pushed into the distance. But you
saw your breath in the air and knew you were there,
the farthest ever from home. There were trees to turn
green come spring. It was sunny, from high in the sky.
There'd be flowers. When the Kwantung Army commander arrived to greet them they stood at attention,
every one of them. In his uniform and peaked cap he
stood stiff and taller than he was, knowing that as a
Japanese he held up the future of all Asia; the gold hilt
and chain of the sword at his side caught the sun. But
then he bowed, low and quick enough to show that he
was not afraid but he didn't trust you not to slice his
head off if you were the enemy, whether samurai, rebel
Manchu or Red Russian bandit.

That girl's daddy was his—Buddy's—buddy, he
thought, and laughed at his own sixty-year-old joke; the
many years gone by; the memory of how shabby and
motley they both were before that officer's gleam. They

both made up their minds to sign on, if not that day, then soon. They both had the feeling that so much was in store for them in this New World. They signed onto their family registries to become official subjects of the emperor, who was civilizing Manchukuo: ridding it of bandits and thieves, making it safe and happy for everyone, even Boy Scouts from America. They didn't think once of going back home. Why would you leave utopia once you found it?

Mas and Buddy worked a few months in an auto repair shop on the outskirts of Mukden, the headquarters of the Japanese imperial forces. They serviced trucks for the Kwantung Army. Mas stayed in Mukden for a time but left long before the Russians came.

It was funny to find out that Mas had later earned his way as a car mechanic in Toronto. Buddy had to admit that it pleased him to know this: Mas, the failed kamikaze, a lowly mechanic all these years. That was what he'd been good at from the start: fixing engines.

Mas finished high school in Tokyo, wrote his entrance exams for university and got accepted; Buddy got his red papers. Even now he was measuring them up side by side, their two fates, as he always had. Through the nisei grapevine Buddy had heard that Mas was at either Meiji or Tokyo Imperial University. They lost touch, the grapevine shrivelled.

Buddy could've gone that route too, if he'd wanted. But everyone's red papers came sooner or later; Mas's when they began drafting even university students, younger and younger, at twenty, then nineteen. Even fifteen-year-olds were getting send-offs at Dairen Port. Students were the elite. They could learn fast. They got the chance to sacrifice, to die in glory. *If I'd gone with your daddy, I'd have been one. I'd have been lucky.*

The red-rice send-offs came back to him, the pier an ocean of red dots bobbing on sparkling white squares—children waving flags, hoisted in the air filled with cries. The sennin-baris with the thousand red stitches given to young brothers, husbands, sons, by some pretty young girl; the red-ribboned hanks of hair, dolls the size of two fingers to pin into their jackets. He never had such a send-off; he had no family there, no sennin-baris to bind his belly and protect his spirit. In the end, they'd kept him stationed in Manchukuo anyway.

What a waste, Buddy thought, drawing a bitter breath. *Mottai nai.* Dying was lucky; was divine. Mas never did believe. He thought luck was something else. Buddy believed, always; before he knew there was an emperor, and after, when the emperor was reduced to a girlish-voiced mortal on the radio. He knew he wasn't bottom of the heap, just some yellow skibby; he knew someone smarter and powerful would tell him so. A woman sidling up to the counter in the now crowded department store smirked right then. She had a bulbous mole under her eye; her lashes brushed it when she blinked. She was old enough to remember. His age.

So much mystery! Where did that five years go? Into the dank concrete corridors, out and round the high fenced perimeter of the prison yard, arms swinging in the dust raised by his marching legs. When did he cease his morning recitation of loyalty oaths to Hirohito? When did he break the habit of saluting every fellow prisoner he marched past? When did Manchukuo become a hazy dream adrift behind him, instead of

ahead? He shut his eyes but he wasn't certain if he
wanted to remember or forget.

Did he do something bad? the girl, Hana, had wanted
to know. The other one wanted to know too; he could see
it in her eyes. She'd even grabbed his sleeve. Kiku had
never been like that with him; she had never been vulgar.

Of course, it wasn't darkness Buddy was seeing with
his eyes still shut, or blankness. It never was. It was mottled with bumps and craters and hairy protrusions; it
was that woman's mole pressing in on him. The sunny
feeling he'd had was gone; it never stayed for long. That
pure warm feeling from his time in Manchukuo had
never really come back; only his remembering it. He felt
heavy and out of breath, and how he knew the particular heaviness of a breathless body, the caved-in middle in
a shapeless sack when your foot still burned from kicking it, and the squirming weight of a body burning on
your shoulder and back, so that it took you by surprise
that rice water could nourish flesh, could keep prisoners
just enough alive; the eventual lifelessness he heaved
onto the back of a truck, though the heart might still
pump like a useless contraption. The heart of a Chinese
coolie, a true yellow skibby. Why couldn't the rest of the
world tell the difference?

Buddy remembered riding silently with the driver
through a night as dark as that woman's mole, then arriving at the hospital door: the relief of seeing those clean
bright-tinged figures in white, trimmed with ribbons of
red. The Red Cross nurses lit at the threshold, ready to
receive with their quaint fifteen-degree salutes, their
high singing voices and their rattling empty gurneys.
Navigating through a maze of hospital corridors into a

sparse clearing of white drapes, a room clean and filled
with humming light, though windowless; everything
hung crisp and certain, even the smell of anesthesic.
The gurneys with their soiled bundles disappearing
swiftly behind white. Once, when he asked if he could
stay to watch, they stared at him as though he were a
monster. As if what they did was different from what he
had done: their gloved hands prodding those breathing
bodies with a scalpel, observing each twitch to advance
medical science.

Buddy had heard the stories long before about parts
being taken out of prisoners while they were still alive;
he'd believed them. After the war he heard about the
nurse whose Class B war crime was eating the liver of
one POW in Kyushu. He'd believed it because you never
knew what you could do under such circumstances; you
never knew what fuelled you to do what you did, and to
be pure and strong to fight for the divine emperor.

"What was your crime?" that Hana had brazenly
asked him.

His own mystery had only been spoken in the kangaroo court.

He was not a monster. No one was a monster. They
were all ningen, all human beings. He had learned that
when he was a boy. Maybe it was because of his mother, who'd soothed him and tried to make him see, if only
so he wouldn't hate his father. He had remembered it
when someone in the ranks sniffed him out for his
accent or bow or salute and called him gaijin, the worst
name to be called: *not one of us*; a foreigner not fit to ride
the roomy streetcars of Dairen. Not fit to utter the oath
of loyalty to the emperor, even when it became shameful.

A monkey in a kangaroo court. A Class B war criminal convicted for torturing prisoners. He hadn't done much: a taunt, a kick, not much more; he had only made them suffer, just as he suffered, for being dirty yellow skibbies on the wrong side of the the war.

Kamikaze could never be gaijin or even ningen. You were spirit, not human. You had no war crime. You were pure. You were blood, air, fire, flower.

Miyo spent the night in Hana's apartment with Ryu, and she slept in his and Hana's futon. The phone rang almost every hour, and each time Ryu sprang up from the corner of the room where Miyo had slept when Hana had been there. Each time it was Setsuko checking to see if Ryu had heard from Hana, or if Miyo had come knocking. Miyo pushed away the receiver, not wanting to talk. *I nai yo,* he said to Setsuko, shrugging. Finally he told her that Miyo had arrived and gone to sleep, and he hung up the phone.

"She is going home to Toronto," he told Miyo. "She says you have something that belongs to her."

Miyo touched the bag with her father's urn, which she'd set down beside her. She pushed Setsuko from her mind. Even as a child, Miyo had not allowed herself to depend on Setsuko for anything; she'd felt no less alone being with her in Tokyo, and she felt no more so at the thought of her leaving. She curled into the futon, which she imagined smelled of Ryu and Hana, faintly of Rinzo's skin and cologne, and which reminded her, less pungently, of David's and her own mingled scents.

She and Ryu woke early on opposite sides of the room, shy in the morning light without Hana between them. Ryu rolled up their bedding and tidied the place while Miyo slipped into the studio to dress, steeling herself for the sight of the red bundles and her father's pocked face once more. But they were gone. The photo hung tattered, flapping at the spots where the bundles had been sutured in, then snipped out. The face was no longer recognizably a face, much less her father's.

When she came out, she saw how bare the place was—what neither she nor Ryu had noticed the night before, with only traces of what had been removed. Ryu was standing in front of the mural, before the cherry blossom, fingering the spots where the soldier's portraits had been stripped from its stamens. Even the odour Miyo had first smelled was faint now, no longer the scent of anyone in particular. "I knew she would come," Ryu said.

They followed the map on the back of the card that Buddy had given them, and took a long ride to the end of the purple subway line. They surfaced onto a wide street with cars whizzing in both directions. They crossed to a narrow road that wound its way into a wooded enclave of houses, the sound of the traffic muffled by thick leaves that cooled the shadows and dappled the light. It seemed an unlikely spot for an art gallery, but finally they arrived at a large clearing at the end of the road and, in the middle of it, a low, sprawling white building, sleekly curved across the front, and windowless. Small steel letters spelled out "Ur Gallery," matching the name on the card. The grounds seemed deserted, but a rustling of leaves and a scratch of feet on the gravel path caught their attention; a figure darted along the curving wall to the back of the building. Miyo stopped herself from calling out; it was a woman, but it wasn't Hana.

Just inside the entrance, by Miyo's foot as she stepped, lay one of Hana's bundles of red yarn, partly unravelled. Ryu picked it up and they followed its short trail into a darkened room just off the front hall. Miyo glimpsed bustling shadows as her eyes adjusted to the dark, and a stripe of light across it. Behind the light she heard Hana call out, "Ne-san!" They both stepped into the light and there was Hana's pretty face, and her eyes that could, when they wanted, meet Miyo's—as they did now, with a look that was for her and her alone; that was home. Ryu stepped forward holding the red yarn in his palm, a tentative offering, but Hana bounded up onto him, clamping her legs around his waist and whispering in his ear, making him laugh. Neither of them could stay angry with Hana.

"The obaasans are here too, ne-san, the ladies of Yasukuni." Hana slid off Ryu and squeezed Miyo's hand in hers. The strength in those bony fingers, the surprising pads of fleshiness at the base of the thumb and the heel of the hand, were utterly familiar to Miyo now.

"You left without telling me." Miyo heard herself: childishly needing comfort, as if she were the younger sibling instead of the elder. She sighed deeply, the tremor of her breath released.

"I told you I had to do my work," Hana said, with a coolness, a detachment that was new, as if to make clear that the flesh and blood they shared could not always come first. "It's important. Perhaps you will understand." She cast an indecipherable glance at Ryu.

Out in the foyer, men and women in elegant suits, some holding elderly people by the arm, had begun to arrive, ushered in by a girl in white gloves bowing at the door, her gaze cast low and vacant. Whenever the door swung open, a crackling bellow sounded outside from a loudspeaker.

"Wait for me until it's over, all right, ne-san?" Hana whispered, so close in her ear now, her particular scent returned, that Miyo wondered how anything could come between them. Hana left them before Miyo could answer or ask questions, disappearing into an adjacent darkened room.

"What is he saying?" Miyo asked Ryu when the bellowing outside erupted again.

"'Tenno-heika banzai.' Long live the emperor," Ryu said. "He is crazy old soldier who drives his black bus with the loudspeaker on top, shouting that war is not over until Japan wins. He comes to Hana's show always." He glanced around at the well-dressed crowd filing in and among them, the few stragglers, hair permed into an Afro or matted into dreadlocks, dressed to appear casual, even shabby, seeming listless and distracted. A youthful couple flopped to the foyer floor munching on food, and the white-gloved girl at the door, distressed, discreetly urged them to their feet.

"The floor is dirty, outside space," Ryu explained. "Very disrespectful to sit, but that is why they do it. They think all Japanese traditions are hypocritical."

In a moment, the white-gloved girl was directing Ryu and Miyo toward the darkened room that Hana had slipped into. "Hana said for you to go in," she said in American-sounding English.

They passed through a short corridor that opened onto a stark, bare space. In the centre, a white cloth drooped down onto the concrete floor under a ghostly light. Where it fell across the floor were four blotches of red in a row: Hana's bundles. Four elderly women were seated with the rolled end of the cloth in their laps; their hands worked busily in tandem, solemnly wielding large sewing needles threaded with the unmistakeable red yarn. Under the cold light, four pinpricks slowly grew to bulbous, fist-sized stitches. Once a row was complete, the women unrolled the cloth by two or three feet and resumed their furious stitching.

In a corner of the room, under a hanging lightbulb, lay a small pile of the snipped-out bundles of yarn from Hana's studio that had studded their father's face, like evidence of a crime. After a moment, the four women rose and retreated to the edge of the room, and another four elderly women took their places. They too took up their sewing needles and stitched. As they did, the room was hushed, even as more people tiptoed in.

"She chose four," Ryu whispered, shaking his head. "Each time four." Miyo was bewildered.

"Ichi, ni, san—shi," he said, and wrote a character in the air. "It means four but also death. Always bad luck to have four."

At last, one woman rose while the three others stepped back. She was wearing an exquisite shimmering kimono with pale pink flowers. Her face was reduced to a blanched oval in the dim light, her small features deeply creviced.

"Sakura," Ryu said, and Miyo recognized the look of the five-petalled bloom from Hana's wall. The room grew lighter at that instant, and at the centre a spotlight beamed down. Hana emerged wearing a black kimono. The large cloth now drooped with the weight of the thickened yarn. Hana and the other woman each took hold of one corner and swept it up, like chambermaids expertly changing a bedsheet; they draped it back over the floor, the other side up.

There it was: the hazy black and white, the nostril, the eye, the lip pierced with red; she was again stunned by the sight of her father's face mutilated and exposed. *She's gone too far,* Miyo thought.

The old woman stared aghast at the sheet; she'd sewn blindly, unwittingly. She flapped her arms up and down. "Tenno-heika banzai, " she cried and crawled forward onto the cloth, face-down, murmuring. She tugged at the yarn in spots, then planted her lips on the face. The lips of the image were not their father's after all, Miyo saw; they were full, petulant, with a moustache above them, and around the eyes were wire-rimmed glasses. The gaze was empty, almost deadened; it was the emperor, Hirohito.

Hana moved to the woman's side and tried to pull her to her feet, but she clung to the cloth, crouched. Miyo did not take her eyes from Hana, but watched her shudder at the sound of shattering glass in the next room. The woman began to weep, all the while calling, *Hajime,* and Miyo knew it had to be Hana's Hajime, that sleek young face pasted to Hana's wall.

People began to file out, calmly but quickly, all around Miyo. She lost sight of Hana; Ryu was no longer at her side. He'd gone to save Hana. In the foyer, the young couple Miyo had seen earlier lingered on, no longer list-less. The girl at the door placed a white-gloved hand at her elbow. "Hana said to wait for her," she said.

In the other room Miyo found shards all over the floor. Three large glass domes lay shattered; one remained intact. The fluorescent lights had been turned up bright and the glass glittered under them. A familiar voice and too-strong scent were suddenly at her side: "She never understands." It was Rinzo. He stood beside her and the one glass dome left untoppled and untouched. "This is not art," he announced, flicking aside the broken glass with his fine leather shoe. "Mottai nai," he murmured, the first Japanese he'd spoken to her. "It's easy to show the ugliness of the world. More difficult to show beauty."

He tapped the clear glass with his foot where the out-line of a flower had been fired into it. "The symbol of the tokkotai, the cherry blossom they painted on their planes and bombs and torpedoes."

Miyo bent to study a small mound of brownish curled shapes inside the knee-high dome.

"They are the sliced fingertips of Korean monks—or something that resembles them."

Miyo gasped and reeled back. They reminded her of fallen petals from a fine flower. She recoiled at the beau-ty she couldn't help seeing in them.

"On the anniversary of the surrender last August, the monks protested Japan's war crimes and the victims who have never received restitution," he said. "But one can never recover from the loss and indignity. It's too late."

"Why too late?" Miyo said, just as Ryu came bound-ing in. He stopped when he saw Rinzo with her. The two exchanged glances. "Come," Ryu said. "Hana wants you." He left, as if expecting her to follow.

"You see, don't you?" Rinzo said, shaking his head. "Hana takes away these poor women's peace, their pride, whatever they salvaged from the death of their loved ones sixty years ago. She devastates them."

The sight of the old woman on her knees, crawling, planting a kiss on the punctured face! Her plaintive wail for Hajime. Miyo herself had wound and stitched red yarn in his name, for his death. "I'm sorry," she said, backing away.

"I'm sorry too. I can't sell any of this," he said, and walked off.

EIGHT

THE BLUR of trees and grass and fields out the window took Miyo back to another train ride. It was late summer and she was with her father and they were on their way somewhere—east to Montreal, but he made her sit facing backward, west, to see the sun. Clouds of monarch butterflies hovered beside the tracks and, as the sun sank, disappeared into the blazing orange light. Miyo surprised both her father and herself by falling into a deep sleep from the train's motion.

When she woke up they were pulling into the station, and it was dark like a cave, and dark out on the street where the lamps cast down cones of sooty light. He was taking her to a doctor, *a special doctor* was all he said. They went in through dark gates, along a gravel walkway uphill; they passed under an arch and came to a place she remembered as a huge ancient tree or rock carved out for people to live in. It was hollow inside, stone cold, with hallways that echoed her crooked one-two steps. The stairs were high and steep, the mahogany banisters too wide and thick to hold. Finally he lifted her up and climbed the rest of the way. His breath echoed as her footsteps had, crooked and catching every so often. Lamps on the ends of heavy chains swayed like glass anchors in the air and lit the ceiling's dizzying swirls. She closed her eyes and pretended she was riding the roller coaster in August at the Exhibition—the long, slow uphill chug over the arching rails before the violent, hurtling release—only imagined, only glimpsed from the car driving on the Lakeshore; her father would never take her there.

What else did she remember? Her father taking a seat in a corner of the room after he set her down, his coat still on, his beige all-weather coat over the suit he rarely wore; his face streaming with sweat like rain. *Why don't you take it off, Daddy?* she thought to say, but then the curtain was drawn and she had to lie down as she was told. Her father wouldn't like that, her telling him what to do, and in front of a stranger, a doctor, as if he didn't know how to do things for himself, or look after a mere sickly child.

The doctor pressed up and down her spine, pulled her arms this way and that, stood back and said, *Look at that,* how easily her bones winged and folded. *You're a bird,* he said. He was nice enough; he said *smile* when he went to take a picture of her insides. *I won't take it until you smile.* She couldn't see him where he was standing, away from her and the camera. She was smiling but it must not have shown, because he waited and finally gave a chuckle and said, *Next time.*

On the way back, there were no butterflies. There were whorls of frost on the train windows, frighteningly intricate, with waves and fronds and cells inside cells.

It had turned cold because now she was remembering another ride from Montreal, in winter instead of summer. There'd been many visits, many doctors, and more than one picture-taking; countless X-rays held to a box of light.

They were stopped and couldn't get home. She touched the glass and her fingertips sizzled with heat, then cold. The fluorescent light snaked down through the cars, and she watched faces in the glass until her father moved her away from the drafty window. The butterflies were gone to Mexico, her father said. The engine was frozen, the conductor had told them. Her father's thick navy coat was wrapped over her own, and his gloves were pushed on over her mittens to where the fingers began, brown leather cut-outs with webbed knitting; she tugged at an unravelled stitch when her father wasn't looking. He would sew it up. He would take the basket from the closet and fish out a brown end from the nest and thread the needle. Her father sat in his flannel shirt, blue and green check, his hands one on each knee, looking strong and ready.

Who wants to walk out there anyway? It's the middle of nowhere and you won't get back home, he told her. The harder she looked in the glass, the more she saw herself, how she looked to the world—a terrible truth. Girls with nothing wrong slouched against one another in their seats, singing snippets of "Maggie May" and giggling, and boys shifted sullenly below hockey bags they'd slung on the baggage rack overhead. It was a funny sensation—like a dream, as if she had conjured everything in the train, including these people never seen before, the look of their faces, the things they laughed at, their very thoughts.

She had her pencil box; her father brought it out, and a piece of paper, a receipt he turned over for her, and the serviette given with a packet of peanuts. She didn't know when the box got lost, but even back then it was already no longer brand new. This was after her father painted a picture of flowers on it, and after part of it was chipped and faded to a soiled pink. They weren't flowers any more but smudges, and the bamboo lid didn't slide so easily as before. Her father pried it open and lying inside were her pencils in her colours: magenta, midnight and blush pink. She couldn't help running her fingers over the box to feel the rough bamboo surface, and the raised, polished bits of pink petals; that was how the paint had chipped off, from her touching too much.

The singsong of the white-aproned, bowlegged canteen girl jarred Miyo back to the train present. *Ocha! Kohee!* she sang out as she ambled down the aisle: *Green tea! Coffee!* Two rows ahead, Hana's head dangled over the armrest as she slept and Ryu watched over her. They were going to Hiroshima, Hana's favourite place, where she said you could be sad and disgusted with the world and not have to explain why.

Outside the window were electrical towers neatly fenced off, with houses built tight to them. Miyo wondered if it was true, the cancer that was said to come from the high-voltage currents carried by them. Then came darkly flooded fields—rice paddies. At home—out west, where she'd never been—farmers grew wheat and waited for rain, not too much and not too little; they waited and waited. Here they watered and watered, and never waited. Overhead were icy clouds like lettuce, or maybe it was a waft of pollutants. In the car, above the door, station names ran in Japanese and English, stick figures scurrying along a moving sidewalk, one after another, each disappearing as quickly as it appeared: Yokohama, Okayama, Hiroshima and so on, to Fukuoka, at the tip of Kyushu.

Miyo caught herself napping, head back, then set her chin down; up was too careless, a gaping doorway, an unmade bed. The train was gliding, fast, unlike the quiet chugging of those rides of her childhood. Everything could seem ordinary and well-enough known to her in this place; all anticipated and on time. If she planted her feet on the tile of irises on the station platform, the doors would open right in front of her when the train stopped. Once it was emptied of passengers, a troop of ladies with dusters and mops would file in, then file out, leaving fresh doilies on headrests and a sweet rose scent in their wake. She could predict these things; she could master arrivals and departures almost better than in Toronto, where she'd lived all her life.

Or maybe she was only feeling this way now because she had to be strong for Hana. *She devastates them,* Rinzo had said of Hana and the widows. But it was Hana who seemed devastated.

Ryu gripped her wrist and yanked her up from her seat. "Come!" He pulled down their bags, along with the shopping bag with her father's urn. The train had stopped and a mechanical female voice was announcing Hiroshima Station. "Come!" Ryu repeated. Hana was already out the door and turned back to them, her eyes burning. Miyo snatched up the shopping bag and scrambled out of the train with him just as the mechanical tones and voice signalled the closing of the doors.

The train flew past them with the whirr of steel and faces in windows. The sensation of rushing backwards and forwards, and the wind snatching at her coat, panicked Miyo for an instant. She resisted grabbing hold of Hana, who stood very still, her eyes staring into Miyo's as if the burning in her own might catch in Miyo's. She had never felt such compelling force—not even with David, who seemed with every glance to ask, *What are you thinking?* With Hana, at moments like these, there was no space between, no asking, no thinking: no words. But then the moment was gone.

Already Hana was striding down the platform. Between criss-crossed concrete beams Miyo glimpsed the city below, bustling, not unlike Tokyo; the high-rise buildings not bright, hard and glassy but porous and grey, the giant letters on the Sogo department store across the way dully red and rounded and quaint, as if from another era.

"Where are we going?" she called out, struggling to keep up.

"This is where Hana and I first meet," Ryu said.

Miyo touched her stomach, rising and falling vigorously with her breath, and imagined that it wasn't her own hand there. This was the place where Ryu had met Hana, and where he'd first saved her.

They stuffed their bags into lockers inside the station and boarded a crowded streetcar that crossed the city. The rose-wreathed shopping bag with her father's urn she kept looped on her wrist.

Hana and Ryu both knew the way to whatever place they were headed for; Miyo didn't ask where. Ryu had worked here one summer when he'd left the stable where he'd been training. His weight had fallen too low and he couldn't compete. The sight of food had begun to make him sick. "Too much," he told her with a sour smile, patting his stomach. Hana just listened and gave a wan smile that made her seem brittle and delicate. When a seat emptied, she shrank down into it.

The people here looked a little different than in Tokyo: they were smaller and squatter, more like her father. When the pretty girls smiled she noticed their large crooked teeth, one or two a dead grey, like an old man's, and when they walked in their high platform shoes she noticed their muscular, bowed legs even more, some so short they looked like a child's, though these were grown women. She didn't feel so self-conscious of her own leg, or her limp. People looked a bit shabby, even the girls wrapped in their fine pashmina wool shawls in pink and peach and lavender; it all seemed a little second-hand and faded or frayed and imperfect. Just like her and her father. Waiting for the streetcar, she'd spied a man's ear filled with a ball of flesh the size of a thumb. He had gotten on the same car as them and had stood near the back.

It seemed to be a sign of some kind. Could the man hear all right? Was there more deformity you couldn't see, elsewhere inside his body? Miyo couldn't tell if he moved to things he saw or things he heard.

"Genbaku-domu," Ryu pronounced, like a tour operator, pointing to a structure with a skeletal dome. Miyo imagined it lowered over the head of a giant Frankenstein's monster for the operation to render him human. They'd kept it to show how powerful the bomb was, the destruction. But except for the dome, all it was was bricks and mortar, half come down or half built up; through the blown-out roof and walls you could see unanchored clouds and a big sky that could not have cared less, otherwise cluttered by high-rises, sliced by electrical lines. It didn't disturb her as much as she wanted it to. The streetcar halted at a stop—Kamiya-cho, a sign said—and a woman got out slowly, one step at a time, holding a tiny dog that struggled in her arms, a scruffy wheat-haired mongrel with a patch of face. Miyo saw the woman's face as she passed under the car window; she grimaced in pain or irritation when the dog wriggled in her arms. In every person's face in this city you couldn't help but glimpse suffering.

That was what Rinzo had mistakenly read in her face, on her body. He'd assumed she was one who'd suffered: radiation sickness, rooted in her mother's body, sprouted in her. That word he'd uttered: *hibakusha,* like a taint or taboo; the momentary recoil of his fingertips. Had that been her affliction all along, and she'd never been told? Was that what her mother had died of? All the myster-ies of her life that she'd let lie; that she'd never prodded her father to tell. Now who would tell her?

"Your mother was from Hiroshima, ne?" Hana said, startlingly self-possessed again, possessing even Miyo's thoughts; as if the instances of strength and uncertainty see-sawed between them.

"Yes," Miyo said, but could not bring herself to say more.

"It is pretty, ne?" Ryu said. "You could be lucky." He was pointing at Hiroshima Pachinko Parlour, all candy-pink lights enticing customers to come play, blinking, garish, on, off: blooming and dying in seconds. Beside it was the Hiroshima High Up Hotel.

"Yes," Hana said. "I think she could."

The car rattled to a stop at a large open-air station. They trundled over rails to a track where they boarded a sleek, modern train. It swished forward rather than rattling and it sped down a dark corridor of old houses. Laundry hung on poles across balconies flapped like tattered flags. In the long gaps between corridors, between towns, she glimpsed a shoreline cleaving to small hills; they were climbing steadily and the sea was down below.

When they got off, the roads were paved, the shops and buildings modern and featureless, set back from wide sidewalks, and in the windows were English signs. They could have been anywhere other than where they were. But the soft sea air was unmistakable. The light was changing to a shade of slate that made her wistful for some other night, or moments in it when waiting for the stars might be all she wished for.

They boarded the ferry and Ryu brought them cans of hot tea from a vending machine. It was creamy and metallic on her tongue, and warm in her palms. Hana held the can but didn't drink from it; she silently watched the water churn and stream alongside the ferry's hull.

"Hana likes to come in winter when the tourists are all gone, ne Hana?" he said, trying to lull her back to him. "She likes to come at night," he told Miyo, as if the changing light were signalling the end of day, but it was still too early. "No one comes at night."

They walked to the back of the ferry, the wind snatching at their hair. Hiroshima was to the right, its outline of buildings and the gaps between like a child's mouth with some teeth fallen out, some coming in. When they returned to the bow, there was Miyajima, the nature preserve, its small blurry greenish-brown mound growing more distinct, like dark sand poured out by hand. *Miyo-jima*, David would have teased, the Island of Miyo, just as he'd say the rest of his nonsense under the covers. She did feel like an island—remote from him and, just now, at this moment, from Hana.

There were other mounds too, in the distance, and a way off, another boat was heading in the opposite direction. Back and forth the boats went, who knew how late into the night, like the ones shuttling from downtown Toronto to Centre Island and back, the destination always the same. She could guess why Hana would be drawn here—the workaday dinginess of Hiroshima, its gaping shell of modern avenues and its grey shadows. Then to come to this, the lush painterly haze of islands.

Ryu was staring hard at Hana as she gazed into the churning water. "Don't be sad," he said.

She turned abruptly, her hair whipping her face in the wind. "I should suffer!" she said. "I failed. I wanted to make them see." She crushed the can in her hand and the hot tea dribbled over her wrist.

"No, no," Ryu said. He went on in Japanese. He tried to wrest the can from her, he tugged at her sleeve, but she turned back to the sea.

Miyo left them. She couldn't bear the memory of that old woman weeping over the emperor's portrait. She stood by the back rails, watching the hills of Hiroshima grow smaller and the waves frill in the ferry's wake. Just days before, Setsuko had uttered those same words: *I should suffer,* as if more suffering could heal all that had gone before, and prevent what was to come. An old feeling overwhelmed her: her own hopeless body, the ache and the numbness as she lay in her bed waiting for her father to come. Only now it seemed a doomed body, tainted with a terrible poison, a terrible story, even as she lived on. She felt helpless; what could she do for Hana, her sister?

"He is hungry." Ryu was raking the deer's fur as the animal nuzzled Miyo's handbag and the bag containing her father's urn. There were four or five deer wandering through the ferry terminal among the concession stalls. No one seemed to mind.

"There's nothing in there for you, just bones," said Hana.

The deer's eyes, large and unblinking, reminded Miyo of Rinzo; it was the way the lids were incised on its face, the skin seemingly pushed back with some fine instrument to reveal glistening glass balls.

"Go play with your friends," Miyo chided, nervously inching back, but the creature only nudged forward. Hana grabbed hold of Miyo's arm and used it to shove the deer back. "Like this, ne-san," she said, exasperated. Miyo's splayed fingers sank through fur into flesh and into bone, and she yanked her hand back.

"You cannot be timid," Hana said, at once more cool and detached. "You cannot expect others to look after you always." It was almost an accusation.

"I don't," Miyo protested. She thought to say more—
that yes, maybe that had been true before, she had
expected a lot, having known nothing else. But wasn't
she changing? Hadn't she changed already?

Ryu was calling out to them in English, smiling and
waving. He bounded through the terminal and the open
doors to the empty square outside. He'd forgotten
Hana's despair and his own because he was back in the
place where they'd first met, regaining that feeling. It
had to be rabu-rabu, love-love they shared—what young
Japanese said when they were deeply in love. Setsuko
had used the phrase to convince her of what had been
between Miyo's father and herself: love given and
returned, not one molecule lost in the exchange. She'd
said it the way a Japanese girl would, with a lightly
curled tongue. It was possible her father had truly loved
Setsuko. She would tell Hana just that one day; it might
give her solace.

Ryu called again and Miyo ran from the deer, and
finally arrived outside. Ryu was bounding in circles,
jumping to tag the wooden signposts with his fingertips, even the trash cans, and Hana stood watching.
"Go on," she told Miyo and took her bags from her,
looping the bag with their father's urn around her wrist.
"Nothing will break." She sat down on a bench that
faced out to sea.

Miyo had never moved in such an open, unpeopled
space, and the sight of Ryu in it made her feel miraculously agile. She stepped tentatively onto the pounded
sand and slowly began to run after him, watchful for
pain or resistance from her body, but none came. Ryu
watched, laughing and reaching for her, but she pushed

his hand away. He urged her toward the rocky steps that led down to the water, and the narrow strip of shore where the tide scudded in.

"Kocchi!" he said, lapsing into Japanese, and she was grateful for that—a modest word that she could grasp and that he felt easy enough to let out. Maybe it was because of Hana, maybe he was feeling her thrumming energy all the more for her not being filled with it herself at this moment; Miyo had that sensation too. He was pointing to the famous red torii—the sea-steeped gateway to Itsukushima Shrine, which extended on stilts past the shore. It was low tide so they could easily wade out there through puddles; a line of stepping stones led the way. Miyo stopped to gaze at the lonely structure; viewed from this side, a gateway to nothing but the flat slate sea and, across it, hills and puny villages, and Hiroshima. There were watermarks at its ankles, and the majestic red pictured in guidebooks and on postcards was actually a wan, sun-bleached pink; the wood was splintered. A few uniformed schoolchildren clustered under it, staring up, then raced around its four aged, bowed limbs.

She followed Ryu's jagged path onto the row of rocks. She thrust her arms out from her sides for balance, and the air tingled between her fingers. She shouted for him and Hana to see, though he couldn't know what a feat this was; barely anyone could, except her father and maybe David, who'd be clasping her hand tightly, barely letting her go. And Hana, because it was she who guessed her strength and must know her weakness. Miyo had never felt this blissful cool wind on all sides, her torso buffeted it, her fingers rustling in it.

She stole a glance at herself in mid-air and instantly she faltered; too late she recalled David's *Don't look down!* and her knee gave way. She thudded to the sand and the water lapped up under her. The icy touch on her calves sucked up her breath. Ryu just at that moment turned back from the foot of the torii. She dreaded the look she'd see on his face but it wasn't there; he didn't rush to lift her up. Instead he pointed at her, as he had at the torii, which was ungainly yet graceful, and he waved for her to get up and come over.

Then he forgot her. He chased the children, ran with them and splashed in the puddles; she heard his boyish laugh echo. The cold crept over her buttocks and she struggled, waving her arms for him to see that she couldn't get up; how could she? Someone always came for her, always. David had left her sprawled on the bathroom floor that one time; she'd felt each cold tile under her measuring her disgrace, but she'd waited and he had come, at last sorry.

Did Hana see? Miyo felt ashamed and wronged. Hana didn't know, after all, didn't grasp how it had been, was still, for her. But yes, she was right: Miyo expected —needed—others to care for her.

Hana walked toward her, slowly and deliberately, lugging the bags, Ryu's and hers, and the urn in the now tattered Takashimaya bag. Miyo closed her eyes in relief.

"Up!" she heard, startled. "Get up!" Hana was shouting, without lifting a hand, just as she'd never been given one. "You're not so weak! Stop pretending!" Hana stood tall and mimed pulling herself up: simple. Why all these years did Miyo slouch and bend? It was habit, lazy habit: nothing more, nothing less. *Get up!* Was it true? Had Miyo been fooling her father, the doctors, herself, with phantom pain all this time? The pictures on the lightboxes back then, even when she was a child? The way she thought she could read the doctors' faces if not the X-rays?

But David's fingers crawling in discovery over and inside her; Rinzo's face drawing back in Hana's dim studio, his whispered word, *hibakusha:* none of that was pretend or denial.

Miyo scrambled to her feet, her knee wobbling; the cold, the ache—that was not phantom at all. She straightened her leg and rubbed it and slapped it warm as her father had done, and stood up tall. She made her way toward Ryu without glancing at Hana. He was standing squarely under the torii now, between its legs—the children vanished—and he looked past her to the cable cars climbing up and up to the peak at the centre of the island.

"You need ocha, tea," Ryu said when she reached him. He began a patient, plodding march back to the low bank of stones marking the shore, every few steps checking that she still followed. Hana joined in turn behind her. They sat down on a stone bench and sipped green tea as deer lounged nearby.

"You see how I try to help, don't you, ne-san?" Hana said. "I told Ryu not to come to you."

"Yes," Miyo said after a moment, "I do." She felt heartened; she had been cared for after all.

"I tried to help the ladies, ne-san."

"Yes," Miyo said again. "I know."

"After all these years, they still believe more in the emperor than in themselves."

♥

Miyo spied a red and white cable car emerging from among the trees, and another inching behind, along a thick cable that followed the rise of the mountain Misen to the peak of Miyajima Island. Both cars slipped behind greenery again and re-emerged with slight, short jerking motions, as if tugged by hand, by an invisible string of heaving strongmen. Ryu had operated the cars here, with his friend Juni, the summer that he had met Hana.

"Hana liked to ride when it was dark and cold. We closed at five o'clock but I let her on." He smiled. "Hana likes the monkeys that live at the top. Ne, Hana?" He touched his face and drew his hand over it. "Do you like monkeys?" he asked Miyo. "Pink monkeys?"

"Pink monkeys are happy," Hana said. "We should be like the monkeys. They take care of their young and just live. They don't care about us. Only when we bother them and stare."

"Then they will attack," said Ryu.

Hana still held the bag containing their father's urn around her wrist. "Go see them," she said, "for me. I will stay here and wait." She cast Ryu a stern glance as he opened his mouth to protest.

"I will be here when you come down," she said, and turned her gaze out to the torii and the sea. "I will wait."

Ryu stared down at the shore they'd come from. It was a long way down; the people standing where they'd been looked miniature. The cable car swayed the slightest bit each time he shifted his weight, standing there, refusing to sit. All around were treetops, tall red pines, the car dipping among them. Two empty cars passed on their descent, one after the other. Three schoolgirls were huddled inside a third one, giggling behind their dainty hands. Ryu was captivated. They laughed harder, mouths clamped, as he stared.

"Hana was like that," he said.

Miyo couldn't imagine Hana so coy. But she recalled the photograph from her father's box, the one of a pigeon-toed girl on the sidewalk.

"How could you have known her that long?" He must have been only a baby in his mother's arms when Hana was that young.

"No I didn't, but I know."

He told Miyo how they'd met in off-season, on a coolish day like this but in fall, not spring, the first year he came, right after he'd fled the sumo stable the first time. Nobody would find him here; nobody would care. He went to the clubs at night and boarded the bullet train to Fukuoka to see the sumo matches. Eventually they took him back at the stable, both times, even though he'd returned thinner than when he left. They might not take him back again.

He used to sit in the booth at Kaya-dani station, the first stage of the climb, and stare up toward the second station on Mount Misen, where Juni worked, though he couldn't see it. Ryu's job was to guide the cars in to the station, then open the doors and let the people climb out. One afternoon the alarm light went on and the cable squeaked and slowed and the cars stopped. He came out of the booth and looked down the lines at the parallel cars all empty and still. Except that on the right, halted on its way up, one car was swinging. Someone was jumping from side to side, rocking the car back and forth, banging and trying to pry open the windows, which slid down no more than a few inches. Things began to tumble out— a red patch caught by the net of treetops, then blue, like a jigsaw piece of sky fallen out. It was clothing stuffed through the gap and dropped down, piece by piece.

The swaying stopped. It was a girl—he knew from how slight the figure was, and the hair—and she was clinging to one side, her forearm dangling out the window like a twig. He went to the emergency controls and slowly inched the cable along, bringing the girl closer and closer, the twig still dangling. One empty car swung in, then another and another. The girl was stripped down to her brassiere, one leg out of her jeans, and her cries had grown louder as the car rounded the track inside the station. When she saw him she began to shout, he didn't know what, her forearm flapping from the window, a trapped wing. *Fuck him, fuck him! Fucking bastard,* she was crying, and he took her for an unhappy Japanese American, disenchanted, like one or two he'd met in Tokyo who had come to Japan hoping to feel at home but never did.

"Who? Fuck who?" Miyo asked. When he didn't answer she asked again—one of the rare times she'd used the word. Front teeth sinking into her bottom lip, the cool stream out; it felt good.

"She likes to make herself angry," Ryu said. "That is why she comes to Hiroshima. She comes to Miyajima when she wants to feel better, but she never does."

Miyo looked down to the shore they'd come up from and imagined that she could see Hana sitting as they'd left her, on the stone bench, keeping their father's bones safe for both of them.

"She meant my father," Miyo said.

Ryu nodded. "She looks for new reasons to hate him, always. I don't know what is true but I know what is bad. In war, there are many things to hate."

When they reached the landing, they came out to a hillside, terraced for the monkeys and their babies, who flew down it, stopping behind rocks and peering back up. The mother squatted not far from Miyo, on the ground. Signs were posted all around with cartoon monkeys warning, *Do not look me in the eyes,* but Miyo stared right into the mother's small face, just as Hana had said not to; the pink flesh and the plaintive button eyes.

"I'm hungry," Ryu suddenly blurted. He'd been feeding the deer, he'd even tossed something from a vending machine to the monkeys, but he'd taken nothing himself. His face crinkled up for a moment like a rag and she immediately recognized the bit of pity he reserved for himself, just as she'd seen it in David. The bit that needed Hana as much as Miyo needed her.

There was one monkey, a small adult, that stayed near Miyo, the skin of its little pink face looking sunburnt, or freshly peeled like exotic fruit. It crouched on its haunches, near as it dared, seeming by turns frightened or menacing, childlike or old. The others climbed busily up and down the terraced mountainside, stopping to instantly puzzle their bodies together; to scratch or to nibble, come apart and scamper away, sometimes throwing a backward look. This one stayed put—a female without a child to mind, Miyo imagined.

They're human, she thought, spying the tiny articulations of the monkey's fingers, noting its fingernails, like a baby's; rimless lips quivering away from its teeth. Something in its glance told her it was capable of being mortified at itself. She found herself moving her fingers too—scratching her own arm, shockingly smooth and hairless, and her face, so large and exposed and unprotected. She stood up and the monkey did too. The air rushed down her fast as she rose, like in an open-air elevator, and the blood from her head knocked her back down to the bench. She realized she hadn't eaten. She stumbled toward the lookout, only yards off; if only she could glimpse the smooth sea and the splotch of islands across it; she longed for a scant breeze to skim the water's surface and float up in a mist that would then clear. But the way down was a thick pathless forest, a profusion of leaves. Somewhere below—strewn among branches, rained on, bleached, worn by the weather—were the pieces of clothing Hana had let drop from the cable car two years earlier. Solid, material things didn't simply melt and disappear.

"Come away," Ryu said, and he tugged her back from the precipice by the fingertips.

That song returned to her; the melody sputtered in her head, half a chorus. Something about a stranger in paradise. Buddy and Setsuko had both used that word; bygone Manchuria was paradise, and so was Setsuko's blossom-strewn Yasukuni Shrine, where the spirit of Miyo's father deserved to rest. Miyo could not imagine her father restful. Duty, as David said, always called to him. *It's what I do,* he'd shouted when, as a little girl not understanding, she'd tried to thank him. He had longed for something better, different. He had wanted to live where duty was understood; it made you a man. "Do you believe in paradise?" she impulsively asked Ryu. He shook his head.

"My father was a kamikaze," she said, as if repenting; but she still didn't really believe it. It sounded like a bad movie. As foreign and absurd as before, conjuring an ad she'd seen on the subway of a kooky salaryman piloting a tiny plane, hoisting a canned energy drink in the air.

"You say, but he didn't die. That is true," Ryu said, echoing her words to Buddy, denying it all. There was no honour in sacrifice; no shame in not dying. Everyone knew that now. He served, he sacrificed, was what Setsuko claimed. Miyo still ached to believe he'd done little more than march around Okayama Second Middle School—practising for battle, showing off to the pretty girl who married him, never leaving the yard—although she couldn't recall precisely how this story had come to her.

"He did die," Miyo said. But he hadn't died lucky.

"I don't understand Hana always," Ryu blurted. He was nervous; they both were, passing symptoms caught from each other. She faced him and fastened her hands onto his forearms. "Look," she said, and took a deep breath, as if it were Hana's ribcage lifting and expanding in them both. She looked into his eyes and found the comforting resoluteness that made him seem older than his eighteen years.

She followed Ryu into the cable-car terminal, where there was a small concession stand, a sun-faded display of insects and plant life, childlike, unscientific; who knew how long it had been there?

As they rode the cable car down, treetops loomed, then shrank behind them. The spot where Miyo and Ryu had stood under the red gateway grew larger and larger, pinker and pinker in front of them, and the bench where Hana had promised to wait was empty.

NINE

NEITHER OF THEM remarked on Hana being gone; it was not a surprise. Sooner or later, as before, she would meet up with them again.

When they hiked toward the shore, the place seemed changed. The air was warm. Shutters were rolled up, the darkened shops now opened. Families sat slurping noodles under the trees. The deer were everywhere, walking and sitting, oblivious of the people among them unless food was sniffed in their bags.

"It's a holiday," Ryu said, but he couldn't recall what one.

They passed a crowd gathering around an improvised stage outside the shrine. A boy with a monkey on a leash, both identically dressed in crisp blue-and-white sashed jackets. The boy strewed objects across the stage and sat while the monkey fetched them in its tiny hands. Its face was familiar, and somehow its expression—the monkey who'd hovered by her on the mountaintop—but of course it couldn't be the same one.

"Come," Ryu said with a tug on her fingertips. One of his habits, she was realizing, but she'd never seen him doing it to Hana, him leading her.

On the ferry coming back, they sat at the front of the boat, looking at Hiroshima, where they were headed, instead of Miyajima, left behind. They got off the streetcar at the Peace Park, by the Frankenstein-monster dome. It was understood that they might find Hana here. They bought dainty, cellophane-wrapped sandwiches with their crusts trimmed, and cans of warm green tea, and ate by the river. "Motoyasu River," Ryu said, but didn't answer when she asked what the word meant; as if irritated by her probing for meaning in every little thing. A boy ran past them, trailing a long, translucent white tail like part of the sky. He circled around a nearby tree, round and round and round without getting dizzy, chanting. He left toilet paper streaming up and down the park, among the stone memorials and founts of brightly patterned origami offered like flower bouquets for the dead.

"Hana doesn't like it here," Ryu said as he tossed out his leftovers. "She says there is no peace in Peace Park."

She and Ryu stood by the tree wrapped in toilet paper. "Then why did we come?" Miyo, too, felt irked by the place; something about it didn't seem real or important enough. The world wasn't the better, the safer for it.

"She still came all the time." He sighed. "She liked to make herself angry. She'd go to Miyajima to feel better."

Miyo glanced at the wide block on its narrow base, the museum and the stairs that climbed up into it like exposed vertebrae. "Maybe she's inside."

"No. She doesn't like to be in there," Ryu said. "It makes Hana feel sick." It was the charred children's clothing, molten wristwatches, eyeglasses and lunch-boxes suffocating behind glass; the picture of a shadow left on a building's steps. It was all too beautiful and sad. The doves projected onto a large screen—flying up and up amid a ballad for peace. The parade of visitors hushed in disbelief, in horror, tears sprouting in their eyes so readily. "Hana says Japanese people don't deserve such pity." Ryu felt ashamed of his own feelings, he told Miyo, of how instantly mournful the music made him; of how the fluttering doves made him feel clean and light, and erased from his mind the stained and gnarled items on display.

"Hana likes to say, 'There can't be peace without truth.'" It sounded so clear and true that he never questioned it.

He brought Miyo to Hana's favourite spot in the park, in front of a framed rising sun made of hundreds of folded paper cranes: red cranes forming the sun in the centre, and white cranes all around, each inscribed with the name of a child who'd perished that August in Hiroshima. Somehow the makeshift memorial had survived rainy season after rainy season, the colours staying bright white and blood red. Some days he couldn't get Hana away from here.

"Hana said they folded and folded, even after the war ended." The dainty wings with the children's names on them enraged Hana; their tininess made her hysterical. It was his fault, the emperor's, letting them go on believing, not letting them stop their useless labouring over immaculate red suns. *What about the others, who have no names?* she'd cry. *They're not here.* She meant the Korean slave labourers who had died, whose monument was not allowed in the park. And the others in their own land, in Nanjing, raped, tortured, slain in the name of the emperor! She'd step in front of tourists' cameras, whatever they tried to snap. They took home pictures of a crazy Japanese woman making monkey faces.

He'd have to calm her down, get her home. But she'd be coiled so tight, veins taut and bulging; seized. Her face contorted, frightening him. "She is strong," he told Miyo; the fits gave her superhuman energy. She became stronger than him, and fast. He'd had to chase her down the park once. Then, when he had smoothed her out, she'd whimper to him, drained, except for her fingers, which clutched his jacket tight to her. He could never leave her. She might leave him or order him away, but he could never just go.

"Did she tell you anything else about my father?" Miyo asked. "Our father," she corrected herself.

"Nothing more," was all he answered. Nothing more than the fact that Hana despised their father and pitied him.

Miyo tapped on the framed cranes as if on a window. The slumbering children with their spirits, their long lives folded and pressed to plexiglass. "What about my mother?"

"Your mother?" he asked. He paused.

"Did Hana say she . . . ." Miyo cleared her throat, readying herself to pronounce the word. "Was she hibakusha?"

Ryu was shaking his head in a way that conveyed the horror and shame of it all—or that meant no. He was silent. "She thought so at first. She looked at lists, at names, to see if your mama was in Hiroshima then."

"She was from Hiroshima. My mother was."

"Hana didn't find it. Maybe she came to Tokyo for your father."

"Yes," Miyo said, unsure whether to feel relieved or not.

"My mother was pretty," she told Ryu a moment later, staring him in the face, somehow defiant. It seemed important to tell him.

Ryu brought her to an old low-rise apartment building opposite the train station. Children's underpants and undershirts and dainty coloured squares were strung from a line on a crumbling balcony. "My friend spins here. Juni." He made sliding finger movements to explain. "It's nicer for him in Hiroshima. Tokyo is too busy."

The apartment was cluttered with comic books, CDs and DVDs and crates of records piled high. Ryu made a face at Juni when the tatami mat crackled under his feet, and the two exchanged joking words. "He needs new tatami," Ryu explained. "When tatami gets old, you must turn over or replace." He laughed when Juni answered back. "Juni says everything in Hiroshima gets—" He searched for the word. "Crispy," he finally said, with a sheepish look.

Ryu hardly had to explain about Hana; Juni had seen her when he'd come down from his station on Mount Misen to help calm her. He had given her his shirt to put on, and tea from his Thermos. They had brought her back to the apartment, hobbling in the one shoe she hadn't managed to toss out of the cable car, and one of Ryu's socks.

"In the morning Hana was happy, ne, Juni?" And for a time after, they'd been a happy threesome, eating together, going dancing, falling asleep after a drunken night out, playing pachinko for days. "We got lucky at Hiroshima Pachinko Parlour," Ryu said.

Juni was saying something, touching the space between his nostrils and upper lip and watching Miyo with a careful, intent gaze.

"Juni says you and Hana look the same here," Ryu said, touching his upper lip. "He said you are both pretty."

Miyo fingered her lip self-consciously, the dip down the longish middle of it and the lopsided edges. Hana's lips were dainty, perfectly formed. "Rosebud," she said to Juni, circling her lips with her finger, then louder to make him understand: "Hana, rosebud. Not me."

From the jumble of his things, Juni brought out a small notebook with a cartoon on the cover, and a CD he'd recorded himself. He mumbled something to Ryu.

"It's some things to keep for you, or you can give to Hana," Ryu explained. The notebook was iridescent pink. Miyo read out what it said beneath the cartoon of a girl with round brown eyes, pink hair and fuchsia dress:

Pink Hana always dreams happy dreams with sunny smiles. She will remain near us as everlasting flowers.

Already Ryu had slipped the CD from her hand and was putting it on. The music was monotonous at first, notes climbing endlessly up and down; then she caught a snippet of a sweet melody only to hear it splintered by a voice, a recitation in Japanese, a scratchy old recording of a girl or boy, man or woman, she couldn't tell.

Ryu had sunk to the floor. "This is for Hana," he said, but he seemed crestfallen, as if he had lost his chance to make Hana happy. "Listen close." He rested his hand on her back. "Juni is brilliant. Hana says so," and he couldn't help beaming at Juni. "No one will love this like Hana." He turned to Miyo excitedly. "It's the emperor's surrender speech to the Japanese and *"My Favourite Things"* by John Coltrane and also dance song. They say Hirohito's servant broke the record into pieces because he didn't want the divine emperor's voice to ever be heard again. Juni found it and made it into a beautiful song. For Hana."

"What is it saying?" Miyo asked. They all listened, amid the squawks and the rising trill of the saxophone, to the human voice that was breathing into the instrument, the cry, the lament, more human-sounding than the emperor's mousy drone. Ryu and Juni exchanged glances and nodded. "Bear the unbearable. Endure the unendurable," Ryu said, and even Miyo could hear it skipping back and repeating the phrase she had heard before, until the melody rose up, along with the driving beat over the slow waltz rhythm. *Taegataki o tae, shinobi-gataki o shinobi.*

"It proves the emperor is not divine," Ryu said. "All Japanese people suffered for him. War criminals die or go to prison. Hirohito did not."

"Did Hana tell you that?" Miyo asked.

Ryu thought for a moment. "Yes, but I believe too." He looked away, shrugged and brightened. "Juni wants to know what is most favourite thing to you? Raindrops on roses? Whispers on kittens?"

"Whispers on kittens," Miyo said and laughed. But she could barely think of a thing. Springtime? Sunshine. Flowers. No—Hana's eyes burning into hers.

♥

It was late when they finished eating. Ryu pulled a spare futon from the cupboard and layed it out beside Juni's, clustering everything else at the edges of the tiny room. There wasn't a square of floor visible under their feet. Miyo carefully propped the Pink Hana notebook and the CD beside her like talismans to bring Hana to them. The three lay down side by side, Ryu in the middle.

Juni was soon fast asleep, and the rhythm of his breathing from the other side of Ryu was comforting. Miyo liked the light and the coolness from the street leaking in through the window; to feel the separation of inside from out, and the porousness between them, too, unlike in Hana's apartment, where she had often felt as if they were sealed in, with only the one small window. All the activity had left her wakeful. Everything in the cluttered room was startlingly clear in detail: Ryu as his head fell back and his mouth dropped open, and his body lolled from his side onto his back, his shoulder up against her. She felt his thick arm nudge closer, and his leg crawl over hers. His thigh was surprisingly smooth and soft, less muscular than she expected; his body less different from hers than David's. His breath came in slow, deep sighs, his body expanding and contract-ing. The weight he shifted onto her felt reassuring, a mooring anchor; she clung to him. She saw a tear glint at each corner of his closed eyes, and nothing seemed sadder or truer: to cry in your sleep, muffled and uncom-forted, and to wake uncertain and unpurged.

TEN

THE APARTMENT WAS EMPTY when Buddy came home. He'd never gotten used to his wife being gone, even when he knew she was. Any moment he expected her to come in the door, fussing with shopping bags, shunning his help in her usual way, too busy to look up. All these years, he'd held a picture in his mind of her kneeling in a tatami room, with her sloped shoulders hunched and her hands on her knees, ready to rise, waiting for him, even if he was only in the next room. He might have come home to her once like that, or maybe it had never happened at all.

Seeing Kiku's slippers by the doorway now, and her shoes gone—the hum of the place broken only by his own puttering—he slumped down. He felt lonely for company, and regretted leaving the boy and the girl. Something in that girl made him want to disappoint her, even thwart her. One part of him resented having to speak English with her, but another revelled in it. She didn't try; she just sat there, unaffected, without even a pinch of the pride that had swelled in him when he had first come, seeing nothing but Japanese faces surrounding him. The boy had been courteous but not respectful enough. He was young, with no memory of what it was to do without, or worse.

When he stopped to think how he'd fooled everybody! Every last person he had ever walked past on the street: the woman he bought his newspaper from, mornings for the past forty years; even Kiku, he'd told the girl and boy, but they didn't believe him. The English he'd stopped himself from speaking, in order to truly become a Japanese, had never left him. He spoke it only the odd time, when he ran into a nisei he knew from before the war—and then furtively, because they'd all kept their secret over the years, for themselves and each other. When he did, the words had a taste and a texture, like warm chestnuts with a hard shell and a soft centre; bitten into, they melted to nothing but a stale echo in his mouth.

In the little theatre they'd fixed up inside Sugamo Prison, Buddy had often sat himself near the front but away from the others, as close as he could to the stage. There were many high-ranking officers and bureaucrats among the inmates—some close advisors to the emperor, he'd heard—and at the end of the show they gathered with the performers. Pictures were snapped but he never saw them. They were the ones who still bowed toward the Imperial Palace each morning, and quietly sang the Kimigayo national anthem daily, in a huddled group. Buddy mostly kept to himself, talking and listening only to keep up his Japanese. He watched *Swan Lake*, his first ballet, from the third row. He was close enough to see the strain on the face of the black swan as she lifted her leg and swivelled on the tips of her toes. She didn't look anything like Kiku, but the ballerina reminded him of her just the same. It was in how she strained with each movement, graceful as it was, her face staying very still—frozen for moments at a time, looking delighted, then sad, then vengeful when the white swan fluttered near the prince. He could only think of Kiku going through the motions while he served his time, pretending to get on with her life, vigorous and determined, never stopping to rest, when in her heart she'd come to a standstill, waiting for him, though she always denied it. November 12, 1950, he'd written in the diary he kept, the day he saw *Swan Lake*. Then he had drawn the black swan in her tutu, with just a few clumsy strokes; he barely gave her a face, let alone Kiku's. Just enough so he'd remember. Outside, the leaves had turned colour and were dropping. It was his third autumn passed in prison.

One month later, he'd watched the prisoners who'd been granted Christmas amnesty let go. Left behind with two years yet to serve, he walked round and round the yard. Snow was coming down. The white flakes were each so clean, each like a miniature crocheted doily that dissolved when it touched his shoulder. Others fell to the mud at his feet, instantly soiled. He saw the relatives of the released men waiting by the fence, women and children and an elderly couple obscured by the snow-fall, light as it was. His own parents and sisters were far away; he'd stopped sending letters home long before the end of the war, and their letters had stopped too. He'd known that sooner or later there'd be news they wouldn't welcome. He saw some of those pardoned appear in the newspaper not long after, accepting posts in the new government; he watched others languish inside for years, never brought to trial, forgotten—then on a lark, let go. Some of the Korean nationals who were convicted served time and were later sent to the Chiba National Treatment Centre for the insane.

There were shows once, sometimes twice a week— more than he would see, or could afford, if he were on the outside, free. Finally he was becoming cultured, refined. If only Kiku were sitting here with him, could see this, he often thought; especially the young Misora Hibari in her top hat and tails, with that clear, keen voice and the way she moved her hands to express the meaning in the songs. So knowing—there could be no mistake, the way she sang of her feelings—yet innocent, as if those feelings were hand-me-downs she couldn't fill out yet. When the Misora girl was a toddler in top hat and tails people said she was kawaii, more endearing than Shirley Temple; but when she grew into a woman, to Buddy she was Judy Garland, with her wide-open, wide-set eyes glistening at the wonder of a faraway world. It was selfish, he knew, wishing Kiku here in this prison with him, even though it was more comfortable than he ever could have imagined. He ate his meals alongside men who'd done brutal, vile things because they'd obeyed the orders of their superiors. Like everyone else, Kiku had pledged loyalty to the emperor—she would have died for him, she said. But nothing had been asked of her. Her belief was her only war crime. Buddy had done things too, but only because he'd listened to his own voice inside, and obeyed, though the voice had only spoken to him once or twice, then never again. He'd tried to explain at the trial but his Japanese words were badly translated into English. He knew but he couldn't speak up. When it was clear what was going to happen, that he'd be punished, he confessed to the officer that he wasn't Japanese; he almost shouted it, the only time he'd given himself away since leaving Vancouver. It was the thought of going to prison, or worse: wriggling like a worm on a hook, not a man, so shameful for all to see his body betraying him, even in death, unable to clean himself up. But the man—a nisei from Canada just like himself, but whose Japanese was shabby—whispered back that he was lucky; the Americans might give him a few years to set an example, but the British would hang him for treason, just as they did Inouye, the nisei they called the Kamloops Kid.

Kiku stayed with him, by his side, all through it, in her way. She'd been with him as the black swan; he'd glimpsed her in the cloud of adult emotions hovering over Misora's face as she sang "The Apple Song," which entered his heart with its snaking, lonely melody. But when she started with "The Sad Whistle," he felt as if he had a hole in his heart and it was Kiku blowing a cold wind through it. A month later, when the geishas from Yamaguchi Prefecture came, they looked so tired under the thick white makeup; their skin was pocked and the ends of their kimonos were frayed. They made him think of Kiku's vow to perform her dance to call up the spirit of her fiancé at Yasukuni Shrine.

The next month, dancers pranced across the stage with bare breasts. They looked too thin from not eating enough during the war; they looked hungry. One dancer's listless gaze reminded him of Kiku again. In her look he saw embarrassment, as if she longed to steal away from herself in that moment; to be free of herself, of him and everything else.

He knew exactly when it was that Kiku began to grow fond of him, even as she resisted; she knew it too, sitting there with him on a park bench in Manchukuo, reading the latest letter she'd received from her fiancé, who was off at war.

She said she'd never thought twice about him during his five years in prison. She told him she was mourning her fiancé, as she would always do, even after Buddy was released and she became his wife. She would always be that young, waiting bride-to-be. She never visited, never wrote, but he understood; in his notes to her he could have been no more than a flimsy shadow of her fiancé, Hajime, whose letters were fierce and desperate in every line. But the day Buddy was let out, Kiku was waiting for him, her hands in short white gloves clinging to the fence as he'd seen the other wives do. It was April. The cherry blossoms were in full bloom, he noticed bitterly. It was Hajime. Hajime, Buddy made himself say and write over and over. Because Hajime was dead, but more alive as a spirit than he had been as the man who wrote those letters to Kiku. At last Hajime had come home—bloomed—just as all the songs and poems promised.

The first time he'd seen Kiku, he had been struck. She was sitting on a park bench, head bent over a letter, hair partly hiding her face; with the way she held herself, her posture so tall and erect, such self-discipline instilled in her body, it seemed she could sit like that forever. He felt something for her that he couldn't describe. When he found out her name, it seemed to fit the indescribable something. Her parents were fervent believers and had named her Kikuko for the white, bulbous chrysanthemum that symbolized the emperor. And she was sixteen, for its sixteen petals.

Like that flower, she seemed simple, with so many plump but dainty petals disappearing into a centre. Each flower petal was the same, white tinted with the green it had sprouted from; you could hardly believe it was real. Her skin was very white then, and thick: opaque. You couldn't spy her veins at the temple, as you could on almost any other face, even a child's. Back then she had stood out on the avenue in Dairen with her pale skin against her kimono, apart from the other Manchukuo-born Japanese girls with their bobbed hair and bold glances, their casualness that could be daunting, heartless even. But Kiku was no longer the fresh girl he'd met in the park that summer. She now wore Western-style dresses, like the ones they wore back in Vancouver, and was almost middle-aged, just like the countless other middle-aged women in Tokyo. Her skin had grown ruddy, dark and weathered. She wasn't any longer the beauty he'd nursed in his mind. *She's no beauty*, he'd in fact mutter to himself and to others before he introduced them to her, if only to remind himself that she wasn't such a prize after all, if she ever had been; wasn't so above him. He had discovered, too, that there was a complicated, even frightening part of her bundled inside, unsprung. It didn't make him happy any more just to feel lucky. But she was still Kiku.

It had taken him weeks to approach her. He tried to tell himself she was just another girl, another Mitsuko, sitting in shabby Oppenheimer Park instead of the grand park at the centre of Dairen, the city they called the jewel of the east, where the roads radiated out sunnily and the mountains sat way off like the Rockies in Vancouver. He liked this park. It was the one place in Manchukuo that felt like home but better; like himself but a better self. The possibilities were there, wide and open; no one road the wrong road; for the first time, he was forging a path that left nothing behind that he would not come back to and claim. He'd shadow people and mimick them to polish his Japanese. Alone at night in his room, in the mirror: *Boku wa, Boku wa. I,* he declared. *Kuroda-san wa,* in the deep gruff voice of commanding officers. It was like sloughing off a dead self and stepping into a new skin, and he did it. He bowed to himself and couldn't help a private little smile of recognition at his old feet, straining at the width where his bunions bulged: the same as ever.

Before long, the two were happening to find themselves at the same bench at the same hour each day, after Kiku finished her shift at the factory, where she sewed parachutes. Big, white, fat pie-cut skirts to cup the air and float flocks of men to safety. She wasn't very good, she confessed, sometimes stitching two seams together at the wrong place and ending up with a two-headed monster that could plummet a man to death. She used her hands to try to describe the misshapen creature she'd created, and tears sprang to her eyes when she told him how her superior had scolded her for not trying hard enough. The woman questioned Kiku's loyalty to the emperor. That was when she'd whispered, "I would die," close to his ear, "just as my fiancé will."

Buddy wanted to cry with her and lose himself, but inside he was still that boy in Vancouver reading about Japan and Manchukuo as far-off, exotic places, seeing the pictures, and now here he was, inside the picture! That part of him kept a secret smirk for this girl eager to give herself over. He'd never met anyone like her, anyone called Kiku; he wondered if it was even a proper name. Yet he knew it had to be the most glorious name he'd ever hear.

He would die too, he told her, but he knew he wouldn't be called on for the ultimate sacrifice; he would never be truly tested. But he could rise and prove himself to the emperor he'd let into his heart—just as if, like Kiku or Hajime, he'd been born to it. He heard schoolchildren here marched to the front of their classrooms and kissed the emperor's portrait, smudging the glass fifty times over with their small lips and the hot breath that streamed through them. He could believe too.

Buddy cajoled her into sharing one of Hajime's letters with him. She consented, touched that he wanted to hear. Carefully she tore off one end of the envelope, bit by bit, unfolded the letter and read.

Dear Kiku,
The maple trees are turning colour now. I remember how we sat, side by side, very close, but never touching. Why didn't we touch? Now when I think of you sitting under a tree somewhere, I imagine I'm a red leaf falling into your lap. I'm touching you.

Hajime

♥

She reddened like that leaf, her voice shaking as she glanced up, sheepish, with his name in her mouth, and right then Buddy realized that she was in love. With his letter Hajime had boldly taken a part of her without asking, then given it back with a part of himself mixed in. Even Buddy, who could never have written such a letter—of how a fall leaf could express desire—could grasp that, and felt sorry he'd coaxed her into reading the letter at all.

"He's different today," she said when she received another letter, a week later. *Why glory for just some of us?*

Then came a gap in a sentence, blackened by the censor's pen.

"The enemy could guess where they are or what they're planning," Buddy suggested, though he could only wonder how letters were delivered, intercepted, translated. He wondered if Hajime had written careless, even unpatriotic words, that they should be hidden from Kiku.

Hajime was a Special Flight Officer Probationary Cadet, recruited from Tokyo University for the Special Attack Forces. The tokkotai. On the survey they were all given, he had circled *earnestly desire: I earnestly desire;* circled it twice, three times, to show how earnest, how desired. He could have chosen *I wish* or *I do not wish*, or left the page blank with only his name written across the top, but, like the others, he did not. The brightest would be first to go; and the training period was much shorter now than at the beginning of the war. He had the seventh-highest marks in his class, and was one of those selected, given the choice, the chance for a meaningful death.

"He'll be happy forever," Kiku said through her tears. "If he stayed in this world with me, it could never be that way. There might be happy days, and sad ones, but mostly ordinary days when you don't feel anything." When she peered behind Buddy to the flat grey sky, tears streamed down her cheeks. She wept so easily in those days. He knew what she meant by the small, nothing feeling of ordinary days, of those days when he was nothing more than a yellow skibby on dreary Powell Street. He tried to touch Kiku then, put his hand in her lap like Hajime's red leaf. We will all die, he thought. But first we have to wait.

"We must every one of us sacrifice," Kiku read from Hajime's letter. He asked that Kiku say hello to their friends and to her parents, and to her new friend, Koji. Koji, that was him; Buddy was long gone. Kiku had written to Hajime about him, her new friend. Now he thought half his spirit might fly with Hajime to Yasukuni Shrine, while the rest of him lived on with Kiku in a victorious Japan and a freed Asia. Was that so selfish of him?

One afternoon in summer, when the sky was cloudless and the sun burned like a torch and there was no escaping it into shade, Kiku brought out a tiny pair of scissors from her bag and placed them in his hands. "Please," she said, and turned the back of her head to him, loosening her bun and pulling out strands of hair to let him cut a lock close to her neck.

At the same time she read from the letter, low, as if she were the one being taken: *I will be called soon.*

Buddy snipped, the silver metal flashing in the sun. Kiku tied a white ribbon around the lock of hair—white for the emperor, for Kiku. There was a single grey hair in with the others which she weeded out, and she smiled wanly at him: a widow aged before her time.

I have no special nostalgia for this world.

"That doesn't sound like him," she said, puzzled. She looked sixteen again, buoyed by panic. "He's forgetting me. How will he meet me in Yasukuni if he forgets?"

The next day she was late. From the entrance of the park he spied her weaving through it, from bench to bench. She was holding out a needle and red thread and a length of white cotton to each girl or woman, asking them to make a stitch and knot the thread; to ensure that her fiancé's fate would be to die, not needlessly, but taking a thousand enemies down in fire with him, with this cloth tied around his belly.

Her eyes were dry and dark even under the scorching sun. "I believe," she pronounced, so quiet and fervent that he had to come close, and he smelled her, her sweat from the heat, not sweet and flowery as usual but slightly sour. "I believe in the sun even when it isn't shining." She looked up to the sky and blinked, as if guarding against something falling from it. He tried not to see her as a little silly and half-hysterical.

"He's afraid," she said. She could tell, even when so much of what he wrote was blackened in his latest letters. "He isn't ready. He isn't happy." He was far away now, in that spot by the ocean where the planes took off and their roar was like insects buzzing. *I will die a glorious death. I will bloom in the sky.* His voice in the letters grew distracted and faint, the writing slighter and less deliberate on the page; the hand that wrote it less loving, less familiar.

His time hadn't come after all. He seemed to shrink away from her. *Isn't it human to want to live longer, even for a little bit?* Others were in line before him and they were ready. "Hajime, Hajime," she repeated, as if chiding him, his name an irony. To initiate, to be first, it meant; as in hajime mashite: meeting for the first time, the Japanese greeting that Buddy had learned in his Vancouver schoolroom. Still Hajime's time didn't come; others went. *I only wish to be the best human being I can be, and to have time to develop myself in that way. Is it wrong to wish for that?* he asked in a later letter. Buddy understood; hadn't he wished to be a human being too, and for others to see in him his humanness and only that? *Only now do I realize, Kiku, for the first time in my life. Now that it's too late.* Kiku seemed pierced by Hajime's relief at being delayed, even shamed.

This time of year, for the past five years, she'd be gone— three, sometimes four days at the height of cherry-blossom season. Ever since she'd met up with an old friend in the basement of a department store, a friend she hadn't seen since they were both fourteen-year-old girls in the same village in Yamanashi Prefecture, cheering their brothers and fathers and boyfriends off to war. The woman introduced her to the others in their dwindling cherry-blossom group. Who knew what exactly the ladies busied themselves and each other with for three days each year? They called it their most painful time, when they would poke and prod at their sorrows, keeping the wounds fresh.

In the bedroom closet there would be an empty spot where a few changes of clothes had been removed, including Kiku's two favourite dresses, her handbag and spring coat. She always tried to look as nice as the other ladies, not any better, just not shabby; to show she'd done well enough for herself through the years, and lived a comfortable, quiet life that she was grateful for. She never told Buddy when exactly she'd return, but one day he'd come home to find the gaps in the closet filled once again, and soon enough she'd arrive through the door with her grocery bags and her flitting gaze.

Home soon, he told himself, though four days had already gone by. Today was the fifth and it felt different, this one day more with no end in sight. She'd never been away quite this long. On impulse, he stumbled into the bedroom and delved into the closet, swimming past the hems of the skirts and dresses aswish in plastic, to the spot behind the line of never-worn shoes. The box that normally sat there untouched, dusty, discoloured, that held Hajime's letters, was gone. Her kimono was gone too—the wedding kimono with the cherry blossoms, that she'd stored away all these years.

On the train back to Tokyo, Ryu showed Miyo Mount Fujiyama, a triangular smudge at the horizon among clouds and smokestacks. "It's our national treasure," he said. She knew it from a 1977 calendar she'd found in a drawer at her father's house after he died, something only Setsuko could have given him. Under February, there was the mountain: coal-dark and iced with snow in a too blue sky; no people in sight. When she unfurled it across the kitchen counter, the yellowed calendar and its waxy odour had flooded her with old bitterness for Setsuko. The bitterness was tinged with another taste too, of reproach Miyo held for herself, at what she might have done to curdle the love between her father and Setsuko.

"They shut the factories down on New Year's Day so you can see it," Ryu told her. "Fuji-san is beautiful," he added wistfully, as if the mountain were a girl who would always be lovely to him through smoke and soot, like Hana when she stayed close.

Miyo was relieved to see Tokyo's cluttered skyline once again. Setsuko had said they'd rebuilt the city with little care, rushing to make everything new, and of concrete instead of the paper and wood that had flamed and died in the firebombs dropped by the Americans. Every big city in Japan must look like this, motley and jumbled and memoryless, except Kyoto, whose palaces had been spared.

She caught the familiar sight of the glass-boat building floating amid the clutter, the sprawling Tokyo Forum near the Ginza. "It's a cave," Ryu said, without looking twice. "It makes you small." Like the fish that boats mimic, Miyo thought; the inside was the cavern of its belly, the hold. As they passed in the train, panes of glass shimmered with reflections of light and watery sky, and she felt she was inside that belly, mere cargo small as any other. Here in the vast crowd of Tokyo's millions, Hana was small too.

Ryu and Miyo reached the street she'd come to know at the top of the steep Kudanshita subway exit to find two older men, one in a wheelchair, both waiting expectantly as if for them. It was the old-fashioned kind of wheelchair you rarely saw, in Tokyo or Toronto—clunky but skeletal and unpowered. She'd hardly seen people in wheelchairs or with walkers on the streets here; maybe they were cloistered by their families, lonely shut-ins; maybe there were secret societies of them exiled to the city's outskirts. The two seemed to be visitors to the big city, naive about its rules, maybe from a small town or village. They had to be brothers close in age; their faces and expressions rhymed as robust and frail incarnations of one another. "They need help," Miyo said, looking back.

"We don't know them," Ryu said. He moved ahead without her. "Yasukuni is this way." She watched his back as he did, the slow ease of his shoulder blades working. She knew what it was like to need the help of strangers. Ryu didn't know what it was to be weak; no one that strong could. He understood Hana, that was all.

"Please," she said. "Sumimasen." She used her clumsy Japanese so he might grasp what it meant to her. Abruptly he went and took hold of one side of the wheelchair and motioned for the younger brother to take the other.

They went down step by step, wobbling until Miyo took hold of a rung in the back. Ryu didn't ward her off. The older man began to hum and sing in snippets, a simple tune, pounding the armrest with the heel of his hand. The steady beat was like the march of her father's *ichi ni*. He babbled a question over and over until they set him down at the bottom of the stairs. "The ojisan wants to know if you're visiting your father at Yasukuni Shrine," Ryu explained. The man nodded, and his whole body seemed to rattle in its own rickety cage. He clawed at his breast, at the stripes above the pocket there. He was in uniform, Miyo realized. When his hat fell from his lap, she picked it up for him, and looked into his gummy eyes. He could've been the same age as her father. "Iie," she said slowly, shaking her head.

She and Ryu climbed up into the sunlight and gazed down the stairwell. The younger man was setting his brother's peaked cap on his head, the kind of cap Miyo had seen the dressed-up soldiers wearing in Yasukuni. There had to be countless stairways to any destination on the subway. How would they manage?

"Even the son is not so strong," Ryu sighed.

"They're father and son?" Miyo was taken aback. They seemed barely ten years apart.

"He said he brings his father to Yasukuni two times each year, at cherry-blossom time, and on anniversary of surrender in August."

They stood at a bend of the wide avenue she remembered from before—no people now that father and son were on their way, only cars whizzing by, and concrete walls on both sides like those of an emptied canal. She glimpsed the steel torii that rose above the surrounding buildings. Why had they bothered to put it back up, after melting it down into a ship or a tank?

"Hana will be here, you're sure?"

"She will have your father's bones with her," he said, "I know."

Miyo felt as bound and helpless as the man in the wheelchair. This was the place where the dead kami from all the wars rested; where Setsuko had wanted to leave her father. She tried to imagine her father as a Japanese, one of the emperor's loyal subjects, one in a vast, believing crowd; in love with the Manchuria that was no more, hopeful for an Asia for Asians: another Buddy, held down as a yellow something or nothing back home, and yearning for a bit of paradise. That bitter beaten-down feeling fuelling something worse.

"Don't worry." Ryu came closer. "They don't want your father here. He wasn't a hero or a criminal." His mouth seemed to twist into a strained smile. "They will never take him. Hana wants him to go to his home in Canada with you, away from her."

Slowly they walked toward the shrine. The weight of the wheelchair had left her hip sore, but Miyo didn't mind. As before, the grounds appeared deserted, if only because the torii and the statue that loomed beyond dwarfed everything around them. A man in bright orange coveralls appeared beneath the torii, clapped once, then twice, and bowed once, twice, three times. On the roadway behind sat a massive black bus, its blacked-out windows like blind insect eyes, the loud-speaker mounted on the roof the mouth of a slumber-ing beast. Just like the bus she'd heard and glimpsed when they had left Ur Gallery. A burst of laughter came from a clearing in the bushes up ahead, where a young man stumbled about, with a vacant, slow grin on his face; he held his arms clumsily up to the sky. A middle-aged man, his father, appeared, snapped his fingers impatiently and threw a ball. The son stared as Miyo and Ryu passed, and a string of saliva swung from a cor-ner of his mouth. He gurgled with delight as the ball fell by his feet.

When they reached the top of the walkway Miyo glanced back: the father and son had disappeared, and the man in coveralls was small but bright in the distance under the torii, a gaudy figurine until it became a windup toy clapping its hands and bowing from a hinge at its waist, in a ceaseless, soundless jitter.

At the well near the entrance, Ryu ladled out water for her. The iciness made Miyo feel clean and pure for a moment, watching him drink and spit it out. He showed her where to receive her fortune. She shook a dark wooden canister, drew out a numbered stick and unfolded the small slip of paper she was given in exchange. There was Japanese on the front; on the back in English, it said:

No. 48 SMALL FORTUNE

Miyo threw it down without reading the rest; her scant fortune numbered, sized. She wanted a new fate, better chances for Hana and herself; didn't they deserve it? Hana believed in that for Miyo, if not for herself. She'd recognized Miyo's despair right away, and hated it; Miyo did too. She should've tied the slip of paper to the tree Setsuko had shown her before, laden with unwanted fortunes.

Ryu chased the slip down the gravel walk and came back. "Small fortune is not bad," he said. He shoved the paper in front of her and made her read.

"Just like looking at the treasure of other people beyond the valley. Let's stop to hurt your heart and give trouble to your mind. If you have right mind, your request will be granted later on. The patient, the sickness may last long, but is sure to get well. The lost article will be found. The person you wait for will be late. The lost will be found. The sickness will heal." She looked up. "So we will find Hana?"

"She is here, of course," Ryu said.

"And this will heal?" She touched her leg and her temple.

Ryu looked at her, perplexed. "It's not you. You're not sick. The patient is Hana."

"Hana?" Miyo blurted, sounding hurt to her own ears. She recalled the day she'd first met Hana, and the sight of her sinewy body braced boldly upright, showing Miyo how to be strong.

"Hana needs you to be strong," Ryu said. "Come with me." For the first time, he took her hand in his, dry and smooth. They walked past the bench where she'd sat days ago with Setsuko, waiting for Hana. That silly song wafted back: I'm a stranger in paradise. It was from a lonely afternoon spent by the stereo, she and her father listening to one of his old records. The tune was filled with yearning, its key turned minor by the last note, sounding unfinished but promising nothing more.

ELEVEN

THEY STEPPED THROUGH the wooden gates into a wonderland: the sky was dotted with pale blossoms, all blooming, and people—alone and in pairs, in families, with cameras—sauntered under them here and there. The air felt laden and thick, yet there was no scent. It was the pure, white, hopeful perpetual Sunday at Yasukuni Shrine that Miyo had glimpsed in a photograph in Hana's studio.

"How long will they last?" Miyo asked.

"They are blooming all over Japan now." Ryu stooped to pick up a trampled flower that had fallen to the ground unopened; he pressed it into her palm. "The blossom will stay on the tree two or three days, then it will fall. They are early because of the heat."

She thought of the painted branch on Hana's wall, the one drooping bloom that threatened to fall. They sat down on a bench as the Toy Symphony began to play over the PA system; pigeons gathered and pecked at grains scattered on the ground. The flock of them thickened, each bird plumper than others she'd seen. A couple waded past, stepping gingerly, but their young son kicked at the ground and the birds sputtered and flapped.

The sight panicked her: the sleek white heads bobbing, their eyes pink with centres of unfathomable black; the accumulation of things moving in the air and at her feet. Miyo rose and birds flew up at her face. "I want to go back," she said, confused.

"Back where?" Ryu asked.

She didn't know. There was the beating of wings; petals stirring, straining to bloom; and then a figure across the way, thin and conspicuous, darting among a slow throng of elderly women, round-shouldered, bentbacked, open-mouthed. It was Hana.

Setsuko glimpsed the two of them, Miyo at one edge of the garden and Hana in the middle. Neither had seen the other. How was it that the boy, Hana's Ryu, was now with Miyo, and Hana there alone, with only her sad widows?

Miyo's hair had grown in the week since she'd arrived; she had more flesh, too; she was thriving, like a flower greedy for light. Hana was thin, just a stem. In the hospital, Setsuko had told Mas, *Miyo will be just fine*, to ease his mind. He'd asked Setsuko to look out for her; there was no one else. As a child, Miyo had come between them as if she were the little wife instead of the daughter. Up to his dying moment, Mas had had no peace, worrying over her. He'd barely thought of Setsuko, who'd come back to the scraps of him, much less Hana.

People who came close to Miyo felt they couldn't help but help her. Even Hana had been taken in, and now she'd lost Ryu to Miyo. First or only children were like that: they grabbed at everything, because they'd been given the world from the start. It wasn't all Miyo's fault; she didn't know her own strength. She could drown another while saving herself. That was her instinct. Hana was forever on her own, pushing herself to be stronger than the rest; a hard luck case, like her mother, Setsuko thought ruefully. Hana felt sorry for the world so it wouldn't be sorry for her. Hana would have come halfway round the world to Mas for one kind word, for the slightest glance. Why else had Hana studied so hard to learn English? To be close to him, so she wouldn't be a foreigner in his world. Miyo had deserted him when he needed her most.

So Hana had turned to those dried-up lonely women and their ghosts, letting them into her heart with each of their stories until she became just one more in their circle. Setsuko should have been sitting among them with Hana at her side. But they'd never let her in! To them she wasn't pure enough, even if her belief and desire were. It should have been Setsuko's story—Mas's story!—penetrating Hana's heart. But Hana would never listen, convinced she'd found out the truth.

How could the same man be father to both Hana and Miyo? The two were utterly different. Nothing of one in the other. Mas had dared to say that himself. There could be no doubt that he was the father, and he'd never set eyes on Hana to know how different she was.

It was after seeing the pictures that Setsuko put in front of him when they met for the first time since separating. Five years had passed. That was how she told him about Hana, who was by then in school in Kyoto.

Without a word, she slid a packet of snapshots, the first ones in black and white with pinked edges, across the table to him at the diner around the corner from his house. There it was, all that she'd gone through without him. She'd done it most of her life—coped, unlike Miyo, she thought bitterly. From then on, she made a print of every photo she got from Kyoto and mailed them to him, without a return address, so they couldn't be sent back. He might have been a brave soldier, but he could be a cowardly man. She even sent him the odd crayon drawing and old toy so that he would have a touch, a smell of her. She'd found most of these stashed at the back of his closet when she and Miyo had gone through his things after he'd died.

"She looks like you" was the second thing Mas had said, leaning back into the banquette, away from her, another disownment. Nothing like him, he meant. He wasn't angry that she'd never told him; there was no sign, no tic of surprise that she'd deceived him. Maybe he'd suspected long ago, maybe even before the separation, but said nothing. He'd let her go her own way.

"How would you know?" she retorted. She was angry; she stood up and towered over him, sunken in the banquette seat; she shouted at him for the first time and he cowered. He hated to be seen or heard like this among white strangers. He swatted the air with his clumsy hand, for her to sit and simmer down. With kids on the street he could shout and be tough or silent and not give a damn, but elsewhere he was easily humiliated. Instantly she regretted her outburst, because his face puckered in the ugly way that showed his rage and suffering sliced open, raw. In a few seconds that opening closed up and she doubted what she'd seen. Still, it made her remember, and believe more than ever that he was a soldier who'd steeled himself against pain to sacrifice, had fought and survived.

"She's a good girl," Setsuko said, settling herself. "Just as good as Miyo." Better, she meant. She let the knuckles of her hand graze his. He looked older, uncared for. He stared at that grazed hand and didn't look up. He opened his mouth, but nothing came out. "Is she . . . healthy?" he finally asked, and there was an uncertain quaver in his voice; healthy could be either a miracle or a curse. Only she could detect that uncertainty, from three years of practice reading him.

"Gotaimanzoku," she answered, realizing he might not know the expression. "Ten fingers, ten toes," she added, careless of the pride in her voice. Instantly she cursed herself, over Miyo. In Japan there were so many cases of children with stunted digits, twisted feet that couldn't grow. Or things could look fine on the outside but be all wrong inside. Miyo had a little of both. Mas had always believed that Setsuko took it too lightly, Miyo's trouble, while he took it for everything.

"Hana is okii," Setsuko went on. "When she came out, she was."

"Big?" He was incredulous at first. Then he looked at her with gratitude in his eyes, perhaps for the first time. It shocked her to realize that all these years he'd wondered if it might have been his fault that Miyo suffered, and not the wife's. He had never quite been able to blame her, because she was beautiful and flawless in his memory. If she hadn't died, it all would've been different. Nothing lasts, not even beauty. He'd rather hold himself, the gods—anyone but her—responsible, in spite of the deaths in her family, the weakness and slow, withering ailments that couldn't be pinned down in their bodies, like bats flapping inside a cave.

"She hardly cries."

"How would you know?" He turned on her just like that. He could never face up to what he was truly guilty of, and what he wasn't.

It was a fact that Setsuko hadn't seen Hana since her sister had taken the infant from her arms and boarded the plane to Japan. But once a week she'd listened to the changing noises, the gurgling voice shaping words inside a tiny, not quite human mouth, among sprouting teeth—a tongue thrust over a curled ledge of lip—all growing so wilfully at the other end of the telephone. Setsuko had the photos, the exercise notebooks, the drawings. Already there were thoughts erupting, a telling glance, a person so suddenly there. Already it was too late; so much missed that couldn't be made up. "A mother knows," Setsuko had answered. No matter what, she was Hana's mother, and Mas was her father.

One thing Mas was grateful for was having chosen a woman who wouldn't burden him. He could never have raised Hana as his own, as he had Miyo. He would've tried to, responsible as ever, but cheating Hana in the smallest ways, turning his back to tend to Miyo, setting her down to lift Miyo, who'd be older but ganglier, needful, always. These slights, Setsuko knew, would wear a child down bit by bit just as she was struggling upward to become someone. Hana would still be an orphan, just like her mother.

Mas forever measured Setsuko against his first wife, with Setsuko coming up short on every count. It was easy to see why: the woman was beautiful, Setsuko was not. She was a lady, born and bred in Japan; Setsuko was not. She—Setsuko refused to let the name ever cross her thoughts or lips—was dead, and Setsuko was not. The moment Setsuko glimpsed that picture, the first time Mas invited her into his living room, she knew. It was easy to stay in love with someone who wasn't alive, someone lovely and now young enough to be your own daughter; someone who'd grown along with you from child to adult, your very first secrets hers, and hers yours.

In his sleep, lying beside Setsuko all those years ago, he'd given over his secrets to her. By then, she'd found the box at the back of the closet. She knew his wishes better than Miyo, better than even he had known them, and now he was waiting—not at rest yet, fool that he was—and only she could help him make his way here. *Yasukuni?* she'd found scratched in an old notebook on an otherwise blank page; Mas wondering if this special place might be at all within his reach.

The women were seated in the garden on old fold-out chairs. Those grey heads of hair, pinned in buns or cropped short, were dowdy and unfeminine; likewise their drab suits and the handbags that drooped from their arms. People here wore their age like a uniform. Setsuko kept herself up, even with Mas gone; even if they'd stayed married, she never would've let herself go. She kept her hair black because it had always been a naturally deep blue-black—her best feature—so much so that people used to ask if it was dyed. Mas had liked her girlishness, even if he was clumsy in showing it. He'd grown tired of the humiliation of trying not to be awkward, and long before had given in to his own roughness, just as she had. She liked that he'd never pretended; that he wasn't capable. She knew he'd liked her hair on his pillow, and he'd liked her face scrubbed clean at night for bed—to see the difference, what was stripped bare and private for only him.

Setsuko lost sight of Hana just as the music over the PA started again, only this time it wasn't the same old tune; it was "Sakura," a song she knew from way back, from the good old days of camp and before. Of course, there hadn't been many good days; only hours of hard work, loneliness and uncertainty. She was struck by how sad the song sounded to her at this moment, one note then another plucked on the koto, and how little that sound suggested cherry blossoms in her mind. *Sa-ku-ra, sa-ku-ra.* Each note seemed distant from the one before; that was what gave her a lonely shiver when she heard it.

A girl was dancing to those sad notes. Her shoulders were slight and bony through a kimono that wasn't particularly ornate or special, but an old-fashioned grey and pink with blossoms painted on it. Still, it hung nicely on the girl's slender frame. Setsuko had studied dancing as a girl but had finally given it up. She would never be very good, and in the internment camp there was no proper teacher, and she didn't want to bring out her one good kimono, which had been her mother's, for fear of getting it muddy or worse. She was too big-boned and undainty for it; she wanted to hide the broad hands holding her fan to the sky, and the broad feet poking out between the skirts of her kimono. In Japan, as long as she was among the others who'd come from Canada as so-called repatriates, she was fine, but later, on the Ginza, she stuck out as foreign-born. She could see the superior look people gave her when she walked and when she talked, when they heard her telltale accent and poor vocabulary. And it wasn't just that. She and the other repats had come back to take what little food and shelter there was to be shared. It was terrible to see the accusation in people's eyes.

She would give almost anything now to be dancing for Mas, dancing the Eternal Shrine Dance as the scroll bearing his name was tied to the sakaki branch and placed inside the palanquin, then carried into the inner sanctum. He'd be enshrined forever at Yasukuni, and at last a kami, a god like the others he'd fought with. It was only fitting after the suffering he'd seen, after he'd embraced his own death for the emperor. It was for the one hundred million hearts as one human bullet that he'd volunteered himself to be for Japan and all of Asia. That was what they used to say; she'd read it in years-old newspapers she'd uncrumpled, papers that had insulated her aunt's rickety house through winter; when she'd smoothed out the sheets used to wrap precious teapots that had been stowed away, then brought out to be sold, there were smudged pictures of crowds chanting at embarking ships. She'd come to believe, if only for him, as Mas must have; hers was one gone astray of the hundred million hearts that belonged ultimately to Japan, even in defeat, and even in the emptiness of her daily life, estranged, across the ocean.

No one except the ones who'd had to return to base, like Mas, knew what it was to fail. To be given your orders and be unable to fulfill them—denied the glory— it had to be the cruellest thing. *Disgrace! They beat me for coming back alive and I don't blame them!* This she'd read in Mas's youthful handwriting on a scrap with other scraps in the box. He never spoke the words. He must've hid the scratchings because if they knew he was from Canada, knew he was not one of them, despite all the care he took with his accent, he'd surely be beaten. But he had to release his thoughts somehow, didn't he? He had to scrawl them in his own tongue, closest to how he felt. In bed, half-asleep beside her, thirty years after, he sometimes fidgeted and muttered, "Disgrace!" "Coward!" Silly dream, she'd thought at first, not knowing anything. But to come back after drinking the farewell saké with your comrades and commander, after donning the clothes you chose to die in, tying the sash around your belly, knotting the headband whose red sun had been made with blood from the pricked fingertips of young girls—how could she imagine this humiliation? This much she could understand: that he'd chosen to die a Japanese for Japan; and in the end, she would help him do that.

He'd given as much as any of those war dead whose widows gloried in their sacrifice year after year. From the contorted grimace on his face the day she told him about Hana, and her being raised by Setsuko's sister in Japan, she knew what he was thinking and feeling. He knew he wouldn't see Japan for a long, long time, if at all, and maybe he'd never even see Hana. It was because of Miyo. His duty to her had kept him away, given him his excuse, was his punishment for coming back alive, was his shame. For the longest time, she'd hated Miyo for being that.

When Setsuko first came to Yasukuni, it didn't seem so special that all the kami would be drawn here, it had seemed to be just another shrine. But with each visit she had grown more enchanted, seeing the doves flocking all together like nowhere else in Japan. She could never leave Tokyo until she saw the cherry blossoms bloom to their fullest in Yasukuni and slowly fall, and rot on the ground from pink to brown. She was held by some sweet and bitter desire, as if she were saying to that woman to whom Mas had first belonged, *I'll have him to the end.*

She'd begged Hana to dance for him. It was expecting too much, she knew, but she couldn't help herself. Hana had her own crazy ideas about her father and the war. "There are no bad things in war," Setsuko had tried to explain.

"You want me to dance for my daddy?" Hana taunted when Setsuko told her he was gone. "I'm glad he's dead!" Still so angry. She twisted her body lewdly, shaking faster and faster, kicking and flinging her arms until she was streaming with sweat and grinning, ugly and wild—possessed!—and Setsuko could only stand back from that heaving, feverish body, frightened and repelled.

Hana had gone around digging up whatever she could about Mas at the Diet Library and the old military archives. She'd met up with some strange characters, like the infamous nisei who'd served time—Kuroda, his name was, the war criminal from around Oppenheimer Park. Back home in Canada, old Vancouver families remembered him from before he'd gone to Manchuria;

before the war and everything else. Setsuko only vaguely recalled the younger brother who was close to her age. They all said the elder one was mean, even as a boy; they said they always knew he was different. They were shamed because they were, they'd say, Canadian, no longer Japanese, and to them Kuroda was a dirty traitor, as bad as the Canadian government made every one of them out to be. A man like him, Setsuko figured, had to be petty and fearful, with no higher beliefs; he did what he did to get by on either side of the fence. If he were a true Japanese, he'd have done the honourable thing in the final moment. But he had let himself live on; he was the true coward, not Mas.

Setsuko was relieved to find both Hana and Miyo at Yasukuni, and told herself that, once she got Mas's urn back and pleaded his case again to the shrine officials, she could go home. Hana was a grown woman now; Setsuko couldn't forever be chasing after her, trying to make up for what was already lost. Miyo would be fine too, with Ryu to look after her. She'd make her way home soon enough; she didn't belong here either. But the blossoms hadn't fallen or rotted yet. Of course she knew that it was hopeless, that Mas had no business being enshrined in Yasukuni when he'd died so very ordinary a death, without choice or glory, too late and too far from Japan.

Hana would always be fine and Setsuko knew it, from all the times before, waiting for her to come back. Because at heart Hana didn't believe in self-sacrifice. She gave her love and pity to the widows, but considered them stupid and vain for what they'd given their husbands to.

The girl in the pink and green kimono kept dancing. Girls often danced for the spirits of their fathers, uncles, grandfathers, or to celebrate their graduation from some elite university like Keio or Waseda. Setsuko crept to a closer bench to watch, wishing she hadn't forgotten her glasses. The girl's arms looked frail; her step faltered. Even the young ones would be so full of emotion spilling out in this nostalgic scene. But then the girl bent at the knees in that familiar posture, holding her fan up toward the sky like an offering, and pivoted, trembling, and she wasn't a girl after all but a woman, an aged woman, older than Setsuko. The arms the kimono sleeves slid back from weren't slender and smooth but brittle and spotted, creped; the hands and wrists held to the sky were branch-like, a little gnarled by arthritis. Her hair was too black and her skin, powdered white, was puckered; her lips were drawn in the old-fashioned way, from long before the war, when all lips were to be a dainty rosebud shape. *Is that how I look?* Setsuko couldn't help but wonder, shuddering, touching a hand to her own powdered cheek, her dyed, done-up hair and lipsticked mouth.

Finally the dance ended, and the small audience clapped politely as the woman fluttered a fan at her face in the humid air. Hana ushered her onto the path that led away to the other buildings. Setsuko strained to see the colourful back of the woman's kimono slither away like some exotic animal, one of those iguanas or chameleons, disappearing amid the shrubbery. Seconds later, from across the garden, Miyo was running after them—running!—swiftly, oblivious of the doves that flew up around her feet. *It's true,* just as she'd told Mas. *The girl is strong, she's even quick.* Tears rose in Setsuko's eyes to see Miyo move like that; stung like soap, or bile; she had to look away. All these years! She'd always known but had never seen it: the girl had never needed Mas, not all of him; she could've let him go, just a little; that would've been enough.

The Shinto priest followed at a stately pace, his robes rustling, so clean and pure; his face serenely expressionless. It wasn't fair that Mas's spirit could not rest here when she sensed him flapping around her in his clumsy, angry way; cheated, always cheated, his whole life given over to duty, both glorious and shabby. No one else could know how unfair it was, except maybe Miyo.

The air in the museum was cool and clammy, as if they were inside the hold or the hull of a ship, but not a light-filled glass ship like the Tokyo Forum. The atmosphere was not fresh; it felt very still and old, like the water of a stagnant pond. Miyo felt conscious of her breath, measuring it in and out, tasting each time its dankness. The corridors were dark too, shaded, and the objects inside the display cases and even the person behind the ticket counter seemed to shrink away from any light or sound. She followed Ryu, who knew the place.

A clatter of feet and voices echoed from the main hall, and there was the click and flash of cameras. Two Japanese tourists, pudgy men in plaid shirts, stood in front of a long, dull steel cylinder tapered to a rounded point at one end: a giant bullet. "Kaiten," said Ryu, "torpedo." It was a human bullet deployed from a submarine. The steel might have come from the gates they had taken down at the shrine entrance. It had been found at the bottom of the ocean when the war ended. "He couldn't find his target," Ryu explained; he, the kamikaze marine, who, like the others, must have worn the cherry blossom on his collar proudly. "He sat and suffocated."

"They're crazy," Miyo whispered back, not knowing who "they" were. She felt she'd have to touch the crusted surface of it to believe, but didn't move toward it.

The tourists were taking turns snapping pictures of one another by the torpedo, then beside a plane with a large red sun painted vividly on one side. It was strange, the sight; nothing looked real—not the rickety, flimsy machines, not even the two men. With its high ceilings and greenish walls, the room felt like a hangar, or a factory where once these very machines might have been built. At the far corner there were miniature planes, Japanese zeros and American B-29 bombers, suspended with invisible wire against a cracked, painted sky inside a glass case. That was how she preferred to think of all this: everything miniature, smaller than life; child's play. The hall was now empty except for them; no sign of the woman or the priest, and the other figure she was sure had been Hana.

"Hana says that all the time—we Japanese are crazy," Ryu murmured, then pulled Miyo back out to the corridor. She cringed at his warm hand on her and wanted to push him away. For an instant she felt glad not to have been born here, not to speak the language, and not to have to wonder, or be sorry, or atone. She wasn't one of "we Japanese."

Ryu raced toward the staircase just as the swishing robes of the priest disappeared up a second flight of steps.

Music faintly played as Miyo and Ryu climbed to the second floor—marching music, the music in her father's *ichi ni.* The march whined on, scratchy and thin, as if coming from some remote place and made to travel far, like the emperor's voice on Juni's CD. They came to a wide, well-lit corridor with black-and-white photographs on either side, crowds with banners on sticks touted high above, or the lone tear-stained face of a child. Down at the end, the hall telescoped into another long corridor, and another, narrower and narrower. At the far end, Miyo spied the kimono of the dancing woman, the same woman from the gallery who'd stitched Hana's red yarn to the face of the emperor and cried for Hajime. The pink and grey silk spilled on the floor, and the woman slumped with her palms and cheek pressed to the glass of a display case, as if to a cage, desperate to be let in, or for whatever was inside to be let out. She was weeping, not loudly, but each sobbing breath was amplified into a hollow din that reverberated down to them. The priest was there, and two others, a man and a woman with their backs turned, all very still and quiet.

There was Hana reaching down to comfort the woman. Miyo knew to go no closer; it was a kind of ceremony, private; perhaps sacred. Ryu went rushing headlong but she grabbed him in time. "Wait," she whispered, bringing him back. Grasping his wrist, she felt his frenetic pulse and his body, a single muscle held in check.

The man, small and elderly, went to the woman's side and pushed Hana's hand away roughly. He gave the woman's shoulder a tentative but familiar pat, fingers clustered like a paw. That ungentle but hesitant hand could have belonged to her father, Miyo thought. But then she knew it. "Buddy," she whispered to Ryu. Now, here, he was Koji, Kuroda-san, and the woman kneeling had to be Kiku, his wife.

Her sobbing went on. The priest stood apart from the others, blind and deaf to it all, his white robes immaculate, austere, ornate brocade folded inward; he was quietly babbling with half-closed eyelids, not in Japanese, not in words. He was chanting from ancient scriptures in a form of Japanese from another age, old enough that it was no longer written, let alone spoken, and no one could understand it.

Ryu's hand slipped from Miyo's grasp and he went bounding down the corridor. Miyo raced after him. He arrived breathless before Hana, stopping short of touching her. Hana gazed up unsurprised, and shifted her eyes to Miyo just behind; Hana's face was gaunt, pocked with dark shadows. No, she wasn't all right. She held herself tall but she was sunken-chested, and her hair hung coarse and clumped in her face, unwashed.

Yet she was smiling a deeply sad smile, beautiful, bruise-eyed, right into Miyo's eyes, telling her, *You're here, you're here,* with relief, though she'd done nothing to let herself be found. No one ever looked at Miyo the way Hana did; not even David yearning to burrow all of himself inside her. Hana had given herself to Miyo, wholly; broken her heart and instantly healed it over with just that look. It was and would forever be, Miyo knew, her most favourite thing.

"Ne-san," Hana sighed. Miyo fell into Hana's arms, the same flesh and blood finally near, ready to let herself be held tight. But instead Hana pulled her toward the glass case, down to the ground beside the kneeling woman. She urged her closer, until Miyo smelled the woman's perfume full in her nostrils, sweet and quaint, like roses or violets. "This is Kiku-san," Hana said, and Miyo looked into a wizened, tear-streaked face with small sunken eyes and a smudged blot of red at her lips.

Inside the glass case, among the rows and rows of young faces, Miyo recognized Hajime from Hana's wall, the diamond pinprick eyes where the light seemed to catch, even though the photo was very tiny and very old.

Miyo recognized seven of the widows from the gallery now seated in a circle around Kiku. They sat silently, as if in prayer or sleep, as Kiku began to read from letters taken from the box propped on her lap. Beside Kiku was Hana, who sat by Miyo whispering spurts of English into her ear, as if she were a medium straining to receive whatever unearthly message might be relayed. Hana had hastily introduced them to Miyo one by one, but she'd barely apprehended the names as sounds. She looked from face to face, anxious to identify something particular about each of them, to imagine them young with their young men, with black instead of grey hair, long, short, straight or curled. But at the moment, with their eyes sunken shut, they receded into themselves far away from her.

Setsuko sat outside the circle and apart from the others, alone; Ryu stood off a way, as did Buddy, like men keeping out of women's business. Ryu looked lost, too large to comfortably fit into one of the miniature chairs, yet young enough for it. He didn't take his eyes from Hana. Buddy fidgeted at the sound of Kiku's tremulous voice, stealing the odd timid glance at her, as if, after nearly fifty years of marriage, he barely knew her.

Am I a monster? Miyo felt Hana's lips brush her ear with the strange stream of words, this Hajime's words from his letters, read out in Kiku's voice and funnelled by Hana into her. He was asking Kiku once, then again: *Am I a cowardly monster?* And then Miyo heard her father's name uttered, *Masao,* a young man from Canada whose secret must be kept; whom Hajime called in his letter *the first person I've made friends with . . . .*

TWELVE

OCTOBER 12 Tuesday—Clear

Kiku,

I woke up this morning from the strangest dream. I never remember my dreams, but here, where I try to escape my daytime thoughts (except of you and the fall leaves—right now they're burning with colour), I wake up with them fresh in my mind. They cling to me, or I to them. In my dream, I was with the other officers, feeling carefree because we were off duty and we were distracted from our usual sentimental thoughts of leaving this world behind. We were riding in the back of a truck, and all around the streets were covered in dark soil and uprooted plants—pine trees, I think—left by a recent devastation, and the whole city was being remade into a garden. We were searching for some lost thing, I don't know what. Something caught my eye and I jumped down to retrieve it. It was an arm, a woman's. It wasn't bloodied at all, but intact and clean and pale. It was easy to spot in the black dirt. I think it was yours, Kiku, the way I imagine it under

the sleeve of your blouse or kimono, the inside velvety
part. The fingers were curled. They didn't move but the
arm seemed alive because it was warm though bloodless.
I held it carefully in my arms, and the skin was so soft I
couldn't help brushing it against my cheek. The strange
thing was that I felt my own touch. I mean, I felt the arm
on my cheek, and at the same time I felt my cheek on a
part of me. It was unmistakable, the sensation of my own
flesh to flesh. Was it my own arm? It was but it wasn't.
I wanted to understand what it meant. After all, it was my
dream, coming from someplace inside me. . . .

Tonight, just as I was returning from dinner to finish
writing this to you, I understood: it was your arm, and it
was mine because you are a part of me. Doesn't that
make sense?

Hajime

October 15 Friday—Rain
Dear Kiku,
It's growing colder here. I feel dampness in my bones.
But it's familiar, like an old friend who knows he's a
nuisance. To feel warm and comfortable without you
would seem wrong.

You asked me what happened next in my dream and
I'm ashamed to say. I gave the arm to a fellow officer,
who put it inside a flimsy box meant for food and sent it
off. The box may even have been stained and smelly
inside. Why did I do that? Leave the lovely arm that
might have been yours or mine inside in that filth? Yet
I felt relieved, because its softness was making me weak.

I was afraid that I wouldn't take good enough care of it, that I might drop it or let it get bruised. I do have a strange imagination, you always said. I lack discipline and fall short even in my dreams. But you said that, if I focused my mind and my spirit, I could accomplish all you envisioned for me. I do cling to your faith in me, as I believe in the sun, even when it isn't shining and the skies are dark and angry, and it is impossible to see the battleships below that we are to fire at, the ships we will one day be asked to plunge ourselves into. When I flew an escort mission the other day, I was caught in thick cloud and suddenly came out of it and one of those new formidable B-29s was right there, banking close and then away, and I thought I saw a face, an American face, large and deep, and a toothy bright smile flashing. I know that sounds like my imagination again, because I've never seen an American, and the sky is so vast and we are travelling so fast, but those machines, you don't know, Kiku, they are just metal not much thicker than cardboard, that buckles and wobbles. You feel the engine inside your organs, vibrating as a part of you. There is barely more than air separating them from us.

I don't mean to frighten you. I won't fail, I promise. I won't be a senseless casualty before my moment arrives. Yesterday, I heard of one pilot who mistook a small island he was flying over for an American battleship. He disappeared into it in a puff of smoke and mist. I pray that he left something of himself, a lock of his hair or his nail clippings, to give to his family.

That reminds me, Kiku. I must remember not to cut my fingernails too soon before my mission. I heard of one pilot—his name was Sekiguchi, I think—who was always

very fastidious, and when his time came, his hair and his
nails were too short to trim anything for his loved ones.
I'll wait as long as possible, so that my family will see
I was healthy and thriving and grooming myself right up
until the final hour. I have been practising my calligraphy
to leave a poem for them. It isn't original, you know I'm
not a poet. Actually it's words to a song I heard one night
outside, or thought I heard—you see, I can never hide
from you how strange I am. It sounded like children
singing, very faintly, somewhere in the distance outside
our quarters. I swear to you I heard them but when
I asked the next morning, no one else had, and no one
knew of children or a school nearby. But this is what
I heard: "You and I are only ephemeral cherry blossoms.
Even if we die separately, we shall meet again and bloom in
the garden of Yasukuni Shrine—the haven of all flowers."
The voices were childish and frail, almost, but brave.
I hope you believe me.

Yes, the training has been difficult, but I know it's
making me a better, stronger person, whose beliefs will
not waver. One man broke down and cried, and it
angered me. He'd been made to lean over and be
beaten, but not undeservedly. The tears were only for
himself. I don't know if I can love the emperor and
sacrifice for him, but I will do my best for my mother
and father and sister, and for you, Kiku. Is this wrong?
Do I disappoint you? I think of you not so long ago, when
you were still in school, how you would kiss the emperor's
portrait and sing your songs. Just a girl, but so dutiful.
The look in your eyes—you were lost in your love for
him, and all I could think was, would you ever look at
me that way, and press your lips to my picture, or to

me? I think of you now, doing your duty in Manchukuo, building the new Asia, your fingers sliding the white parachute silk under the sewing needle. You always sewed so perfectly, the collars you mended for your father, and then for me.

I am also doing this for Japan. So Japan will grow and, with all of Asia, be released from the hands of the Americans and British, which we are told are wicked. It must be true. I dream that Japan will someday be as great an empire as Great Britain was in the past. I don't know what will come to be true, Kiku. But I do fervently wish for Japan to be Great. I long for the world to know that we are superior human beings who can walk in any nation proudly, because we are humane and compassionate and learned.

Yoshimoto, Honda and Sato didn't come back. I knew they wouldn't, and there was no time to be friendly with them. The truth is, I never felt comfortable enough to join in with them, but tonight I regret their absence. I pray they are happily on their way to Yasukuni.

Hajime

November 3—Clear
Kiku,
I've been sending you my thoughts every day because I'm greedy for yours. I have a gnawing ache in my stomach when I wake up each morning that stays even after I've eaten. It only goes away once the mail is given out and I have your letter in my hands. Sometimes two letters come at once, and I savour them, vowing to myself that

I'll save the second to read later in the day, or even the next. But many times I can't help myself. When nothing comes, I feel empty and I start filling the emptiness with useless sentimental thoughts. You hate them, I know. You hated it when I said I could sit with you on that park bench forever, watching the maple leaves fall as they are falling now. I told you I'd stay there until the cherry blossoms arrived in spring, feeling you at my side, with nothing changing except the weather. I wouldn't need to touch you. Our natures are so different. You hated that I had no ambition greater than myself. But you were wrong, Kiku. Haven't I proven that to you?

I won't ever see you again. You tell me to gaze up to the clouds. See you in Yasukuni, you keep writing. Have you nothing else to say? I repeat the same words to myself. I heard them, didn't I, out of the dark night, from the mouths of children? Maybe it's true what you say— that this, what I have faithfully given myself to in the name of the emperor, means so much more than an hour sitting with you at my side, the two of us with the sun shining in our eyes at the same time, apart but together— barely an inch apart, my sleeve very near yours. But at night, when everyone should be sleeping, I'm holding the arm as I was in my dream, the arm that was yours though I didn't quite know it. I imagine that, so many miles away, in your bed in Manchukuo, you feel it, but so gently that it doesn't even wake you.

The next day . . .

Did I tell you that when we were back in ███ and enroute to ███, Commander Okamoto said we would fly over Tokyo, low enough over the streets that we could wave our silk scarves in the air so everyone could see

and cheer us on? I fooled myself into believing that
you'd still be there, and you'd see me swooping down
from the sky over our old neighbourhood. You'd see what
a skilled pilot I've become, and you'd see my smiling
face for the last time and know that I was happy and
honoured to be a member of the Special Attack Forces.
Kiku, I know what I wrote yesterday may have sounded
shallow and foolish, to hold onto fleeting sensations
when there is something much more precious and lasting
at stake. Still, I don't take it back, I'm still sending this
letter as I wrote it. I do long for your touch, and I do let
myself dream.

When I see the fall leaves, I remember the cherry
blossoms. I think of the wind, which we can see only
because of the blossoms and the leaves it carries.
Otherwise it is silent and invisible. This tells me there
is a greater power I can believe in.

In the end, we had to fly high above the city to make
up for lost time. I didn't glimpse a single human face.

Hajime

December—Cloudy, snow
Dearest Kiku,
A light snow fell and covered everything, but melted away
before noon. The fall leaves are just in my memory now.

How I miss you, and how I miss my books, which used
to keep my thoughts busy so I wouldn't miss you quite
so badly. Did I tell you they took them away, my precious
Stendhal and even my tattered French dictionary? I didn't
want you to worry, since only you and my mother know

how much reading comforts me. I was making my way
one word at a time through *La Chartreuse de Parme*.
I think I told you how much I admired the character of
Fabrizio. He let his passions get the better of him at
times, but he was always pure and honest. I miss him!
You were with me the day I bought the book. Do you
remember the shopkeeper in Ochanomizu? You said he
lit up when we came into his dusty, lonely shop, and you
felt bad when we had to leave. We even lingered a while
longer because you couldn't bear to see the smile drop
from his face. How kind you can be to strangers! Kinder
than to me!

Sometimes I wonder why I spent so much time and
deep thought on such frivolous books. Why didn't I study
to be a doctor instead, and live a simple, useful life
without these complicated thoughts, away from war?

I don't want to be weak, but is it weak to hold onto this
life and to you? I look at everything around me knowing
I will never lay eyes on it again. Ordinary things one
never thinks of, but each becomes special in its own
right. Even my dear old pillow where I'd laid my head all
these nights, waiting for my last. It has a homey look and
smell to it. I am hungry for words. In addition to your
letters, which I pore over again and again, I read labels,
scraps of newspaper my shoes are wrapped in, anything
with words to occupy my mind. Bits of old news from a
world I'm already half gone from.

When I first said the word *love* to you, you turned
away. How very un-Japanese of me to say that word so
baldly, and now to write it down. But then you asked me,
what is love between two people? You asked, how can it
compare to the love we have for our divine emperor, and

our divine nation? I know you didn't want or expect an
answer. As you say, we are two hearts, but merely two out
of one hundred million hearts across all of Japan, beating
triumphantly as one.

This heart whispers good night.

Hajime

December—Cloudy
Kiku,
Today I brought out the thousand-stitch belt you sent my
mother to give me at my send-off. The others have been
wearing theirs for their escort missions but I've saved mine.
I wonder which stitch in this thousand is yours. Can you
recall? I feel I should be able to recognize it. Is it the first
on the corner where the cloth is a little frayed? There is
something of you in that stitch. It's neater and more precise
than the others. Maybe you've forgotten. I don't blame you.
I'm much too sentimental over things that hardly matter.

It wasn't that long ago that I completed my training
and was flying over Tokyo. Everything below was very
tiny, the people like insects. It is easy to drop bombs and
not feel anything. In fact, the more the insects scurry, the
more you want to obliterate them so not one is left to
burrow into your brain at night, to torment the inhuman
monster you've become.

Am I a monster, Kiku? I fear I'm something greater or
lesser. I always strove to be a superior human being. But
superior to whom?

I swear I saw another face in the skies yesterday, an
American, but not smiling this time. He had no expression

at all when he flew past, then disappeared below into a cloud. I think I was the one who hit him, but later Hasegawa boasted that he did it. I secretly prayed that it was him, not me. Am I the coward you always believed me to be? A cowardly monster? I have nothing but questions for you today—questions that make no sense.

I don't know my feelings any more. My thoughts are often jumbled, without you to order them for me, but my feelings I can always sort out and keep close. Maybe it's only for today they've drifted away from me, dropped into the clouds like that American plane. When I'm way up in these clouds, nothing has substance. Not even you. Nothing matters. I hope I don't upset you writing this. I must be pure and honest with my words. I pray that you'll understand.

I always say I don't mean to worry you, yet that's just what I'm doing! Please be assured that I will fulfill my mission in glory. I'm never lost for long—only minutes, if that—seconds, even—before the clouds clear and the islands reappear below. From up there, they look like an ancient creature's bones that were tossed into the sea and worn smooth. Once I see them, I can make out the home base I'll return to, perhaps for the last time.

Today, when I came back, I took out your picture and the lock of your hair you sent me. Then I drew a map of our great empire of Japan. I wasn't sure why, but then I suddenly understood. Do you remember the book I bought in that old bookstore with the lonely owner, the very last time we went? It was one of the frivolous books they took away from me, but I remember parts of it by heart. It was *Clélie: histoire romaine,* by Madeleine de Scudéry. Inside was the *Carte du Tendre,* a Map of

Tenderness. That is what I've drawn, Kiku. A map of the feelings between us, so that when I fly through the clouds, perhaps for my final sortie, I'll look down and see you and me and the love that Stendhal wrote of, that crystallized between us, and the path it took. How sentimental I am! But I can't help it, and I won't! I've enclosed the original I first drew, and I've made myself an exact copy which I'll tuck inside my thousand-stitch belt on my final mission. I may be suspected of giving away secrets. But they're only secrets of my heart, to be deciphered by you and you alone, Kiku. I pray you receive the map intact, without any black marks blotting out pieces of my heart.

Please forgive my jumbled thoughts. I don't have you near to chastise me for my lack of discipline.

Hajime

December Tuesday—Sunny
Kiku,
I've just learned that it is my turn to go tomorrow! I will bathe and groom myself with extra effort tonight. I look forward to my cup of saké with the commander and my fellow pilots. I can already see their faces—Sumida, Hanada and Yamamoto—and I imagine their awkward smiles, their quivering lips they'll try to hide. Together we'll shout, *Tenno-heika banzai!*

I feel separate from myself at this moment, but I'm also feeling my mind growing tranquil. Yes, I am determined to bring glory to Japan tomorrow, and I am serene in knowing I will fulfill my mission.

I will write to you once more, in the morning, and enclose my will for you to convey to my mother and father. I don't want these to be my last thoughts to you. There's so much more to say—why have I been writing gibberish to you all this time? I know you want me to be alert for my final mission. I don't know if I will sleep but I'm suddenly tired. I must at least close my eyes.

Please know that I am serene.

Hajime

December Wednesday evening
Dearest Kiku,
I'm sending this letter off to you as quickly as I can. I am still in this world. Something strange happened at the base in ███ and two squadrons from there just joined ours.

Hajime

December Thursday—Windy with rain
Dear Kiku,
This is what I've been told: eight planes had just taken off for their final sortie from ███ when one suddenly turned back. At first they thought he had engine trouble and was trying to land again. But he kept coming, too fast and too high. They shouted to him and waved but it did no good. He plunged into the main hangar, where thousands of gallons of fuel and maybe twenty planes went up in fireworks. It must have been quite a sight. Beautiful is

what my new friend, Masao, who saw it all, told me.
Apparently the man was crazy. He'd broken under the
pressure of waiting for his turn. That will never happen to
me, Kiku, don't worry. The man left a note behind saying
that he would save his comrades from senseless death,
that Japan would not win this war. But of course even I,
with all my doubts, know that he was a fool. It's impossible
for us to fail. We are a divine people with the gods on our
side. Isn't that so, Kiku?

Masao is the first person I've made friends with here.
He's an odd fellow, but so am I. Maybe that's why I feel
at ease with him. His accent is a little strange but he
won't tell me where his family is from. He's been to
Manchukuo and he told me how happy he was there. He
said he never felt more at home anywhere, not even in
Japan! That makes me happy, knowing you are there.

Hajime

December Monday—Sunny
Dear Kiku,
They are bringing us a new kind of plane. These planes
are better than any others that have ever been designed,
even by the Americans.

I wish you could see how beautiful they are, like mother
and child. As I write that, I can't help thinking of the
child we might have had together, but I'm to climb down
when the mother plane reaches within ██ feet and I'm to
die inside this structure. I am the child. Isn't it strange?
In a way, I feel as if the mother plane is the emperor
sending me off into the afterlife, on my way to Yasukuni.

Masao, the mechanic I've become friends with, keeps to himself, but he is good company just the same. He is so stoic he once fell asleep before his mission! But at the last minute it was aborted. He said he fell asleep out of fear. I had to laugh at that. He's a mechanic by training but he doesn't want anyone to know, because he wants to fly like the rest of us and not be left behind to service the planes. He is afraid he'll be the only one left, all alone. He couldn't bear that loneliness, he said.

I'll tell you a secret he told me. He is a nisei born in Canada. I am not allowed to tell the others. Masao said the officers were cruel the last place he was stationed. They strapped pilots in so they couldn't escape their duty. I don't believe it, Kiku, do you? Masao is afraid that, if they find out he is not a pure Japanese born in Japan, they will strap him in too, not trusting in his honour and love for Japan and the emperor.

I don't want to believe any of it, but I know that Masao is faithful and true, and he will fulfill his mission in glory.

Hajime

December Saturday—Cloudy, cool
Dear Kiku,
I haven't received a letter from you in five days. The mail must be slow. Though the letters from my mother have been arriving regularly, now that the family has moved to my aunt's. I hope you receive mine in the order I wrote them.

I'm sorry, Kiku, I don't mean to doubt you. I can't say how, but the tone is different in your last letters, and they've been shorter. I can't help noticing, and I must be honest and pure and tell you. I've been rereading each letter, and it seems to me that you changed around the time I sent you my Map of Tenderness. Is that it, Kiku? Was I presumptuous in some way?

In my book, the narrator warns her lover to go by way of Great Heart, Honesty, Generosity and Goodness, for if we part from Great Spirit, she says, we go to Neglect . . . and if we continue this deviation, we go to Inequality, thence to Lukewarmness, Lightness, Oblivion. I don't know why these words stay in my head. Masao says it is because it took me so long to translate. I feel it was for a reason.

Let us not go to Oblivion, dear Kiku.
See you in Yasukuni!

Hajime

THIRTEEN

KIKU SAT ON the chair with her feet tucked under her and under the folds of her kimono, quiet and small, as if nesting there. She held Hajime's last letter in her hands, the box containing the others balanced on her lap. Her face was closed: eyes downcast, mouth pursed to nothing; she was no longer the girlish woman who'd danced and wept an hour before.

On the floor were a pair of silver zori, her Japanese slippers. Hana's fingertips nearly touched them as she knelt before Kiku, palms down, head deeply bowed, not moving. "Gomenasai," she said, just above a whisper.

"Gomenasai," she said again, louder. It was an apology, Miyo understood. The widows averted their eyes, and Miyo had to as well. It pained her to see Hana this way, made to be still and unwilful, and contrite for doing what she believed in. At last, after another few minutes, Kiku spoke to her in Japanese, and Hana rose from the floor.

Kiku began to weep again, and Hana went to her side. It struck Miyo as grotesque, the spectacle of this wizened woman sobbing for her baby-faced lover, now too young even to be her son. She turned to a glass case to distract herself. Inside were more pictures, clippings, soldiers' drawings of various weapons, and a coconut, obscenely round and large and featureless except for the message carved into it by a boy who'd starved to death in the jungle. It had been found years after the war and delivered to the boy's mother, who had wept and carried it here, an offering to the gods of Yasukuni. Beside it was a curled newspaper clipping that showed the aged mother cradling the coconut in bony arms.

They were all dead. Every mother of every boy, dead. Wives, fiancées, sisters, all dead or soon to be dead; and daughters like Hana and herself slowly dying off. Who would come to visit the gods of Yasukuni then? When Hajime wrote *See you in Yasukuni!,* when all the young soldiers were promised this paradise where they would reunite with their loved ones, was this what they envisioned? That those loved ones would weep before a tiny untouchable square of photograph, an obscure grey gnarl of a human face under glass, one among thousands—millions?

Miyo would never leave her father here to be just one more.

As if reading Miyo's thoughts, Setsuko suddenly bolted to her feet. The widows were gathered around Kiku and everything was over for another year. She grabbed hold of Miyo as she tried to sweep past.

"Where is it? Masao—" Her voice broke. "Hajime told the others about Mas not being one of them. It wasn't his fault," she said, and glared at the widows consoling Kiku. "They still look down on us."

Hana went to her, and Setsuko fell into her arms even as she fought Hana too. Just as Setsuko had fought David the last afternoon at the hospital. Miyo felt sorry for her, as she hadn't that day.

"I have Masao's remains," Hana said, and cast a glance from Miyo to Setsuko. "I will give them to you."

Miyo ran down the corridor. She could not bring herself to look back at Setsuko in Hana's arms—the first tenderness she'd witnessed between them, the first complicity, spiting her own wishes and her father's.

Photos on the wall blurred past: tearful orphans; shabby sumo wrestlers hauling rubble from their bombed-out stadium; ravaged faces among the throngs after the surrender. More cases with bloodied sashes and flags, and soiled frayed uniforms, curiously small. She was passing through this dust-filled air like nothing; and if dust, as David had once told her, was moulted human skin, then she was breathing in the fleshly residue of these soldiers from the things they'd worn and the things they'd touched.

Her father was not one of them. She was overwhelmed by the place: the smell of it, its bodily dankness, the hollow din of her own marching footsteps down its halls; she would never let her father remain here, among ghosts. She turned off the corridor, slammed into the washroom, heaved over the sink and sank to the clammy floor. More than anything, she wanted David to come for her. If he made her come home now she would not resist, nor would she despise herself for it. The military march droned on outside the door, and her heart kept matching its beat. She willed her heart to slow and fall out, but it marched on.

❤

When she came out, Setsuko was gone. Hana sat alone with seven empty chairs between herself and Kiku, seated with one last widow; the others had left and Ryu and Buddy were nowhere in sight. The sunlight from the corridor had disappeared and Hana looked thin and wan; her gaunt face drew in all the shadows. She sighed exhaustedly when she saw Miyo. "There used to be many more of us."

"They're old," Miyo said. "You're not one of them."

Hana shook her head vigorously. "No, that's not it."

The last widow left Kiku's side and came to Hana. "This is Kawara-san," Hana told Miyo. The woman replied in Japanese, taking Miyo's hand in both of hers, smiling blindly. All Miyo could do was stutter an apology for not understanding: "Gomenasai."

"Her fiancé was in the Imperial Navy, ne Kawara-san?" said Hana. The woman didn't understand and Hana didn't bother to repeat herself in Japanese. That unnatural brightness was growing in Hana's eyes; she spoke rapidly, staccato: "He volunteered to test a new suicide weapon, ne Kawara-san?" She let go of the woman and latched onto Miyo. "They put him in a frog suit and attached explosives to the top of a bamboo pole. They ordered him to wait in shallow water to attack enemy landing craft."

Hana's iron grip tightened as Miyo tried to move away. "He waited for the enemy like a good little frog," Hana went on with a morbid smile. "The secret attack weapon was not successful. The impressive technology that was to win the war for Japan—it failed!" There was hysteria in her voice now, and Miyo's wrist ached and burned. She pulled away again; abruptly Hana let go.

"But he died a glorious death anyway, ne Kawara-san?" she said, standing apart.

The woman smiled indulgently and waved a frail hand through the air, as if turning something aside. "All," she struggled to say through a thick accent, "gone." Then she slipped away to join another widow waiting down the hall; the two bowed and left.

"They're going to see the model of the Fukuryu Tokko Taiinzo, the little frogman back there," Hana added. "Every year they sit in front of it for one hour. She says the face inside reminds her of her fiancé."

Once Hana had given her that flimsy shopping bag with Mas's urn inside, Setsuko had gotten up to leave; there was nothing to stay for. Miyo had left. But the one chatty old woman had lingered with Kiku and came to talk to whoever would listen about her husband. He'd been in the navy, one of those suicide sailors. Setsuko had seen the model on the way in. It was a ridiculous-looking miniature green figure made of some kind of rubber or plastic, and resembled a GI Joe only bigger, in exotic underwater gear like nothing she'd ever seen. How could the woman imagine her husband dying gloriously in that? How could she imagine him bursting like a cherry blossom in three feet of water, clutching that pole? How messy and undignified a death he must have suffered. Nothing like the glory that might have belonged to Masao high in the sky above everyone, close to heaven, already among the gods.

It was her first time inside the museum. She had never known it was here, hidden behind the bushes, a nondescript concrete building obscured by cannon and plaques and display cases dating back to the wars of the Meiji era. She'd been content to wander back and forth by the cherry trees and the well just inside the gates, where she could cleanse her hands and mouth with its cold, clear waters. She would peek inside the shrine's inner sanctum, envious of those allowed in, whose shoes she saw lining the front vestibule. This was where the scrolls inscribed with the kami's names were kept— along with, she'd heard, the remains of many high-ranking officials convicted as war criminals.

But why was the museum so empty? She would've expected it to be swarming with visitors every day. Except for the widows, it was deserted. When she walked down the hall there was an awful echo that left her lonely. She had expected devoted workers polishing, scrubbing, dusting constantly, the way they cleaned the handrails and steps and entrances to banks and department stores; even in the subways there were those ladies with dust cloths in their chapped hands, climbing up and riding down to clean the escalators. She might have been one of them, had she stayed here instead of returning to Canada.

Inside the cases, the items had grown yellowed and dirty; the displays looked like school projects done by children on cardboard. Some cases were labelled in English and Japanese, others in Japanese only; hand-printed strips of paper were haphazardly taped down in yet others. Nothing, she realized, had been properly cared for. The red stitches on the sennin-baris were bleached by sunlight, and the uniforms seemed destined to turn to dust—even that of some great admiral of the Yamato battleship. Only the hair stitched in braids to the Hinomaru flags remained black and lustrous, as blue-black as hers had been when she was a girl.

Down on the first floor there was a plane—not the one Mas would have taken his final mission in, but one he might have flown earlier in the war. She was surprised by how puny it was, not so much bigger than herself, and the metal thin enough that she could dent it with her thumb, and the wind would wobble it. On its side someone had painted a cherry blossom, plain and simple as a child's drawing. Not at all the beautiful flowering blossom she'd always pictured. Nothing like the lush blossom Hana had painted on her wall.

How dreary the whole place was. There was nothing particularly glorious about it, she had to admit; nothing that hinted at the promise of a dream larger than herself, larger than the Mas she had known as stingy, too proud to ask for more, who had lived a petty life with no glories great or small. Was there not some beauty and grace to be had, if not in this life, then in the afterlife waiting for them? She'd always pictured it in Yasukuni. Maybe it was nothing more than an image in her mind, or the feeling she'd have watching the doves fly up and hearing the coo from their plump bodies, or imagining a cloud of floating petals. But that picture in your head, and that feeling could make you forget everything, if you were ever hungry or cold, humiliated or lonely, or if you didn't know where home was.

The only glory in this place seemed to come from the words of that man Hajime. Mas had always been a practical man who said little and put himself out little. He could never write her sweet, soft, learned phrases; it wasn't in him. She had only his scraps to piece together;

there was no poetry, no serene thought left to her. She had been taken aback by the anguish Mas had scrawled: *Do not fail! I am not one of them. Coward! Disgrace!*

But didn't Hajime seem regretful to leave this world and its pleasures? *I won't ever see you again,* he had written to the woman. *Why didn't we touch?* And when he wrote *See you in Yasukuni,* didn't he sound doubtful and afraid, longing to be reassured?

Across the room, a man stood by the huge rusted torpedo, resting a hand on it. It was the man from upstairs, who'd been with Kiku, loitering near their circle, listening in as she read. It was the same man she'd seen speaking with Hana the day she'd brought Miyo here—one of the old soldiers who came to tell their stories to whoever would listen. Of course, Hana would only hear what she wanted to. But as she watched him now, something else struck Setsuko. She sensed that he was like her, a nisei who didn't quite belong. Something self-conscious in his walk told her that he wasn't at home in his skin. Mas had been like that too. His Japanese had been good, as good as anyone's here, but he hadn't been able to bow like a man born here, without the humiliation of feeling like somebody's servant.

When she started toward the man, he walked on. Yes, there it was—that bit of hesitation in his step—and when she crossed his path, surprising him, he lowered his head crookedly, almost like a boxer protecting himself, evading her instead of greeting her. "Sumimasen," she began, then "excuse me, but—"

A flash of recognition passed between them; she caught it before it died in his eyes. It was Kuroda, the war criminal. The younger brother had those same watchful, thin eyes. This was the brother they all talked about, the shame of the community, the skeleton in the closet.

The man's eyes were deadened. He muttered back in Japanese to say he didn't understand. "Sumimasen," he said back to her, bowed stiffly—correctly this time, a military bow—and walked off. Through the room's high doorway she watched him leave the building. Yes, that had to be him. She could spot it a mile away: the broken, wayward pride in his step, the unease of trying to be what he thought a man should be; the bitterness that could turn ruthless.

She came out to the front steps and saw him make his way back to the garden. She wanted to ask if he'd known Mas, if the two of them had ever met up in Manchuria. Yet she didn't know what he could tell her that she'd want to hear. Mas had never talked much about the place—Manchukuo, it was called then—but she knew it had once been a special place for him, the home he'd wanted, because it was where all races mixed together, and where he could be, if not on top, not at the bottom of the heap either. That was before the ugly things began to come out: hideous things that could only make him wonder if it was something in the Japanese, something inhumanly cruel, in Mas and in her too, that just might show up one day. It had shamed him, she knew, though they never spoke of it: what was done to the Chinese, to the POWs; to the women.

Whenever they had a fight, he looked at her as if he didn't trust that this cruel something wasn't lurking inside her too—especially when she was around his little girl, his Miyo.

One thing she knew: there was nothing special, good or bad, about the Japanese. They were people, and it was war. There was something small, slight, occasional, but monstrous all the same in everyone. It was carried by each child coming into this world: a hard nut of cruelty, a callus on the heart that either grew bigger or stayed child-sized, but never disappeared. It was the same with kindness; it could grow or wither.

Setsuko sat down on a bench in view of the cherry blossoms, Mas's remains at her side. She was startled by a hand on her shoulder. Miyo slid in beside her and they sat together in silence, watching the breeze whittle the odd petal from a blossom and skip it along the gravel.

"My father doesn't belong here," Miyo said after a bit.

"I know," answered Setsuko, with a sigh she could not stifle.

"He chose to leave Japan. He would have stayed if he had wanted to."

Setsuko was about to say that he had wanted to come back, and that he would have if not for Miyo. But she stopped herself. She wouldn't throw that in Miyo's face as she had before.

"He would never want anything he didn't deserve," Miyo said.

"But he deserves something," Setsuko said. "A little honour." With that, she stood up, leaving the bag where it sat. "You look after your sister. She needs you. You are her ne-san."

Setsuko had recognized that nisei in the museum the same way she'd spotted Mas all those years ago, on a street in her neighbourhood in the east end of Toronto, in front of the garage where he worked then. There was a lonely look to him and the way he walked. Of course, she knew he wasn't looking for anybody. She'd have to work to make him see that he needed her, or that she needed him. The next week she took her rundown car out of storage to the garage to get it fixed. He liked that it was old, a 1960 sandy-beige Rambler, and he worked away on it even when she couldn't afford to pay. That was his nature, and the only way he knew.

Setsuko passed through the shrine gates and back out to the wide gravel avenue. She stopped at the towering statue. It was Omura Masujiro, the Vice Minister of War in 1893, the sign below said. Farther on, three soldiers carrying bombs were carved into bronze—*nikudan sanyushi*—human bullets from the Sino-Japanese War. Setsuko had passed the memorial a dozen times but had never stopped to look. Three boys forever charging into a dream of blossoming in this dismal place.

Could Masao's spirit ever be at rest here, even if they did want him?

She took the subway to Shinjuku station and got out on the Kabuki-cho side. Out-of-work salarymen were already roaming the streets, past clubs whose neon lights had begun to flash. It had been nothing like this when she or Mas lived here, but she felt completely invisible and at ease walking. There were the red-faced men leering at anyone but her: at tender young girls parading on the sidewalks with their pink or orange hair and chalky lips, selling their underwear or themselves. Hana could've easily become one of them, but she hadn't. That much Setsuko had made sure of.

She gazed at the blinking neon, all colours glittering in the distance. Was this what they sacrificed for? All the kami of Yasukuni Shrine, and all these salarymen working to make Japan rise again—were they any different?

Mas had known better. He was smart and kept quiet and he worked, and he saw things for what they were. He always did what was to be done, without expecting much in return.

But would he ever have been fool enough to give his whole life for nothing, for no good reason? For a country that wasn't really his own and didn't accept him as he was? Japan had never believed in him. Maybe he had chosen not to believe in Japan.

Miyo found Ryu sitting on the steps alone. "I go home now," he announced irritably. He nodded at the bag she held. "You see, she gave it back to you."

"Yes, you were right." She smiled and drew the bag closer. "Where's Hana?"

He pointed upstairs, then let his hand drop. "She says for me to go back to sumo stable."

"But why?"

"Because she cannot look after me now. This is what she says to me." He guffawed. "But it is I looking after her. You see?"

Miyo nodded, "Yes, I know."

"Will you look after her?"

"For as long as I'm here, I will," she answered.

He brought out a piece of paper he'd written an address and phone number on, and scribbled a small map, then slipped it into an envelope. "This is to find stable," he said, and dropped it into the shopping bag. He bolted down the stairs and across to the exit without a glance back.

Miyo felt old and abandoned sitting on the cool, hard steps, clutching her bag, watching him and hearing his quick, boyish steps in the deserted hall. It only then occurred to her that Hajime had been about the same age as Ryu when he flew his final mission.

The two girls had stayed behind with Kiku when the widows went home to whatever family they had. They had walked her back to the hotel, holding her on either side, afraid she might fall. Of course, she was an old woman to them, and her knees did ache. But the truth was, she felt exhilarated, bristling. These few days of the year were the time of her most intense life—the time when she felt the welling of feeling inside her, sensed an inner rapture blooming across her. As she read Hajime's letters to the ladies, even those that shamed her, she felt herself flush from pale and dry to fiery red in her cheeks and nose and down the small of her back. She felt a brief, stifling claustrophia of heat enveloping her body until she broke out in sweat; she left moist fingerprints on the withering paper that Hajime had written on.

Each time—each year, after it was all over—she felt ready to die. *Let us not go to Oblivion,* Hajime had written to her. Oblivion was her numbed life, all the rest of the days of the year she must return to.

This time Koji had almost ruined things, following her here. The letters were not for his ears and this was not his place. It had been a mistake to share them with him all those years ago in Dairen. She had been lonely then, and it had soothed her, even excited her, to hear herself read them aloud, to hear Hajime's words of devotion with someone else hearing them too, a witness to her suffering and Hajime's coming glory.

I am tokkotai! You are tokkotai! he had written. She had never felt so proud of him being one of the Special Attack Forces; her love for the emperor and for Japan having burgeoned inside her. To be part of the ichioku gyokusai, the one hundred million that would shatter utterly, like a beautiful jewel, in the final suicidal battle. She would die for the sacred homeland alongside Hajime, with a clear and bright heart.

Yet she could not; she was helpless, could only wait for her life to be taken from her, and it never was. She wept and wished to be sacrificed, but in the end she remained one of the lesser living, the surviving inglorious, as did Koji. To live through the terrible moment when the voice they said belonged to the emperor came from the radio. Could this be the descendant of the Sun Goddess proclaiming his humanness to them, ordering them to surrender in so timid and ladyish a manner? This was not at all the supreme ruler she'd glimpsed in pictures, majestic on his magnificent horse, White Snow. "You can gaze upon the lords," her mother would say, "but looking at the shogun will make you blind; and the emperor cannot be seen at all." She had found herself telling this to the girl, Hana, who had been kind to her as no one else had. So tender and rapt listening to her letters, always curious, asking questions; Kiku should have known better.

But then there he was! Kiku had told Hana—the Showa emperor walking among the people, in a commoner's Western suit, short and slight with drooped shoulders, tipping his hat, waving and stopping to chat

as American soldiers marched and hovered behind him
wherever he went. He'd been made into a human puppet, mortalized for the Japanese people once and for all.
But for Kiku he was now an ethereal, otherworldly soul,
tragically vulnerable in this cruel new reality.

Ever since she'd confided to Koji her long-cherished
wish to join Hajime, he'd grown more obsessed with the
letters over the years, and watchful near cherry-blossom
time, when she was preparing to leave. He'd buy her
extravagant gifts of silk shawls in her favourite colours,
and pretty French cake slices. She'd have to slip away
when he was on one of his outings.

It was true she'd been deeply depressed when she
had met up with Koji again at the end of the way;
she'd succumbed, like so many others, to the kyodatsu
condition—sheer exhaustion and despair. Koji had been
shocked by her appearance the day he found her.
Everything that had sustained her until then had been
wrenched away.

She had never told Koji what it was like in those days
after the surrender. She had told Hana a little of the
awful confusion in the avenues of Dairen, the things
trampled, looted, people scrambling without pride, cart-
ing off as much as possible—even the Kwantung army
officers in their sullied uniforms, scrambling pitifully to
escape, and the Russians with their jangling coats, their
pockets brimming with pillaged watches, guns, knives,
even hair ornaments. The straggling Chinese, runaway
house servants and others streaming in from the north,
bedraggled and bone-thin, screamed and lunged at food
and whatever Japanese got in their way. There was
uncivilized hate in their eyes now that they were let

loose, no longer under the roof of harmony, within the sphere of co-prosperity so nurtured by Japan. It was ugly and barbaric and frightening.

She had thrown away all but one kimono—the one she was wearing today—and fled. It was repugnant to her that she could be spared by pretending not to be Japanese, by being taken for a third-country person, Chinese or Korean. She ran clutching a small bundle of belongings. When she reached the park she found the lovely grass torn up, flowers and bushes crushed; the benches where she'd sat with Koji overturned and splintered. She thought she saw blood and, on the far side of the park, crumpled heaps. It was too quiet.

It would pain Koji to know even this much: what had become of the park where they had sat under a white sun so many afternoons reading Hajime's letters. She had had such a cloudless heart in those days. She had never told him, though he must have heard the stories that made the Japanese into crazed monsters.

He had kept his secrets from her too; there was no need for his war crime to be spoken of because, whatever he or anyone else had done, it had been in the name of the emperor, for the good of the Japanese empire and the great Yamato race. "There are no war crimes," Kiku had explained to the girl when they first met. "Your father fought for Japan. Given the chance, he would have died, proud and honorable. He did not fail." The war had simply ended before it was his turn.

"You don't know the truth," the girl had said. She'd stood before Kiku with bowed head, like a misbehaved child pleading for forgiveness while not truly repenting. The poor girl, torturing herself for no good reason—that was what Kiku had thought at the time, not realizing to what lengths Hana would later go with her strange and hideous artwork, or how naive and fierce she was. Kiku would never surrender her belief to such a slip of a girl, though she recoiled at the memory of having unknowingly pierced the emperor's face with her needle. Kiku should have realized that a person so young understood nothing of war; she'd never learned to stay silent; she had no gaman, no perseverance.

"Your father was not a bad man," Kiku had told Hana more than once, and she believed it herself. She knew Masao from Hajime's letters, and from after the war, when he'd come to her with the belongings entrusted to him by Hajime.

No one would blame Kiku for succumbing to the kyo-datsu condition when, all around her, people had been hungry and wretched. She had fought it as if it were the new enemy that would defeat Japan, or what was left of the great nation that might, some day not too distant, rise anew. Kiku was taken under the wing of a poor family with whom she stayed in the barracks of Shitamachi. She barely recognized the place. Whole neighbourhoods had vanished; she tried to find the street where her parents' house had been but every landmark was gone, with hardly a cindered trace. Mere months before the surrender, a thousand B-29s had come in the night, and it was said that by morning a hundred thousand were dead—as if the numbers were magical, mystical. All the houses of wood and paper went up in flames, but the people inside went slowly—not as many as in Hiroshima, but more than in Nagasaki. She tried not to think who might have been among them: her parents, aunts and uncles, class-mates she'd fallen out of touch with.

In those days it seemed that all of Tokyo was sinking into the same marshy depths of the lower city of Shitamachi, with diseases breeding in every puddle and river—tuberculosis, smallpox, polio, scarlet fever. You had to keep up your strength to guard against them, because once you fell ill you were shunned, along with the hibakusha who had the radiation inside them yet to erupt, with their telltale darkened skin and patches of baldness. As if that illness were contagious too.

It took a day to gather food for one meal, wherever one could find it: acorns, grain husks, grasshoppers, along with rationed rice watered down into gruel; once they fermented sawdust to make bread. One day she heard a rumour that the crown prince's dog was missing and feared eaten; she was grateful not to have come upon it, not to have had her piety tested for a piece of dog meat. She sold cigarettes made from butts she collected, and sewed the dowdy monpe pantaloons that women took to wearing out of practicality and, it was said, to ward off the unwanted attentions of American soldiers.

Night falling was a gift, an end to the harsh drudgery of the daylight hours, and sleep.

Every day she walked past street urchins playing in the puddles, mimicking the one-legged soldiers hob-bling past in their threadbare defeat suits, or the gaudi-ly made-up panpan girls. In the first days after landing in Tokyo, she'd see motherless children wandering the docks with labelled boxes of their families' remains hung round their necks. She'd check the posted signs for news of her parents, relatives, anyone she knew, but each day amid all the clutter there was nothing, and no response to the signs she'd put up.

The one hopeful vision that burned in her head was the wondrous sight of the Blue Sky black market in Ueno, by night, with lights strung up around it, the pots and pans that had been scarce during the war now glimmering under them. In each of the stalls were endless rows of items for sale, things she did not recognize, like old machinery parts from airplanes or trinkets and clothing from GIs. People were busy and industrious once more, buying and selling—their faces, despairing by day, for the moment lit from within by the undefeated Yamato spirit.

Sometimes she'd hear snippets of a certain song that played over the radio, and she couldn't help but be buoyed by its simple melody and lyrics. *Apple's lovable, lovable's the apple,* she found herself humming. The song seemingly urged her to see and taste the loveliness in small things that might come her way in a day of dreariness.

Even the torii at the entrance to Yasukuni Shrine, taken down for its metal late in the war, was soon to be rightfully restored, she heard, and this heartened her.

Then one day there was her own name, posted by Masao.

Shamefully, she wept when she saw him—the friend Hajime had written of with such fondness, in his badly frayed uniform that he'd somehow managed to keep reasonably clean. The buttons at his collar, with their cherry-blossom insignia, were badly tarnished. He bowed deeply to her and handed her Hajime's lunchbox and a box containing his hair and nail clippings. He also gave Kiku an envelope with the last letters Hajime had written to her. There was his seal on it.

Masao bowed deeply again and hid his face. "Forgive me," he said, then left her, walking briskly into the crowds.

July—Clear, sunny
My dear Kiku,
Every day we hear terrible news. We are hearing that our forces are being devastated utterly, and that Japan may surrender.

Of course, you know I don't believe Japan will ever surrender. Every one of us will fight on until we die, because we are the Yamato race, and even if we are defeated today, we will naturally rise again tomorrow.

I cannot bear the thought of coming home to you in my defeat suit.

Don't worry, Kiku, and don't doubt me. I will complete my mission for the emperor, for Japan and, most of all, for you. I know you hate me saying this, but these three are inseparable in my heart. To me, you are everything that is the beauty and goodness and strength of Japan. I am weak but, as always, I must try to match your strength.

Hajime

Dearest Kiku,
I must be honest and tell you that I am fighting my doubts daily. You would be both shamed when I waver and proud when I embrace my belief once again.

Masao and I often have long talks into the night while the others sleep. He asks me questions I often can't answer. If you were here, I know, you would tell me what is true and right.

He asks me, if the emperor is the one divine descendant of the Sun Goddess, then how can we all become kami in the spirit world? There can be only one God and that is our beloved emperor. And why is the emperor the greatest kami of all and we are all lesser? Masao says it doesn't make sense. I don't understand it myself, Kiku, I must tell you. Will you explain it to me in your next letter?

This questioning is upsetting to me. It is disloyal, I know. I must put down my pen now and try to sleep. Last night I hardly shut my eyes. I will finish this letter tomorrow . . .

Later:

I have tried to avoid Masao for the past two days. We have both avoided each other. Maybe we remind each other of painful thoughts that shake our belief and courage.

Hajime

Dear Kiku,

Masao and I are friends again. We both need the comfort of each other's friendship. He has stopped asking me the questions that were upsetting me.

Sometimes, in the night, we are the only two awake, and I feel less lonely even if we don't speak. I know it will make you happy to know I have such a friend.

Hajime

August

Dear Kiku,
Masao says that the war will soon be over and we cannot win. He has lived in Canada and has travelled in America, and he knows what a vast continent it is, with so many more people and resources than we have. He says the Americans are much taller and stronger than us too.

He says we are no match for them even with our Special Attack Forces. It's true that the B-29s are much faster and more powerful than our airplanes. Sometimes it is frightening to be in the skies with them, but all I fear is that I will die without fulfilling my mission.

Even if what Masao says is true and our great nation is defeated, I will not disappoint or shame you. I will die in glory and we will meet in Yasukuni.

Hajime

Dear Kiku,
It will be Masao's turn tomorrow night for his final mission. He cried to me, Kiku, and I understand why. He is afraid of death because he can't bring himself to believe that he will flourish in the afterlife. It was difficult for him in Canada, where he was trampled on by the white race all his life, from birth. He did not grow up under the protection of our loving emperor.

He says he is not a pure Japanese. He feels he stands apart from the others, along with his impure thoughts. He cannot be at the heart of the ignorant crowd, he says, though he longs to be one of the one hundred million who believe.

To me he is not a coward. How can he believe when everything and everyone conspires against his faith? The others have been cruel to him at times. I have seen it. It's true that they don't consider him a pure Japanese, and it's possible he won't be granted entrance to Yasukuni. Can this be right, Kiku, when he has returned to embrace Japan as his home?

I don't blame Masao for his fear. I am only grateful that I have this belief instilled in me, and that I've had you to quell my doubts.

Hajime

Kiku,

Masao believes that Japan's surrender will come any day now, and that it is his cursed luck not to be later in line so that he can be spared. He is clinging to this life and this world so desperately. I am deeply sad for him.

I am going to give him my place. He will fly the mother plane and I will pilot the bomber. I know that in my heart that this is the right thing to do. I know he will decline at first, but I will insist and convince him of how much it means to me. He will see it in my eyes.

This way he will have a chance to stay in this world a while longer. In case the war ends before it is his turn, I am entrusting these letters to him to give to you after I'm gone. I want you to read them intact. I will put them my lunchbox. It isn't much of a memento of me, but this is all I have besides my clippings of hair and nails. My books, as I told you, were all taken long ago. You have the map I drew for you, that proves our love is as deep and wide as the empire of Japan.

When you meet Masao, I know you will see in him what I see, and will become friends, with my spirit joining the two of you together.

I love you, Kiku, more than I love the emperor. I know I mustn't say this but it's true, and I must be truthful in my final hours on this earth so that I will come to you with a clear, clean heart.

At the very moment when I crash into my target and sink a great American battleship, I will be a fiery blossom lighting the sky. Even as I am scattered across the infinite sea, I will be thinking of you dancing for me in Yasukuni at cherry-blossom time.

Hajime

P.S. I have asked Masao to paint a cherry blossom to give to you. It is just like the one he painted on the nose of our bomber. It's beautiful, isn't it? This is how I know his heart is pure.

FOURTEEN

WHEN KIKU REACHED home, she was exhausted. Koji was not there yet; perhaps he was out buying her more gifts. The exhilaration she'd felt earlier was gone. She was tired of talking, tired of the two girls.

It was true that there was so much more she had never told Hana and Miyo, especially about Miyo's mother and how she had come to marry their father. Back then, Kiku had agreed to accompany Masao as an informal go-between at the group marriage meetings held by the Maruko Bridge, on the bank of the Tamagawa River. There were rows and rows of desperate young women and men with numbers pinned to their shabby Western suits and dresses; no one wore kimonos any longer. Among all the many women and the outnumbered men, those two had found each other, each having thought the other had died.

Kiku almost envied them their happiness, and what for her had been traded away. It was a small bright miracle in the midst of so much dreary darkness. She remembered, for a frightening moment, thinking she'd glimpsed Hajime's face in the crowd.

Kiku had never told Miyo about the illness that had weakened her mother. There were diseases breeding everywhere, and she was frail, not hardy like Kiku, and young, not much older than a girl. She was, Kiku thought, perhaps more like the woman Hajime had always imagined herself to be. He'd treated Kiku so gently, as if she were lovely and fragile instead of enduring and magisterial, like the chrysanthemum, her namesake and the emperor's symbol. It had seemed only fitting to give Hana and Miyo their father's painting of the cherry blossom, which Hajime had enclosed with his last letters.

She sometimes worried that the letters might lose their magic to call Hajime forth, to conjure that time for her in all its perfect sadness. She was afraid that she might not see him again in Yasukuni; that he'd leave her to her own vanity and selfishness.

Carefully she retrieved the last letter he had written to her. He'd tucked it inside the bottom of his lunchbox, and she wasn't certain if he had intended for her to find it or not. In his delicate calligraphy, he'd written out his final will, with expressions of filial piety to his parents and sister and brother. He'd asked Kiku to convey these expressions to them and to forgive him his shortcomings.

But perhaps it was he who had never forgiven her. In those early days of the war, married men and eldest sons could not be tokkotai, and she would not consent to marry him.

It was only recently that she had noticed faint circles around certain characters in this letter. Over the years, the circles had almost disappeared. It was a love puzzle. Eagerly she had copied out each circled character. Assembled, they formed his final message to her:

I know you love me more than you love our great emperor, and that is why you have sacrificed me.

FIFTEEN

THE TAXI LET Miyo off in front of a house that resembled a bungalow in the suburbs of Toronto, except that it looked brand new and unrooted, plunked down on this quiet street in the middle of Tokyo. When she rang, no one came. She checked the address Ryu had written down, rang again and waited and was about to give up when someone emerged from behind the house.

"Ohayo," he called out. At first she took him for Ryu grown larger. It was an odd sight: a young man with long hair tied on top of his head, wearing only a brown triangle of cloth, lumbering toward her on this street that could be, if she blinked, in suburban Toronto. Another figure came out behind him. It was Ryu.

Ryu smiled sheepishly. He had gained weight; barely two weeks had passed but he seemed more a man. He said something to the other young man, who disappeared back behind the house. "Hana is not here yet." He tilted his wrist and glanced down at his bare arm and smiled. "No time," he said.

"Will she come?"

"Will you come into heya to see sumo?" He gestured to the house.

She shook her head. "No time."

"Hana will come soon."

They waited in silence. Anything Miyo could think to say seemed unnecessary. She wondered if this last minute visit had been a mistake. But in another minute Hana appeared down the road, striding toward them. With each step closer her gaze came into focus, meeting Miyo's with that special look for her alone.

Hana sent Ryu inside, and she and Miyo sat on the stoop.

"I stopped to get your fortune," Hana said. "That is why I'm late." She searched her pockets and brought out a slip of paper. She cleared her throat and turned the paper over to read the English on the back. For the first time, she seemed shy.

"Fortune is good. Wish will be fulfilled but be careful. Expected visitor tells in his or her letter he or she will come soon. Missing thing you will find before long. Believe in love. In business you will get some profits. Take good care of yourself. Walk don't run, and be religious. Travel is no problem."

"That's good, isn't it?" Miyo said, and laughed. "What about yours?"

Hana shrugged and handed her a small package. "Open later, on the plane," she said. Before she went in to join Ryu, she directed Miyo to the main road, where she could catch a bus or taxi back to Setsuko's house.

❤

Dear David:

I'm writing this on the plane bringing me back home. My fortune says that an expected visitor tells in a letter he or she will come home soon. Is that you or me?

I have my compass and my map, my whistle and my twenty-five cents to call you when I land. I write this now because I don't know if I'll give you this letter or not. I'm hoping that by the time I reach the final line, when I write my name, I will know.

Here it's been so unusually warm that the cherry blossoms came out early. All of Japan was in confusion, because cherry-blossom viewing is a national pastime. When I left, the blossoms were already scattered on the ground. It was sad to see because they're so exquisite and delicate when they're in full bloom on the branch.

Before I left Hana, she gave me a pencil box that our father painted with cherry blossoms a long time ago, when I was a child. It belonged to me in the beginning, but Setsuko gave it to Hana, who had nothing from our father. Setsuko saw it in my bag and said under her breath, *Yes, that's yours.* Then she told me not to worry, and that Hana will always be fine. I'm not so sure, and I know Setsuko isn't either.

At Yasukuni Shrine, Hana and I lingered inside the wooden gates. There were blossoms at our ankles, already brown and trampled—so many that it felt as though we were wading through them. When she looked at me, I knew that my heart is breakable but also strong. She sees me as no one else can, not even you. I made her promise to call me whenever she feels sad. Ryu will always save her, I know, but I will too. She laughed at me for saying that, but I know she knows it's true.

For the first time since I've been in Japan, I tried to imagine your life without me. I think of it as spartan and purposeful as ever—you willing those people who sit before you, a little lost, back to gainful employment. Just as you are willing me back to you with a few choice trinkets and a few words. I picture you in the kitchen alone, chopping things up in your usual efficient way. Your routine without me.

It seems lonely.

In all my time here, it never once occurred to me that you'd find someone else to take my place. Was that foolish? Was it that I didn't care enough? Many nights here I couldn't sleep. I'd toss and turn in whatever new bed I'd been given to lay my head on, and I would wonder if I was truly missing you, or if it was only your body withdrawn from mine that I suffered, and nothing more.

But then I remind myself that it was you who'd urged me to come to Japan for the sake of my flesh and blood, my Hana.

And it was you who wondered about my father in that old photograph. I know now that he was a pilot in the Special Attack Forces of the Japanese Imperial Army. He survived, but another man died in his place.

Setsuko and I sat in silence on the plane for the first hour of the flight. All that time, she stared out the window at the see-through clouds and I knew she was thinking of my father, and that she's forever imagined and wished him suspended up here, his spirit serene and proud. But instead we are bringing him back to be buried alongside my mother. We have both convinced ourselves that it would be his wish to be planted in the earth and not sent to drift in the wide open skies.

I told Setsuko that I knew she loved my father
and that he loved her. She never turned away from the
window and the clouds, but gave a little nod of her head.

One of the widows at Yasukuni Shrine mustered two
words of English to say to me: *All gone*, she said.

It can't be all gone, can it?

Love,
Miyo

Miyo folded the letter and sealed the envelope. On
the front she wrote

and put the letter in her bag, beside the envelope that
held Ryu's address and telephone number. On it, he'd
written her name in Japanese, in dark strokes. For the
first time, she imagined the beautiful night she'd been
named for.

ACKNOWLEDGMENTS

I AM GRATEFUL to my father and mother for the sustenance and faith that enabled me to write this book. I thank Gordon Hideo Sakamoto for taking me to see his father's Japan, negotiating the distance with me through one less degree of separation. I thank Teruko Sakamoto for reading countless drafts, and for sharing with me her insightful intuition which has enriched the manuscript on its way to becoming a finished book. I must remind myself more often that I live the privileged existence of a writer because of how hard my parents worked to offer me a world of wider possibilities than was given to them.

My appreciation to Richard Fung for the ethical and political compass that steers me toward a brighter horizon and new ways of seeing. My love to my sister, Laurie, who has always believed in me. My admiration and gratitude to Dr. Margaret Whitfield for her wisdom and compassion.

I am surrounded by loving friends and enjoy the company of brilliant minds. I am deeply grateful for the spark of their ideas which challenge my own. My love and respect to Dalia Kandiyoti, Ruth Liberman, Lynne Yamamoto, and Ellen Geist who read and read, and buoyed my spirits throughout. Thank you John Greyson and Stephen Andrews for incisive comments, and thank you Helen Lee, Susan Maggi and Cameron Bailey, who also read or listened to parts of the manuscript along the way.

Special thanks to Lynne Yamamoto for the inspiration of her sublime artwork and the idiosyncrasy of her vision. Thank you John Greyson for showing me Madeleine de Scudéry's "Carte du Tendre." I am indebted to Mona Oikawa who gave me the issue of *Amerasia Journal* entitled, "Beyond National Boundaries: The Complexity of Japanese American History," which shed light on the experience of nisei in Manchuria and Japan during the Pacific War. Thanks also to Setsu Shigematsu for sharing with me her translation of "The 'Emperor's Heart' and 'Mother's Heart': What Gave Birth to the 'Mothers of Yasukuni,'" an article by Kano Mikiyo.

John W. Dower's seminal works, *War Without Mercy: Race and Power in the Pacific War* and *Embracing Defeat: Japan in the Wake of World War II*, were indispensible to me in writing this book, as were Haruko Taya Cook and Theodore F. Cook's *Japan at War: An Oral History*, Roy Ito's *We Went to War*, and *Listen to the Voices of the Sea: Writings of the Fallen Japanese Students* compiled by the Japan Memorial Society for the Students Killed in the War—Wadatsumi Society, translated by Midori Yamanouchi and Joseph L. Quinn. *The Japan We Never Knew: A Journey of Discovery* by Keibo Oiwa and David Suzuki, *Religions of Japan in*

Practice edited by George J. Tanabe, Jr., and *The Wages of Guilt* by Ian Buruma were also helpful, among many other books and articles.

With affection and respect, I thank Denise Bukowski, my life-transforming agent and stalwart friend. My deep gratitude to Diane Martin and Louise Dennys for their faith in this book when it existed as mere fragments. Special thanks to Diane Martin for guiding me with a subtle and gentle hand, which helped to make this a better book than it might have been. Thanks to Gena Gorrell for her uncompromising rigour, and to Andrea Schulz for her helpful suggestions. Thanks also to Elisabeth Schmitz for her comments on an early draft.

Very special thanks to Professor Ayako Sato for her incredible generosity, support and friendship in Japan, and to the rest of the Sato family: Susumu, Takeo and Yuta. Thank you to Yuta Sato and Yoshio Wada, my chaperones through San'ya and Kotobuki-cho. Thank you Ted Goossen and Toshiko Adilman for reading a draft with careful eyes. My appreciation to Lynne Kutsukake, Yusuke Tanaka and Yosh Inouye for their kind assistance with my research.

I am extremely appreciative of the funding support I received from the Canada Council for the Arts and the Ontario Arts Council which allowed me the time to write this book. A generous fellowship from the Japan Foundation granted me twelve precious weeks in Japan.

Finally, my love and gratitude to Daniel Tisch for the glass half full.